LAMAAR RANSOM
PRIVATE EYE

By the same Author

MELODY JONES (IN *NEW WRITERS 12*)
A FAMiLY ALBUM

Lamaar Ransom
Private Eye

BY

DAVID GALLOWAY

JOHN CALDER · LONDON
RIVERRUN PRESS · DALLAS

First published in Great Britain in 1979
by JOHN CALDER (PUBLISHERS) LTD
18 Brewer Street, London W1R 4AS
and in the USA in 1979
by RIVERRUN PRESS INC.,
4951 Top Line Drive
Dallas, Texas 75247

ISBN 0 7145 3686 5 casebound

Library of Congress Cataloging Card Number
79.63414

Photoset in Baskerville 11/12pt by
Specialised Offset Services Ltd., Liverpool
Printed in Great Britain by Whitstable Litho Ltd.,
Whitstable, Kent

For the conspirators:
Douglas, Maureen, Michael

1

IT was noisy with the top down on the car, but the wind helped keep me awake. For nearly an hour bright green fields went spinning by like overgrown checker-boards on both sides of the highway. What came from them wasn't quite the scent of new-mown hay. It was more like the smell of cow shit, and it suited my mood. After one of these divorce set-ups a little spiritual gangrene always sets in, but twenty-five bucks plus expenses at least puts a dent in the overhead. And there's a lot of overhead. One by one the fields began to surrender to clumps of Spanish bungalows with rickety carports attached, and the traffic was heavier now. The world was off and running for another day of hump and hussle in L.A.

A highway interchange rose up on the horizon like a dirty wedding cake, and I swung right to line up for the access ramp when a truck came farting out of a gravelled side-road and nearly amputated the right side of the car. I gunned the accelerator, and if the little Plymouth didn't exactly leap ahead, she gave it at least two-and-a-half cylinders. It was enough to lay some rubber in front of the truck, and I could hear a nice close-harmony quartet of brakes behind me. I raised the middle finger of my left hand in salute to the guy's lightning reflexes.

It was 9.20 when I pulled into the parking lot beside the Cahuenga Building. I should have gone home first, I guess, what with the latest slumber party keeping me up all night, but I still hoped I'd walk into the office and find some million-dollar baby waiting for me. I sure hadn't found her at the five-and-ten-cent store. The elevator jerked me up to the sixth floor and the doors did their usual spasm before they opened enough for me to squeeze through. The first

7

thing you see when you step out is the sign on my office:

LAMAAR RANSOM
PRIVATE EYE.

The location is supposed to be very choice, and I guess it's better than the one at the back of the building that belongs to my competition, the great unwashed keyhole-peeper. Still, people don't exactly tumble out of the elevator to hammer on the door.

When I walked in Lavender gave me his best piano-keyboard smile. You need sunglasses when he really turns it on, so I knew his night had been jollier than mine. He was wearing his favorite powder-blue lounge suit, and against his charcoal skin it made him look a little like a fresh bruise.

'Mornin', boss,' he said, and stood up to make me a minstrel-show bow.

'At ease, Mr Trevelyan.'

'Get another picture made for the society page?'

'Yeah. There were so many flashbulbs popping it felt like the Fourth of July.'

'I don't see why nobody wants to photograph *me*,' he said. He smoothed back his marcelled hair and sent fresh waves of Dixie Peach floating my way.

'They don't want to photograph me, either,' I complained. 'They only want to photograph *part* of me.'

Lavender tapdanced round the desk singing, 'All of meee ... why not take all of me?' He signed off with a brisk bump and grind.

'Christ, you must have gotten your rocks off last night.'

'Don't be coarse,' he pouted. 'I'm in love!'

'Again?'

'It's like it never happened before.'

'I hope your pecker's longer than your memory.'

'No complaints from the Department of Weights and Measures, honey. All certified and grade-A-approved and classified as highly desirable. And I'm savin' it all for Mr *Right*.'

8

'Well, save a little of the jazz for him too. My pre-frontal lobes can't quite take it this morning.'

'Was it rough?' he asked, really concerned now.

'No, just a routine motel entrapment, but it makes me feel like I need a bath. Maybe that's because I need a bath.'

'How's about some java?' he offered.

'I've got enough in me now to corrode a battleship. I think a cuba libre is more what the doctor would order.'

'Ugh!' he said, and made a disapproving face. 'That's so *sweet.*'

'I know. It's sweet and dark and soft – just like you. That's the reason I love it.'

He hustled around behind his desk and started opening and shutting drawers.

'The rum's in my filing cabinet,' I said.

'Actually, I've been rearranging things,' he answered, holding up a half-full bottle of Ron Rico. 'The coffee was a little weak this morning.'

'And you fell in love last night, yes?'

'I fell in love last night, yes. He's a Pfc. and he has blue eyes and dimples.'

'O.K., O.K., I'll read about it in the gossip columns.'

He looked hurt when I shut him off, but some very limber guys in my stomach were having a hula contest with some very limber johns in my head. Besides, I could count on Lavender to tell me all about it later, whether I wanted to know it or not. It was part of the dues I paid for having a secretary-receptionist, errand boy, assistant, and sometime photographer who would work for the cheesy salary I could pay.

He poured an inch of rum into a glass and cocked one eye at me. I nodded and he added another inch. Then he folded back the screen concealing the old G.E. refrigerator that wheezed away in the corner. It should have been sent off to a home for the chronically ill years ago, but it had grown attached to us and didn't seem to mind working overtime. Lavender slammed an ice-tray on the desk until he managed to bounce out a couple of ice-cubes, dropped

9

them in to the glass, and topped it up with coke. He held up a chunk of lemon that was wearing a furry green evening wrap.

'Skip it,' I decided. 'I don't want to live quite that dangerously.'

He heaved the lemon across the room, and it banged into the metal wastebasket.

'Thanks,' I said, when he handed me the glass. 'Give me about ten minutes and then we'll look through the appointment calendar, I'll dictate a few letters, and we can rake the book-keeper over the coals.'

'Sure,' he agreed, in a voice that reminded me that the phone hardly ever rang unless Conchita wanted me to pick up a dozen eggs on the way home. It began to look as if I was type-cast for the motel circuit after all.

I opened the door to the inner office.

'Keep smiling,' he said.

'Fuck you, baby,' I answered, and closed the door behind me.

It felt good to be back in my retreat, even if it wasn't exactly *House and Garden*. It has a desk, a pair of filing cabinets, two straight-backed chairs and one swivel-chair – all metal, all color-coordinated in swamp green. The furniture is set off quite smartly by the jaundice-yellow walls, I think, and no doubt would be described by those in the know as having a tailored, understated chic. And there's just enough dust to make it look lived in. I flopped into the swivel chair, angled my legs up onto the desk, and took a long, thin swallow of the drink. The ice-cubes made nice music against the glass, and the cobwebs in my head began to thin out a little. Ten minutes later they had disappeared along with the drink, and I reached for the telephone. I dialled the number without looking and listened to it ring with three long catpurrs before Conchita answered.

'Good morning, baby. Sleep well?'

Her voice had a sexy heaviness that told me she was still in bed.

'*Sí*,' she answered.

'Miss me?'

'*Sí*. Very much. You have bad night?'

'I have mucho very bad night, but I also have twenty-five clams, which are better than twenty-five tortillas.'

'You want tortillas for dinner?' I had obviously disturbed her beauty sleep, but she can do without it anyhow.

'What I really want for dinner is you.'

'You make me very alone when you go away,' she whispered.

'It makes me alone, too. I'll see you tonight.'

'When you come home?'

'Not later than six, unless the client of my dreams walks in. If he does, I'll call you.'

'I make you dinner,' she offered.

'I'll make you for dinner, thank you.'

'But you no cook even leetle bit.'

'Go back to sleep, sweetheart. See you tonight.'

I hung up the phone and sat there for a minute, wondering why she always sounded as if she had a vacant lot between her ears. She was, in fact, a very smart cookie. Maybe she thought I liked it when she sounded dumb and helpless. Come to think of it, I like it when she sounds dumb and helpless. I guess it brings out the man in me.

Lavender was hunched over the morning paper when I opened the door to the outer office.

'Gary Cooper's going to star in *For Whom the Bell Tolls*,' he said.

'The news does not move me.'

'With Ingrid Bergman.'

'That moves me a little more – but a very little more.'

'You've seen *Casablanca* three times,' he challenged me.

'Conchita has seen it three times. I've seen it once and slept through it twice. There's no accounting for tastes. Have you seen my handbag?'

He nodded at the coat-rack where I must have hung it when I came in that morning.

'Feeling better?' he asked.

'I may rise from the tomb at any moment.'

'Hallelujah!'

I hooked the bag off the rack, opened the door, and walked down the hall to the john. The mirror told me I was not the fairest in the land, and maybe it was just as well a client hadn't come in that morning. I scrubbed my face with cold water and soap that smelled of Lysol, put on a little lipstick, and brushed out the worst of the tangles the wind had woven in my hair. When I went back to the office I didn't exactly feel like a new woman, but as if I'd had a decent re-tread at least.

As I crossed the outer office the telephone exploded like an anti-aircraft barrage. It was so sudden and so piercing and it happened so rarely that even Lavender shaded from charcoal to slate-grey.

He picked up the receiver and spoke in a clipped imitation of Ronald Coleman. 'Lamaar Ransom's office. This is Miss Ransom's private secretary, Lavender Trevelyan. Would you hold the line a moment, please?'

He cradled the receiver against his shoulder and winked at me. I went to my desk and sat down without waiting for the second-act curtain.

Through the door I heard him say, 'Terribly sorry to have kept you waiting, but Miss Ransom was on the other line. I can connect you now.'

We don't have a buzzer, so he hammered a couple of times on the connecting wall, and I picked up the telephone.

'Lamaar Ransom here. Can I help you?'

The voice at the other end of the wire oozed stale cooking fat.

'This is Louie Minsky,' it said.

'What can I do for you, Mr Minsky?'

'I seen you one night in a club on the Strip.'

'Very interesting.'

'You're some swell-lookin' babe.'

'I'll send you an autographed picture.'

'Naw, you really are, and I think you're just the ticket for

12

this little job I got. Interested?'

The more I heard, the less I liked of Mr Minsky, and he was beginning to demonstrate a pronounced Cheyne-Stokes tendency in his respiration. Still, there might be a legitimate job in there somewhere.

'If you're looking for a private investigator, I've got a license. My usual fee is twenty-five dollars a day, plus expenses, for ordinary investigative work.'

'Fifty!' he shouted.

'What?'

'You do the job right and I'll give you fifty a day and maybe a little bonus.'

He was breathing heavier now, but maybe it was just the strain of holding the receiver.

'It must be a difficult job.'

'Naw, it ain't hard. You come over to my place, baby, and we'll talk about it.'

'That's what I rent an office for, Minsky. You come here and talk.'

'Well, sure, but it ain't a good idea for me to be like seen comin' to your office.'

'Then maybe you'd better state your business now.'

'It's kinda confidential, but it's real easy. You just gotta put on some kind of fancy clothes and go to a few night clubs with this guy I know.'

'And somebody happens to take a few pictures of us, right?'

'Classy lookin' dame like you, somebody must take pictures all the time,' he suggested.

He went right through the pith to the nerve with that one.

'You wouldn't be trying to put the pressure on somebody, would you, Minsky?'

'Naw, naw,' he reassured me. 'Just persuade him a little.'

'Look, buddy, hire yourself a nice dumb little taxi-dancer.'

'But you're a private dick, ain't you? An' you got real class.'

'So long, Minsky. See you in the funny papers.'

I slammed the telephone down and sat looking at the top of the desk. The landscape wasn't too good. There was an unpaid phone bill, a notice for three months' back rent on the office, and a friendly little electricity company reminder that I hadn't bothered to open yet. Lavender pushed the door open and stuck his head in.

'Prince Charming?'

'No, he smelled like overripe limburgher.'

'Tough,' Lavender nodded.

'Very tough. Capital V, capital T. Fix me another drink, will you?'

'Right away, Miss Scarlet.'

He had just closed the door when the telephone rang again, and this time I got it myself.

The woman's voice was as carefully inflected as a radio announcer's.

'Lamaar Ransom?'

'Yes,' I answered.

'You are, I believe, a private investigator.'

'That's how I'm listed in the phone book.'

'Well, it *is* somewhat unusual to find a woman in your position,' she suggested.

'It takes all kinds.'

'Indeed it does. And I am pleased to have located you since I require assistance in a somewhat delicate matter for which a woman might prove rather more tactful.'

'Listen, lady, if it involves dressing up in a baby-doll nightdress or putting the screws to some lovelorn husband, forget it. I've just retired from the greasy-collar trade.'

There was a long, stony pause before the voice spoke again.

'This is a matter involving a missing person, and it must be handled with intelligence and tact. If you persuade me you possess those qualities, I am prepared to offer you quite attractive terms.'

'Then we should discuss the matter, by all means.'

'I am pleased to find you so reasonable. Would it be

14

convenient for me to call on you this afternoon – say between two and two-thirty?'

'You can make an appointment with my secretary. One moment, please.'

I walked over and cracked the office door open. Lavender was just stirring my drink with a pencil, and I high-signed him to the telephone.

'I think it's a live one,' I said.

He picked up the phone with one hand and pushed the drink toward me with the other.

'Miss Ransom's secretary. May I help you, please? ... This afternoon? That will be rather difficult, I fear. Let me see. No, we do seem to be booked up for the day. Would tomorrow morning do as well? ... No? ... But of course, if it really is *urgent*, we might try to cancel one appointment ... In that case, two o'clock would be best ... Yes, of course, but please try to be prompt ... And your name? ... Yes. Yes, thank you.'

He hung up the phone.

'Her name's Ann Shoemaker, *Miss* Ann Shoemaker, and her accent's phony, and she's coming at two o'clock.'

My drink and I went into the office to wait for Ann Shoemaker. If we'd had any sense we'd have beat it out of there and joined some safe, cozy little kamikaze squadron.

2

ANN Shoemaker was a large, raw-boned woman, but she moved with careful, calculated grace, and when she took the chair facing me she eased herself into it as if it just might contain an overlooked land mine. She was what is known in some circles as a lady of a certain age – somewhere beyond ripe but still this side of withered. Her battleship-grey hair was plaited onto the top of her head in tight braids that disappeared beneath a green felt hat topped by a great flourish of purple feathers. With her carved, impassive face, she resembled the radiator cap on a very expensive automobile. She wore a tailored green gaberdine dress and no jewelry, but the alligator handbag she carried was big enough to conceal the arsenal for a revolution in some semi-tropical republic. I wouldn't like to meet her in a dark alley, and I wasn't too sure about meeting her in the light of day, either. She wasted no time in sizing up the opposition.

'I must confess that I am somewhat surprised by what I see,' she said.

'You expected a lady wrestler, maybe?'

She gave me a heavy dose of silence then, and when she finally replied, she chose her words with careful deliberation, like someone picking out his favorite bon-bons from a Whitman's Sampler.

'No, not precisely. But I had imagined you to be more – well, frankly, to have a more masculine air.'

'You should be around when I work up a sweat.'

'You are aware, no doubt, that such remarks are simply a defense mechanism.' Her entire face hardened with reproach, making her look like a cross between the head nurse in a booby hatch and a very tough marine sergeant.

'Do I need to defend myself?'

'That, my dear, is your problem. I have come to you with a business proposition, and one which necessitates considerable tact. It is surely not surprising that I am interested in your general attitude and in your demeanor. Furthermore, in my profession an appraisal of feminine beauty becomes more or less automatic, and you are a very striking woman.'

Lavender was right. There was something phony in the accent; it was too clipped, too carefully enunciated. I would have wagered a sawbuck that her birth certificate was filed in the Bronx. Meanwhile, her drill-sergeant approach was leaving me a little cold.

'Listen, Lady Shoemaker, if your business has anything to do with a photographic surprise party, forget it. I just hung up my peignoir.'

'My name is Ann Shoemaker. Miss Ann Shoemaker.' She pronounced the syllables very carefully, very distinctly, with a slight warning hiss that wouldn't have been out of place in the cobra house at the zoo. 'The problem which I have brought to you is somewhat delicate, and a woman will no doubt be able to explore it more freely than a man. I am therefore pleased to find you so attractive – not only because it may be of use to you in making certain inquiries, but also because I enjoy working with persons of pleasing appearance. It helps to compensate somewhat for the inevitable unpleasantness with which one is daily confronted.'

She was off and running, and I wondered if I shouldn't try to catch a little cat-nap while she finished her oration.

'Might I make an entirely personal inquiry?' she asked.

'Fire away,' I said. Trying to stop her would obviously be like stopping a Panzer with a feather-duster.

'Do you always wear trousers?'

'No, not always. Sometimes, if the occasion calls for it, I've been seen in drag.'

'In drag? It is a word whose meaning I fail to grasp.'

'O.K. Listen, if you want a fashion show, you've come to the wrong address. I wear pants because I feel good in pants, but if I have to be incognito, I put on a dress. Simple? Besides, I thought Marlene Dietrich had made it all so chic that even such arbiters of fashion as yourself wouldn't be surprised any longer.'

'Marlene Dietrich is a peasant,' she hissed, and then her face shut down hard. It must be a little like that when they close up the vault at the Chase Manhattan Bank.

'Listen, Miss Shoemaker, I very much enjoy our cosy fashion chats, but I feel guilty about taking up so much of your time.'

'You have spirit,' she snapped. 'I like that. I like that quality of resistance. You might do very nicely.'

'Why don't you check out the Powers School first, or central casting at M.G.M.? They might have something that would suit you better. Unfortunately, I have another appointment at two-thirty,' I lied. The only appointment I had at two-thirty was with a lot of unpaid bills and a half-bottle of rum.

She ignored me while she opened her purse, carefully studied its contents, and then pulled out a long white envelope. She laid it on the desk and with one hand made a fan of hundred dollar bills. There were five centuries protruding from the envelope, looking as fresh as the first crocuses in spring.

'It is,' she said, 'a matter of a missing person.'

The sight of those pretty greenbacks blooming on my desk made it a little hard to swallow, but I swallowed and told her, 'That's a matter usually handled by the police.'

'The intervention of the police in this instance would be unthinkable!' she barked.

'Let me explain it to you, then. The police have access to information I couldn't touch with a barge pole. They get full reports from hospitals and morgues and boobie hatches, and they've got an information network that stretches across the entire country. Me, I've got one assistant who's just fallen in love again and probably wouldn't recognize your missing person if he fell over her – or him.'

'I like your integrity, and I am grateful for your clarification. Nonetheless, this is not a police matter. You have, of course, heard of the Fairfield Academy?'

'No,' I said, and the answer seemed to stun her momentarily. It was just as well I didn't add what crossed my mind then – that it must be one of those classy riding academies out in the Hollywood Hills.

'The Fairfield Academy is an institute dedicated to the training of actresses and models.' She sounded like a full-color promotional brochure. 'It provides both private and group instruction in the thespian arts, as well as counseling on career opportunities. Our graduates have won considerable distinction in the field of fashion, the theater and motion pictures.'

I wanted to say, 'Name two,' but those five green friends

on the desk anchored my tongue.

'Our reputation is such that no scandal must attach itself to the Academy. Is that clear?' she asked.

'Uh-huh.'

'Your inquiries must therefore be discrete.'

'Inquiries about whom?' I gave her that final 'm' with real gusto so she wouldn't think I was just another high-school flunk-out.

She went back into the Carlsbad Caverns of her purse and came out with another white-as-the-driven-snow envelope which she slid across the desk to me. I opened it and took out a glossy photograph, the kind of side-lighted, stardust-sprinkled shot that's supposed to say 'Hire me!' to agents and producers. The woman was only conventionally pretty, with dark hair that fell softly down one side of her face in a kind of modified Veronica Lake-look. There was nothing outstanding about her except her chest, and that was so outstanding it began to do things to my respiratory rate.

'What's her name?' I asked.

'Her name is Yvette LaFlamme,' Ann Shoemaker answered with distaste. Obviously she didn't have any luck in changing it.

'And when was she last seen?'

'She was in our group acting class on Saturday morning. She should have had a private singing lesson that afternoon, but she failed to appear.'

'So she's been missing for two days.'

'Yes, and quite unaccountably missing.'

'Maybe she had a date with a boyfriend and lost track of time.'

The iron mask snapped open. 'She had no boyfriends!'

'That's a little hard to believe, with the kind of front she puts up.'

'Our girls are permitted no outside interests, no distractions which would in any way interfere with their studies. We are a highly professional organization.'

'Still, girls will be girls,' I theorized.

19

'There is, to be sure, that eternal weakness to be reckoned with, but to the best of my knowledge there was no young man in Yvette's life. No older man, either,' she added, shooting down my objection with a hair-trigger flick of her right eyebrow. 'Furthermore, nothing has been removed from her room. All her personal effects, including make-up, are there. It is unlikely that she anticipated such a lengthy absence. And she was one of our most serious students, if not one of the most talented. There was, as you can perhaps see from the photograph, a touch of coarseness in her, but we were beginning to handle that quite effectively.'

I took another look at the glossy 5 x 7, and thought I wouldn't mind handling a little of it myself.

'What else can you tell me about her?'

'She came to us three months ago, claiming some experience as an extra in motion pictures, as well as a dancer in Reno. She gave her age as twenty-one, which implies she was at least twenty-five.'

'Parents?'

'On our registration form they are listed as "deceased".'

'And you don't believe it?'

'Let us say, simply, that from the beginning Yvette struck me as a young woman who might well have had something to hide.'

From what I'd seen, she wasn't hiding very much. 'You don't give me a lot to go on, you know.'

'I am prepared to pay well for that omission.' She fingered the bouquet of centuries across the desk in my direction. 'This,' she said, 'is only a retainer. I will, of course, expect to receive an itemized bill for your services whenever the case is closed.'

'My fee is $25 per day, plus expenses. And if the case is never closed?'

'I will pay you your normal rate until such time as you have exhausted all reasonable possibilities. If Yvette's whereabouts are then unknown, we will consider the case closed. If, on the other hand, your efforts meet with success,

I am prepared to pay you a bonus of $500. Is that satisfactory?'

'Entirely,' I said. I reached over, plucked two of the bills out of the envelope, and slipped them into my shirt pocket. 'Two hundred is a standard retainer in such cases,' I told her. Two hundred was also the biggest retainer I'd ever had, but I didn't tell her that. 'When this runs out, you'll hear from me.'

'I hope to hear from you before that time,' she said, laying a business card on the desk. 'Naturally, if I can be of any help ...'

'You could help me right now by telling me about any particular interests, any quirks, any associates, any hobbies that might help me get a lead on your Miss LaFlamme. For example, where did she work in Reno?'

'She declined to tell me, saying it was a part of her past she preferred to forget. She was very serious in her ambitions as an actress.'

'How can I talk to her drama coach or her singing teacher?'

'That, for the moment, is out of the question. I have announced that Yvette was called away on urgent family business, and the presence of a private detective would naturally discredit that announcement.'

'Didn't she have any friends in Los Angeles?' A girl like that, I thought, must be in plenty of little black books.

'If so, she no longer saw them. Outside of occasional visits to the cinema, her time was entirely accounted for in the three months she spent with us.'

'No Thursday night bowling team? No quilting bee? No bridge group? Nothing?'

'Nothing!' She underscored the answer with a faint grunt.

'Then you have no idea where I should start?'

'If I had an idea where to start, it would not be necessary to employ a private investigator.'

'O.K., it's your money.'

'It can be yours if you earn it.' As though to spur me on

21

to my most heroic efforts, she gave me the gift of a smile. It was about as cheery as a freshly dug grave. Then she gathered her purse against her chest with her left arm and stood up. 'I shall hope to hear from you in the very near future.' She shook my hand with a grip Joe Louis would have envied, then turned and walked to the door, but paused there with it half-open and looked back at me with her screwdriver eyes.

'Are you a natural blonde?' she asked.

'Sure. Can't you tell by my beard?'

She ignored that. 'It is such a fashion today. One never knows.' The door clicked shut behind her.

I sat down and spread the portraits of General Grant out in front of me. It was the first time we'd really seen eye-to-eye, and we hit it off right away. Lavender came in then and whistled in appreciation.

'My, oh my, you've gone and had *twins*.'

'They do favor each other, don't they?'

'And what are you supposed to do for them? Croak her husband?'

'She doesn't have a husband, and you know perfectly well what I have to do. I saw your – pardon me – black shadow against the door the whole time she was here.'

'Well, isn't that what a private secretary's *for*?' He tried to look hurt but he couldn't; he was too excited about the prospect of actually getting paid this month.

'And what did you make of Mount Rushmore?' I asked him.

'She is one very determined person,' he said. 'She is also v-e-r-y ugly. If I was God I'd make everybody pretty.'

'If you were God, Lavender, you'd make them all boys, and then I'd be in a hell of a fix.'

'Don't worry, nobody's offered me the job yet.'

'Well, I've got a job for you.' I handed him the photograph of Yvette LaFamme.

'Some jugs,' he said.

'Some jugs. Flash them around town a little. Go to the big theatrical agencies and see if anyone recognizes the

22

photograph. While you're at it, see what you can dig up on the Fairfield Academy. You can report to me tomorrow morning on the links.'

'Oh, sweetie, not *that* again! I'll scrub floors for you, I'll send your bill collectors chasing off to Pasadena, but do I gotta play *golf?*'

'It relaxes me.'

'But it gives me a pain in the ass. I mean a real pain like the kind that *hurts*.' He put on his most mournful let-my-people-go expression.

'It helps me sort things out in my head, and we may be onto a big one this time.'

'O.K., O.K. What time you pick me up?'

'Eight-thirty sharp.'

'Deliver me from evil,' he muttered, 'and me with a big night at the U.S.O.'

'If you've got a big night at the U.S.O., you'd better shuffle on down to the agencies.'

'You are *right*,' he said, suddenly clutching at his head with hands as encrusted with rings as a Spanish reliquary. 'You are *right*. Feet, do your stuff!' He was off and away with a couple of pirouettes in the doorway, spun back to snatch the photograph off the desk, and disappeared like Tinker Bell.

I thought about fixing myself a drink, and I thought about phoning Conchita again, but instead I got my feet up onto the desk and spent some time contemplating the calendar on the opposite wall. It showed a blonde down on her knees with her arms stretched back over her head to show off her milk farms to best advantage. The background was artfully wrinkled blue satin, but it was the foreground that interested me. Still, it didn't interest me enough to keep me from sawing a few logs.

3

I COULDN'T have napped for long, because when I woke up the sunlight that oozed through the venetian blinds was still laying the same stripes across the center of the desk, and the frill across the room was still holding her arms over her head. Traffic noises washed up faintly from the street, like a lazy ebbtide. The only other sound was my stomach, announcing that I'd neglected to feed it for nearly twenty-four hours. It was beginning to rattle the bars of its cage.

When I left, I locked the door of my inner-sanctum, but left the hall door open, just in case some tycoon might want to cool his heels there while he waited for me. Locked or unlocked didn't much matter. There was nothing to steal but a geriatric refrigerator, and a two-year-old could have jimmied the lock with a tinker-toy anyhow.

The elevator door was jerking open as I left the office, and my competition down the hall came stumbling out with a strip of dirty gauze wrapped around his head. 'It's nice to see somebody's working around here,' I said, but he was trying too hard to get one foot in front of the other to notice I was alive.

Al's Coffee Shop is around the corner, just off Hollywood Boulevard. Nobody seems to remember Al, or to know if there ever was one. Anyhow, the place is affectionately known around here as the Ptomaine Palace, and it's cheap if not exactly cheerful. A Greek named Nick Papadopoulis greases up the food for you, and his wife Electra works the counter. From twenty feet away, the kitchen smells are so strong you could build a bomb-shelter out of them. When I went in, the radio and I seemed to have the place to ourselves. First it told me how Halo would glorify my hair and then how I could help win the war by pledging a regular part of my income to War Bonds. If it depended on a regular part of my income, the boys in black boots would be strutting their way down Sunset Strip any day now. Electra came out of the kitchen then, wiping her hands on a soup-stained apron. It made me feel nostalgic; it looked like the soup they'd served last year on my birthday.

'So how's the keyhole business?' she asked. She automatically heaved a chunky coffee cup onto the counter and splashed mud-colored liquid from a Pyrex pot. What didn't end up on the counter somehow got into the cup.

'It's picking up a little. Trouble is, there are too damned many Yale locks around these days.'

She gave me one of her gut laughs and flashed a couple of teeth at me. I must be getting old, because I could remember when she flashed a good half-dozen. It was getting to be like the last rose of summer.

'Eat?' she grunted.

'Yeah. Let me have a couple of poached eggs on toast.'

She bent over and shouted through the short-order window, 'Gimme Adam and Eve on a raft, and move your tukkas. It's for Sherlock Holmes!'

The door banged open and the blind pencil-salesman who works the sidewalk in front of the Mansion House Hotel came shuffling in. He pulled down his glasses, winked at me, and hoisted himself onto a stool at the end of the counter. Electra went off to give him a lap full of coffee and an ear full of gossip, and I was left staring at half a coconut cream pie under a thumb-printed plastic dome. Overhead, the radio was making with a blow-by-blow description of the Dionne Quintuplets' ninth birthday party. There's no business like show business, I guess.

Nick came out to deliver my order in person, and propped his stomach on the counter in front of me while I ate. After the first mouthful I said, 'Keep up these gourmet standards and they'll offer you a job at the Ritz.'

'You like it?' he asked.

'It's real cordon bleu. This must be one of the few places in the country where you can still get old-fashioned rubber eggs.'

'You don't like it,' he said. He pushed his lower lip out in a pout, but it didn't stop the excavating he was doing with a toothpick.

'I like it, I like it,' I said, 'and even if I didn't, I'd come in just for the atmosphere.'

'You worka too hard,' he accused me.

'The hardest work I do these days is worrying about all the hard work I'm not doing these days.'

'No business?'

'Last night, yes. I gave somebody the business. And today I got a case that sounds like no case at all – tracking down a lady who probably disappeared for perfectly good reasons of her own and wants to stay disappeared. In that case, the only way I'm likely to find her is if she turns up at my door selling Fuller brushes. Still, I may be able to stretch the whole thing out for a couple of weeks and meet the month's expenses.'

'Maybe you should get married,' he sweetly suggested.

'And wash pee stains out of some guy's boxer shorts for the rest of my life? Sorry, Nick, but that's not my poison anyhow. Besides, where would I find such a gorgeous, sexy beast as you?' He was a good-hearted, romantic slob, and he half believed me. At any rate, he stopped the excavating long enough to give me a boyish leer.

'You one good-lookin' dame,' he said.

'And you make Clark Gable look like Frankenstein's Monster.'

'I seen him once.'

'Frankenstein's Monster?'

'Clark Gable. Walkin' down the street like nobody's business. Little runt you could break just like that.' He made a fist in the air that looked like an Armor Star ham. He might have a vacuum tube for a brain, but Nick would be alright to have around if any strong-arming was called for. Or if I wanted to put a steamroller on somebody's front-porch at Halloween.

'You're a prince, Nick. Now give me some more of your witch's brew to float those eggs with.' He aimed some coffee in the general direction of my cup, and I tried to shoot it down without tasting it, but my reflexes weren't quite fast enough. Then I laid a half-dollar on the counter and he stared at it for a while, trying to work out how much change I had coming. He began to sweat a little with the effort, but he finally got it right, and when he laid the two dimes beside my plate he was so pleased with himself he lighted up like a Christmas tree.

As I left the diner, the four o'clock news broadcast on WQXR was reporting another case of industrial sabotage at a shipbuilding yard in San Diego, but outside it was strictly business as usual. The heat hung as dense as theater curtains, there was a rare perfume of automobile exhausts on the air, and on the corner a cop was giving hell to a grandmotherly type who had just backed her Model-T into a fireplug. But I was keeping the eggs down, and that was proof enough of the power of mind over matter.

4

THE movement was so slight and so fleeting that it might have simply been the product of my over-active imagination, or a trick of the light on the frosted glass panel. Still, I felt certain a shadow had moved quickly across the door from right to left. It shouldn't have surprised me – not even in a business where unexpected customers are as rare as hen's teeth. After all, the door was left unlocked so that millionaires with tired arches wouldn't have to stand around in the corridor. But the form had seemed to move so swiftly that it gave me an uneasy feeling. On the other hand, it might be nothing more than the early stages of acute food-poisoning. I approached the door as quietly as I could and slowly twisted the handle. Opening it a crack, I was greeted by the back of a man in a trim pinstripe suit, bent over Lavender's desk and shuffling through the papers there. I

27

swung the door in and leaned against the door-jamb.

'Lose something?' I asked.

The man spun around, fumbled with the knot in his white satin necktie, and then laughed confidently. 'As a matter of fact, I thought I had lost you. I was looking to see if there was anything in your appointment book to tell me when you'd get back. You *are* Lamaar Ransom, I presume.' He was sure of himself now. He shot his white-on-white shirt-cuffs down out of his jacket, smoothed imaginary wrinkles out of his sleeves, and gave me a three-quarter profile that he obviously thought was a dazzler. There was something about him as greasy as Nick's eggs.

'Don't worry about losing me. I've got a way of turning up like a bad penny, and just when I'm least expected.'

'Let me introduce myself. My name is Brand Brockaway. You've heard of me perhaps.'

'Should I have?'

'Well, I have a certain reputation as an actor.'

I hoped it was better than the reputation he was getting with me.

'Stage or silver screen?'

'Mainly the latter,' he oozed.

'Too bad. I don't get to the movies a lot, and when I do I tend to fall asleep. It's a back-to-the-womb syndrome, I think.'

'But the cinema is the first truly original art form in two-thousand years,' he insisted.

I wondered out of what cheap trade paper he'd memorized that old cliché.

'Did you want to discuss your film career with me, Mr Brockaway?'

'Well, no. Frankly, I've come on a rather personal matter.'

He arranged another profile for me, and I discovered I liked him less and less the more I saw his matinee-idol mug. His hair was brushed back in a glossy pompadour, and one eyebrow seemed to be permanently arched in what probably passed in classier circles as a come-hither look.

He was tall and lean, but his face had the plumpness of a spoiled baby, and his long upper lip was intersected by a moustache thin enough to hide under a fingernail.

'If you would be so good as to give me a few minutes of your time ...' he said. There was a slight break in his voice, a sour note to the harmony that didn't go with the suave act he was giving me. The total performance was about as genuine as a Woolworth's wedding ring.

'If it's too personal, I'm probably not interested. If it's middlingly personal, maybe we can do business.'

'I really only need a few minutes of your time, but somewhere a little less public than this.' He nodded to the open door and the elevators beyond, where a brood of pastel secretaries was clucking away while the elevator banged its way up to them.

I gestured at the other door. 'After you,' I said.

He took a step toward it and looked back at me over his shoulder. 'But it's locked,' he protested. Finesse was definitely not his long suit.

'Oh, is it? How silly of me. Just like a woman, don't you think?'

His eyebrow hiked up a little higher and he made a low, murmuring noise that I think was supposed to combine sex-appeal with manly consolation. I unlocked the door and nodded him into the meditation chamber. He stepped inside and stood there for a minute sizing the place up.

'Sorry about the way things look. My decorator got drafted and the Aubussons are held up in customs. You know how hopeless red tape can be.' He tried another of his lady-killer looks on me, but they were already as stale as last week's donuts.

Getting the desk between us helped get Mr Brand Brockaway into perspective, and it showed me he was a pretty cheap imitation of the kind of pretty-boy the ladies seemed to be dampening their crotches for this week. He wouldn't score very high points on anybody's heart-throb meter but his own.

'Sit down, Mr Brockaway. Rest your sex appeal for a

29

while. And maybe you'd like to tell me what your business is.'

'This is all rather awkward, you know.'

'No, frankly, I don't.' But I could hope.

'It is a matter of confidence, you see.'

'A client has my fullest confidence, if he *is* my client.'

The distinction was lost on him. 'That greatly reassures me,' he said, giving me his frankest, most earnest gaze. His eyes, I noticed for the first time, were the color of swamp water. 'All I really require is a brief consultation in a matter of some confidence. What would your fee amount to?'

'If you'll stop dancing round the mulberry bush and tell me what your business is, maybe I can tell you. My usual fee per day is ...'

'No, no,' he broke in with a flutter of pink, well-manicured hands. 'It isn't that at all. I should simply like to ask a question or two. I had hoped twenty dollars would not seem unreasonable for your cooperation.'

Obviously this was my day. The greenbacks were spawning early this year. 'First let's hear the questions.'

That ruffled a few of his well-preened feathers. Apparently he hoped to spend another hour or so waltzing around and stunning me with his good-looks.

'Well, it's difficult to know where to begin ...'

'Then why don't you leave now, take a brisk walk around the block, have a cold shower, think this whole thing through again and come back tomorrow. It's been a long day for me, and I was thinking about closing up shop anyhow.'

'Oh, no, it really isn't quite that bad. I am, however, somewhat ill at ease. This is my first encounter with someone of your profession, and the fact that you are a woman ... well, it makes this all a bit awkward.'

'If you'd like to continue a little farther down the hall, there's a peeper in 608 who might be more to your liking. He's probably in changing his bandages right now.'

'Heavens, no! It's you I have to see. I don't need a private detective. I simply need some information, and I think you can give it to me.'

Getting that much off his chest seemed to charge up his self-esteem batteries a little. He pulled a tortoiseshell case out of his pocket and leaned across the desk to offer me a cigarette.

'No, thanks. I only smoke cigars,' I told him.

'Oh, really? But you don't mind if I smoke?'

'Not at all. Be my guest.' He was already lighting up so the question wasn't, I believe, what the lawboys call a moot one. I shoved a Mansion House Hotel ashtray across the desk in his general direction.

Brockaway sprayed a little smoke around the room and finally got down to business. 'You were, I believe, recently asked to assist in locating a missing person.'

'Was I?'

'I have, well ... some reason to believe so,' he hedged.

'And?' I don't like fishing expeditions, and I sure as hell wasn't going to make it easy for him.

'Well, am I correct in my assumption?' He was puffing faster at the English oval now, and his looks improved a lot behind the smoke-screen.

'If you have reason to believe so, then maybe we should start with your telling me about that reason.'

'You don't make this easy for me,' he sighed.

'You must think me terribly ungracious, but it would no doubt greatly facilitate our little tête-à-tête, Mr Brockaway, if you'd either shit or get off the pot.'

He choked on the smoke and his face got a little disarranged, but he didn't take long to regain his fatally debonnaire composure. 'I am, from time to time, employed by the Fairfield Academy.' He followed the declaration with what was no doubt intended to pass for a pregnant pause.

'Fact one. We're making real progress, Brockaway.'

He was ignoring me now, and his little set speech came out right on cue, with all the proper eyebrow-hoistings, confidential up-from-under glances and rippling cheek muscles. 'It is, you understand, an institute for the training of young women in the thespian arts, but from time to time male actors are required for the acting classes, as well as for the trial screen-tests. Naturally, this is somewhat tedious for an actor of my experience, and yet one owes something to the profession as a whole. At times, too, I direct brief scenes, which help to mature my own theories of the dramatic craft. Recently I've been coaching a new student, Yvette LaFlamme.' He gave a perfectly voluntary stage-shudder that let me know what he thought of the name – and of LaFlamme as well, perhaps. 'She had certain obvious endowments, but acting talent was definitely not among them. Still, I managed to coax one or two quite respectable scenes out of her. We were scheduled to finish a short film yesterday – just a little vignette, really – and she didn't show up. I was informed she'd been called away on family business, but this seemed to me the flimsiest cover-up for some kind of escapade that might embarrass the Academy. And then, this morning, I happened to be passing the office and overheard the director telephoning you. I presumed her visit might have something to do with Yvette's sudden absence.'

The cigarette had burned down to his fingers while he brought forth his little oration, and he lurched forward to grind it out in the ashtray.

'I don't quite see why any of this should particularly concern you, Mr Brockaway.'

'Oh, it doesn't, of course.' He dabbed at his forehead with an oversized monogrammed handkerchief. 'No, of course it doesn't, except that I've invested a lot of time and professional skill in the Academy.'

'And you are concerned about its reputation being somehow tarnished,' I prompted him.

He jumped at that one. 'Yes, exactly. You see why the matter is so delicate.'

I stood up and leaned across the desk so that I could look a little closer into his swampy eyes. 'I see you're nervous, and I don't want you crapping in your pants as long as I'm downwind of you, but if you want to express your concern

in these grievous matters, I suggest you shag your ass back
to the Academy and talk to your gracious director. When I
told you a client's conversations were confidential, I meant
just that. Ann Shoemaker is my client. I'll tell you that
much only because you've snooped around and found it out
for yourself. If she wants you to know anything about the
matter she hired me to investigate, she can tell you herself.
And if I think you can help me in any way, I'll call you.
Meanwhile, don't call us, O.K.?'

His sweat glands were really working overtime now, but
he had at least one more B-movie scene left in him. He
stood up suddenly and tried to come on with a tough-guy
routine. 'Listen,' he snarled, 'I came here with information
for you. Nobody at the Academy knew Yvette better than
me. If you're too stupid to use it, that's your affair.'

Maybe it wouldn't hurt to play straight-man to his
bargain-basement George Raft. 'O.K., Mr Wise-Ass, give
us a little sample of your inside information.'

'Yvette LaFlamme was no goddamned actress.'

'Better keep the secret to yourself. Let it out and every
studio in town will close down.'

'I mean she'd never done any acting. She wasn't what she
said she was.'

'And what was she?'

There was a brief hesitation before he said, 'I don't
know.'

'Your information is so hot, buster, it's likely to melt
every I-beam in the joint.'

'She was vicious and conniving,' he spluttered.

'Since when is that inconsistent with being an actress?'

'She didn't know stage-left from stage-right, and she
froze up whenever there were cameras around.'

'Great. Thanks to you, I know she lied about her past
experience. She wasn't an actress. She only wanted to be an
actress. Thanks for the information. Now what did you
want from me that was worth twenty bucks?'

'Did Ann Shoemaker mention my name?'

'Isn't it on every tongue these days?'

33

'Did she say anything about Yvette and me?' he persisted.

'Even if my conversations with clients weren't confidential, I still wouldn't tell you that.'

'Why not?' He seemed genuinely hurt, as though I'd managed to plant a heel in his ego somewhere.

'Listen carefully, buddy. Let this sink into that sub-pretty, pompadoured head of yours. I wouldn't tell you because in the first place I don't like you, in the second place you stink, and in the third place I don't like you in the first place. Savvy?'

He shrugged it off with a nervous laugh. 'Look,' he said, 'Yvette and I had a little disagreement last week – nothing serious, just a professional thing. She didn't like my performance, that's all, and she got pretty loud about it. Nothing serious. But if anything's happened, I want to be sure my name isn't mixed up in it. I've got a reputation to think about.'

I walked around the desk and held out a hand to him. 'Mr Brockaway,' I said, giving him a firm old-boy handshake, 'you can be assured that this agency will do everything in its power to protect your lousy reputation. No turn will be left unstoned. Now get your butt out of here.'

He stood there, still holding onto my hand, and arranged a pair of bedroom eyes for me. 'Why don't we try being friends?' he asked, pulling me toward him.

'Christ, you're as predictable as a dose of clap, and about as hard to get rid of.'

It didn't stop him. He was getting me off balance, and he was getting me mad, and I decided to give him something to remember me by. I brought my right knee up hard against his groin and watched him collapse from the top down. The body-wave left his pompadour, his eyebrow sagged, his eyes went away somewhere into the back of his skull, his pencil-line moustache hung at half-mast, and then he began to double over. I got him into a half-nelson and out the door without seeing the last of his dying-swan performance.

I needed a drink, and while daylight began to shut down I changed my mind and had two. It didn't help a lot. The trouble with this kind of business is that you have to spend too much time with the losers, with the slobs and deadbeats trying to pull some final, desperate angle, and always at somebody else's expense. There was almost always a little slime around the edges. It was time to go home. I may have bent a few fenders getting there, but it was worth it. Conchita was waiting, and later that night, as I held her firm brown body against mine, I felt clean again. For a little while, at least.

5

LAVENDER was standing at the curb in front of his apartment house dressed in tweed plus-fours, an argyle sweater, and a pork-pie hat, looking like a refugee from an Agatha Christie novel.

'If you think you're going to throw me off stroke with that outfit, you're wrong,' I said as he got into the car.

'Honey, if I can't play golf I can at least look pretty at the club-house.'

'You're too much,' I said.

'On whose scale?' he asked, and pulled the cap down over his eyes to announce he was about to take a little snooze.

I drove west, nosing through side-streets to avoid as many of the time-clockers as possible. The morning still had that cool, damp quality about it when you can imagine the world has been reborn, even if it has just flipped over another page of the calendar. The green lights were all turned on for me. Some days are like that. Most of them aren't. I moved onto the Strip and drove for a bright mile past the well-lacquered fronts of antique shops and decorators' studios. They weren't open yet. Probably the owners were still limbering up their wrists. The famous nightclubs glided by, their neon signs and famous, over-paid chefs asleep now. We slid past rows of airplane-modern office buildings, past the casinos, past the drive-ins where girls dressed as drum-majorettes or Betsey Rosses or prehistoric cavewomen brought hamburgers and plastic smiles and heaving bosoms to shove at the window of your car, always in hopes that a famous producer was lounging inside. Lavender slept, I drank in the morning air that somebody forgot to take out a patent on, and the road drifted along a wide, smooth curve past the bridle path of Beverly Hills. Five minutes later we were parked in front of the club-house. I did my best imitation of a bugle call, and Lavender came awake in sections.

'Do I gotta get up?' he mumbled, scooting even lower into the seat.

'You gotta move that sweet ass, baby.'

'That's what I did all *night!*' he protested.

'Is that so?'

'Dat's so so' I cain't touch it wif a powder puff!'

'Please. Spare me the intimate details,' I said.

'There ain't no intimate details. If there *was* any, maybe I'd feel a little more frisky.'

'Don't tell me it was the old orange-juice-and-cookies routine.'

'Right-o.' He stretched, pushed the cap onto the back of his head and made with a yawn that resembled the Grand Canyon at dusk. Two nights a week he served refreshments at the local U.S.O., and the sight of all those uniforms was almost too much for his blood-pressure.

'I thought there was a new man in your life.'

'There is, but he had to do guard-duty.'

'Maybe you should get yourself put in the brig.'

'They do terrible things to you there. I mean *tur-ruble* things. They all gang up on you, and before you know you've been ravaged. Just imagine that.'

'Sounds grim,' I agreed.

'I wonder what you *do* to get into the brig?'

'First, I think, you have to join the army.'

'But I've checked the *box!*' he moaned.

'Anybody check your box lately?'

'No, that's the trouble. That's why I'm feelin' so ornery.'

'And so horny.'

'Them is definitely the right syllables.'

'Cheer up,' I said, swinging the car door open. 'Just remind yourself you're saving it for the one you love.'

'But what if he don't *want* it?'

'You can always donate it to the church bazaar.'

'You are very sharp this morning. You been eating carpet tacks on your Wheaties again?'

'No, roofing nails. Now get your unloved ass out of that car and lets knock a few balls around.'

'You know how to get a fellow where it *hurts*, don't you?' he shot back.

'Well, I made pretty good work of it yesterday,' I admitted. Brand Brockaway's smug, pampered face came back to me then, and the morning seemed a little stale already. But he had done one hell of a routine there at the end – as if he were a puppet and somebody had suddenly cut the strings. That, at least, had been a pretty sight.

Lavender managed to stumble around to the back of the car while I was heaving the golf-clubs out.

'Flip you for caddy,' I said.

'O.K., if I gotta.'

'You gotta.'

'Call it,' I challenged, tossing a quarter into the air.

'Heads!' he shouted as the coin still glittered in the air. I clapped it against the back of my hand and lifted a finger to peek under.

'I'm caddy,' I said.

He showed me the whole piano keyboard then. 'And I is mighty pleased, Miss Scarlett.'

The coin had come up tails, but he looked to me like he could hardly manage to carry his own plus-fours around the course.

I teed off first, and the ball made that kind of easy, pretty arc down the center of the fairway that takes your breath along with it. At mid-arc the laws of gravity and all the other laws seem to get suspended. It makes for a nice little tingle in the solar plexus, and it's all just that much sweeter when you don't have to pay for it. A lifetime membership is the bonus I got from the club manager for saving him a nasty flutter with the insurance company when his wife's pearls disappeared last year. They turned up in a pawnshop in Sausalito, and the pawn ticket turned up in her purse. Since Mandrake the Magician was out of the country at the time, there seemed only one explanation, and it wouldn't have looked too good on the lady's D.A.R. record. We managed to keep it off.

On the far horizon the ball bounced onto the green, did a happy skip and a jump and came to rest near the flagpole. How close it was I couldn't tell, but close enough for comfort.

'Beginner's luck,' Lavender muttered. He stepped up to the tee and managed to look like something from the chorus of *Swan Lake* as he bent to put the ball on it. He did a pirouette as he swung the club, and missed the ball by the width of a parking space. Turning to look at me with a King Kong scowl, he said, 'It moved.'

'You're right. You're right. It's a goddamned miracle!'

'Hallelujah!'

'May the saints be praised!'

'May they come marching *in*!' Lavender shouted, and took a lethal chop that sent a wedge of emerald-green turf winging through the air.

'Revelation!' I said.

'Constipation!' He swung again, and this time the ball and the tee departed together, but for different destinations.

'Fore!' Lavender called, and the ball swung sharply into the woods. There was a light musical interlude as it went rat-a-tat-tat against the trees.

'Next time you might shout "Tally Ho!"' I suggested, but he was already shuffling off into the woods with a shoulder sag that told me he had had about enough lip for the morning.

I waited for him on the green, watching the bushes near the tee thrashing about as though a wounded rhino were on the loose. Then the ball came sailing along the fairway, with Lavender trotting behind it. A half-dozen strokes later and he was on the green beside me.

'Call it five,' he suggested.

'Five hundred?'

'I think you are impugning my integrity.' He cast injured eyes down in the general direction of his wing-tipped oxfords.

'Never,' I said. 'We don't know each other well enough for such carryings-on. Anyhow, I don't go that way.'

'Call it seven, then,' he said.

'Seven it is!'

A group was gathering on the first tee, so I put my ball into the cup with a nudge of the iron. Lavender chased his around the green a while and then eased it in with the side of his shoe. I signalled the group behind us to play through, and we sat it out for a while on a bench just off the fairway.

'Now tell me all about it,' I said to Lavender, who was busy straightening the seams in his socks.

'Well, he's eighteen and has two sisters at home. His daddy works for the railroad, just like mine used to do, and he has a little-bitty mole on his right cheek.'

'I don't want to hear those lurid stories before breakfast. But I wouldn't at all mind hearing what you happened to find out on your way to the U.S.O.'

'Oh, *that!*'

'Yes, that. Convince me you've earned your handsome salary.'

'Well, I posed as a casting director.'

'Perfect. What's the film? *The Return of Uncle Tom's Cabin?*'

'No, I was thinking more in terms of a musical version of *Macbeth*, with the Andrews Sisters playing the three witches.'

'You're inspired.'

'I'm *tired,*' he groaned.

'Get tired on your own time, handsome. We could use a little information if we want to keep General Grant as a steady house guest.'

'There ain't much information. I said I was *assistant* to one of the casting directors at R.K.O., and that he had sent me out to find some chickie he had seen in Reno that he thought would be just right for a new film he was doing.'

'Did anybody fall for that line?'

'No, but they couldn't have told me anything anyhow. Nobody registered nothin' when they saw that picture. Nothin' but a little old-fashioned lust, maybe. Nobody recognized her. Not exactly,' he added.

'What does "not exactly" mean?'

'Well, somebody at Famous Faces allowed as how she reminded him of one of the girls who used to work at Ma's place. But just reminded him. Probably it was the knockers he thought he remembered.'

'They're not your everyday garden-variety knockers, though.'

'I don't know, to me they all look alike.'

'There are certain subtle differences,' I assured him.

'Yeah? Well, if you ask me, when you've seen one pair you've seen 'em all.'

'But that wasn't the opinion of our buddy at Famous Faces.'

'Maybe not. But he didn't say for sure. He just said that she kind of reminded him of somebody who used to work for Ma.'

'And no longer does?'

'And no longer does. Leastwise, he said he hadn't seen her there in a long time.'

'Well, that gives me the day's assignment. I check out Ma's.'

'Why not me?'

'Because I have, shall we say, a more subtle appreciation of the aesthetics of the knocker. Did anybody bite when you mentioned the Academy?'

'They'd heard about it. Everybody seemed to know it's

some kind of finishing school or modelling school or something, but nobody lists girls who study there.'

'That makes sense,' I said.

'That don't make no sense to me. Who's gonna want to study there if the place don't help 'em get jobs afterwards?'

'Precisely, my dear Watson, and that makes sense because it explains the faint but distinct odor of rat that Madame Shoemaker was trailing along behind her.'

'You are *right*!'

'You bet your sweet ass I'm right. That broad's as genuine as a nickel hamburger.'

The foursome had played through, and we trailed along behind them. The sun had sharpened its angle, and curtains of heat were beginning to shimmer in the air. The girls at Ma's place would be starting to take out their bobby pins any minute now.

6

MA WALLER made her reputation by providing everything the tired businessman needs, as well as a few things it had never occured to him to need. There's champagne, caviar, smoked salmon, steaks that look like half a steer, and that's only for starters. The sexual smorgasbord is the real *piéce de résistance* – male or female in every color, shape and size, and every age from jail-bait to fish-bait. You name it: Ma provides. I'm told there's even a cunning little medieval torture chamber in the basement, and a special room for animal-fanciers.

But it isn't just her Ringling Brothers sense of showmanship that recommends Ma Waller. She does it all with style, and with what in Hollywood even manages to pass for respectability. You may not run into the Vanderbilts there, but you can usually scare a district-attorney or two, an assortment of oil barons and a few

41

studio magnates out of the woodwork.

A liveried gatekeeper, looking like a refugee from Buckingham Palace, stopped me at the gate while he telephoned the house. Then he waved me through with a glance that pegged the price of my loyal Plymouth as accurately as any Smilin' Ed could have done. He wasn't too impressed by what he saw.

The white-gravelled drive wound its way between silvery clumps of eucalyptus trees that shrank back here and there to make way for marble gods and goddesses that all seemed to have lost their togas. Then the drive spilled out like creamy frosting across a velvet lawn. You know the kind. You plant it, you water it every day, you give it lots of California sun, you roll it every week, and presto! In two hundred years you've got just the effect you wanted.

A Negro boy flagged me as I neared the house and pointed me toward a turning that ran away to the left, through a grove of mesquite bushes. There was a row of garages, lined up like overgrown shoeboxes, where customers could tuck their cars away without the danger of having their license numbers or monogrammed hubcaps spotted. It's the little touches that really count.

The only time I had met Ma Waller was in her less grandiose phase, when most of her girls worked the streets and gave curb service. But from the look of the house she was running now, I expected to have a regulation English butler come to the door, someone with basset eyes and a BBC voice. I was disappointed, but not for long. The door was opened by a young lady with more curves than the Brooklyn Dodgers ever dreamed of, and she wore a French maid's uniform that put them all on display.

I stood there for a minute thinking I might pretend to be a customer, but she said, 'You must be Miss Ransom. Mrs Waller told me to expect you. Won't you follow me?'

Follow you, I thought. Straight out across the Mojave, if you're the outdoor type. But she didn't lead me to the Mojave. She lead me instead across a marble foyer that might have had the Hollywood Bowl nestled off in one

corner, and showed me into a drawing room that was all
French. One of the Louies, I think, but I always get them
mixed up. There were damask-covered sofas and chairs
everywhere, gold and crystal sconces on the walls, and
carpets laid on top of other carpets. There were paintings
everywhere as well – paintings of landscapes and of
reclining nudes and of ladies in fancy dress. There were
plenty of lamps, too, and in all the right places. It looked
expensive, but it felt about as cozy as a railroad waiting-
room.

'If you would like to sit down and wait, Mrs Waller will
be with you shortly,' said my French maid. I wondered if
she could use a little help with the dusting, but before I
could ask her she had pulled the barn-sized door closed
behind her. So I twiddled my thumbs for a while, learned
that the leather bindings in the bookshelves were authentic
even though the pages were blank, and helped myself to a
couple of shots of very pale, very dry brandy that was sitting
on a chest near the fireplace. Actually, it wasn't a chest.
When it's got that much inlay on it, it's called a commode, I
think.

I was beginning to get a little antsy when the door drifted
open and Ma Waller came in. She hadn't changed a hair
since I last saw her, and that's no figure of speech. It was set
in those same tight little finger waves that made me wonder
if she stapled it into place every morning. She was wearing
a long black dress with white collar and cuffs that gave her
the solemn air of a Quaker matron.

Her manner was all the gracious Southern lady as she
waded through the orientals and offered me a dry, bony
hand. 'How do you do, Miss Ransom. It is such a pleasure
to meet you again.' Somehow she got a couple of extra
syllables into 'pleasure' that I hadn't noticed there before.

'Then you remember the first time we met?'

'To be sure,' she smiled, 'I remembered so soon as I
heard your voice on the telephone. I never forget a name or
a face or a voice.'

And I'll bet you've got a few other details stored away,

43

too, I thought. What I said, continuing our little garden-party scenario, was 'That's very flattering, and you're most kind to see me.'

'But of course,' she said, and managed to make 'course' rhyme with 'rose'. 'Our business interests are, after all, complementary.'

'Are they?'

'Why, certainly, my dear. We both deal, I believe, in discretion.'

'Then you won't mind, I trust, answering some discrete questions?'

'I should be most pleased to assist you in the inquiries you mentioned. But shouldn't we make ourselves more comfortable?'

'Comfortable' wasn't exactly the word I'd use for one of those straight-backed, hard-assed sofas, but I made the best of it, and Mrs Waller got down to business as swiftly as only a lady used to getting down to business can do.

'This is, I believe, a case of a missing person.'

'Yes, it is.'

'And you have reason to think I might be able to assist you.' Her voice sloped up to a question mark at the end.

'Yes. That is, someone suggested that the young woman I'm looking for might once have been employed by you in some sort of domestic capacity.' I was getting to be almost as good at shoveling the shit as she was. The only difference was that she had a golden shovel and I was making do with something from the Sears, Roebuck catalogue.

'Help is so unreliable these days.' She sighed and rolled her icy blue eyes up toward the ceiling, which was just low enough to be visible from where we sat.

'How true,' I sympathized. 'And of course, with so much coming and going, you might well have forgotten.'

'I never forget a face,' she reminded me crisply.

'Or a name,' I added.

'Or a voice. Now what was the name of this young woman?'

'All I've got is what's probably a theatrical name, and a

lousy one at that. Yvette LaFlamme.' I scored nothing with that one. Ma Waller's face remained as impassive as the Great Wall of China.

'I'm afraid I can't help you, my dear. No one, I think, could have forgotten such a cognomen.'

'Then let's have another try with the face and, ah ... torso.' Torso was the best I could give her in trade for 'cognomen'.

I slid Ann Shoemaker's envelope out of my purse and studied Ma Waller's face while she took it, opened it, and pulled out the photograph. This time I hit pay dirt, alright. She turned the color of pickled beets, jammed the picture back into the envelope, and sailed it in my general direction. But blood will tell, and Ma Waller was a wizard at repairing broken gaskets.

'Forgive me,' she said. 'I rarely permit myself such obvious emotional indulgences.' She smoothed imaginary wrinkles out of her skirt and plucked off the stray bit of invisible lint. 'Now,' she said, 'what can I tell you?'

'First of all, what name did she use when you knew her?'

It wasn't easy for Ma. She looked as though her nose had just discovered a little fresh manure in the very near vicinity. But she didn't get where she was without courage, and she bit the bullet again.

'Blanche,' she said. 'Blanche Framboise.'

'Well, at least she's consistent in a vague French sort of way.'

'And in her unimpeachable bad taste.'

'Then I'm correct in presuming she worked for you?'

'Let us say that I gave her a home at a time when she was in need. As I have given homes to other poor motherless girls.' The way she said 'girls' was close enough to 'gulls' to make someone think Ma Waller ran a bird sanctuary.

'And she repaid your kindness poorly?' I was beginning to sound like a page out of *Redbook* myself.

'She took outrageous advantage of her position in this household,' Ma Waller answered. I thought I wouldn't mind knowing exactly what kind of position Yvette-Blanche favored, but the subject seemed a little esoteric at that moment.

'Could you give me an example?' I asked.

'Details are unimportant. She was able, because of my trust, to learn certain personal facts about my friends, and she sought to use them for her own profit. She pried, she asked unfortunate questions, and she tried to gain access to my own private papers. She was apprehended as she tried to open the safe in my bedroom.'

'And what happened then?'

'She responded with a vulgarity scarcely to be imagined. She also made various accusations against me and against my friends. They were, of course, groundless. Her evil, cunning mind had simply distorted certain perfectly innocent facts which she had learned.'

'That, I believe, is called blackmail. Why didn't you call the police?'

'My dear Miss Ransom,' she began, and then paused. She looked a little like a first-grade schoolteacher correcting an idiot pupil. 'My dear Miss Ransom, my speciality is discretion, and I must spare my friends any possible embarrassment. Blanche or Yvette or whoever she was had neither the intelligence nor the courage to pose a serious threat to me. It is necessary, always, to appraise the opposition.' Ma Waller could give Dale Carneigie a few pointers on self-confidence.

'But what if she was employed by someone else? I mean, she might have been passing on her information.'

'It occured to me, of course. But I shall deal with that problem if and when it becomes manifest. Until then, I can only presume that Blanche was simply a vicious, vulgar, conniving young woman who tried to take advantage of my kindness to her. Furthermore, anyone who would have been sufficiently stupid to employ her in a matter requiring intelligence would himself be too stupid to concern me.'

There was the sound of finely tempered steel underneath the honey in Ma Waller's voice.

'And when did these events occur?' I asked.

Ma didn't even hesitate. The information was all neatly stored away, and it came out as steady as a ticker-tape. 'Blanche came here on January 17th. The following week I first suspected that she was abusing my hospitality for her own purposes. On January 28th she was discovered trying to break into my safe. She departed shortly thereafter.'

Very shortly, I thought, and very swiftly. 'And you've not seen her again?'

'Life has kindly spared me that experience,' Ma purred.

'Do you have any idea where she went from here?'

'She left me no forwarding address. But considering the devotion which certain old friends show me, and their power in this community, she would have been advised to take a rather long journey. Two thousand miles would have been sufficient, perhaps.'

The information didn't exactly help me narrow the search, but it seemed all I was likely to get.

'You've been very kind,' I said. 'And if by chance you or your friends should happen to hear anything about the missing French pastry, please let me know.'

I handed her a business card, and she looked at it with about as much enthusiasm as a pawnbroker inspecting a dollar watch.

'But of course,' she said, and stood in a way that let me know the audience was at an end. 'I'll have someone show you out, my dear.'

I thought I could find my own way, with a couple of reconnaissance maps and a compass, but I let her pamper me in hopes of getting another look at Marie Antoinette. I got a look, alright, but that was all. The 'No Trespassing' signs were up all over Versailles that day.

7

I SLID into the Plymouth and punched the starter button. The motor squawked, spluttered, and began to idle. I let it hum for a few minutes and thought over the little I knew.

Other than a possible but underdeveloped taste for blackmail, Yvette LaFlamme seemed to have no more and no less to offer than the platoons of well-stacked girls that turn up in L.A. every month. And yet she had a talent for going against the grain. Ann Shoemaker, Brand Brockaway and Ma Waller all seemed a lot more worked up about her than they could have been about the average bargain-basement hooker. Ann Shoemaker was willing to part with a good deal of the folding green to have her found. Or did she just want it to look that way? Of the three people who had known Yvette, only Ma Waller had really seemed to level with me, but maybe she was only giving me a sample of her famous bedside manner. The pieces just weren't fitting together.

I eased the clutch out and backed into the drive, then curved again past the marble bathing-beauties. The lummox at the gate waved me through in a way that didn't exactly encourage me to drop in again next time I came beagling through the neighborhood.

By the time I figured out the maze of snaking lanes that got me back to Wilshire Boulevard, the traffic was so thick anyone would have thought gasoline rationing had gone out of style. I clicked on the radio to hear the last bars of 'Bewitched, Bothered and Bewildered' and thought about adopting it as my very own national anthem. Then somebody asked me if I'd taken my vitamins for peace, and Snookie Lanson trilled a little bond-buying melody, and somebody else I didn't know suggested that if I wasn't having success, it might be because of bad breath. He could be right.

The twelve o'clock news had some warmed-over tid-bits about vice-squad graft, a report on the Red Cross blanket drive and some more bitter-pill reports from a place called Attu Island. An industrial espionage trial was cranking up over in Marin County, and an office building had collapsed sometime during the night in Santa Monica. A few stories of brick and steel suddenly turned into crumb-cake. It all made a girl feel glad to be alive. But then things picked up when the Andrews Sisters started thumping out 'The Boogie-Woogie Bugle Boy from Company B'.

By the time I had the car parked, tanked up with some of Al's greasy coffee, and got back to the office, it was nearly two o'clock. Lavender looked so cute sprawled over the desk in his Ronald Coleman disguise that I hated to wake him, but I hated even more to see him sleeping on company time.

'Rise and shine, soldier!'

'What?' He jerked up as though someone had shot a few hundred spare volts through him. 'What you say?'

'I said "Rise and shine".'

'Jest watch who you call a shine, lady.'

'Come on, handsome. I need some company.'

Lavender pawed at his eyes and gave a slow-motion yawn.

'How's business?' I asked.

'What business?' he blinked.

'That bad, huh?'

'Business as usual,' he said.

'Christ, not *that* bad?'

'Worse.'

'No telephone calls?'

'Just Conchita. Wanted to know did you want her to cook some dinner or were you gonna take her out to dinner.'

'In short, she wants to go out to dinner.'

'In short.'

'And that's it?'

'Well, the window washers were here. And the postman brought you something about the Women's Army Auxiliary Corps.'

'I'll join up, I think. At least you get to eat regularly, and who knows what kind of fun and games there are in the showers?'

'Maybe you'll find LaFlamme there.'

'Somehow she doesn't strike me as the type. And there's a good chance she's already headed for the tall timber.'

'Did Ma Waller tell you that?'

'No, but she suggested it might have looked advisable for her to get out of town – a *long* way out of town.'

'Anything else?'

'No, but we've got a new pseudonym to work with.'

'Tell me.'

'I don't know if you're old enough.'

'But I'm real mature for my age.' He pushed his chest out to prove it.

'Are you sure?'

'Sure, I is sure. Lay it on me.'

'Well, hold onto your hat, or your seat, or your pecker or something. Ready?'

'Roger!' he shouted.

'Blanche Framboise.'

'You shittin' me?'

'Nope. That's the name she used during her very brief visit at Ma Waller's.'

'Well, shut my mouth!' he said.

'Shut it yourself, or you'll start catching flies.'

'So now I've got to go back to all those agencies.' He was flying at half-mast again.

'Wrong,' I said. 'I've got a hunch they couldn't tell you any more about Blanche Framboise than they could tell you about Yvette LaFlamme or Framboise Flambé for that matter.'

'Framboise who?'

'Forget it. Take the afternoon off. If you fall asleep on me again I'll probably fire you.'

'You're in a bad mood?'

The guy was a real mind-reader.

'I'm on the rag – spiritually speaking. Somebody's playing me for a patsy, and I want to know why, and I don't know whether people want me to find the vanishing bust or don't want me to find it. So I think I'll just go into consultation with our Cuban friend and see if he doesn't have some ideas.'

'And I can really go *home*?' He was making saucer eyes at me.

50

'Yeah, you're free.'

'Oh, I thanks you, Mr Lincoln.'

'Don't thank me. Everything I am I owe to my dear old mother back in the log cabin. Now just waltz on out before I start feeling witchier.'

He waltzed out then, and as soon as the door closed I was sorry he was gone. But I didn't want him around, either. I didn't want to be here, for that matter, but I didn't want to go home. And I wanted to see Conchita, but I didn't want to be with her until I'd sorted things out a little. I had the feeling I was being set up for something, and that the something was even less pretty than the divorce numbers I'd been drawing. After discussing things with my rum and coke for about an hour I heard a knock at the door to the corridor. I buried the glass in a bottom drawer and went to open up. It was a boy from the Green-Feather Messenger Service, and he had an envelope for me. It was an ordinary, Woolworth's kind of envelope with no return address, but it was a lot heavier than a letter ought to have been. I gave the kid a nickel tip, enough to buy a Hershey Bar to feed his acne with, and took the envelope back to my desk. Then I got the glass out of the bottom drawer and topped it up and sat looking at the envelope for a while. It was too light for a bomb and too heavy for a fraternity pin, and it had a fat little bulge in the middle. Of course, it might have nothing at all to do with Yvette LaFlamme, but I had an uneasy feeling that the old patsy train was building up a good head of steam now.

I slit the envelope with a nail file. There was no letter inside – nothing but a wad of brown paper, and wrapped inside the paper were two keys. They were blunt, with square heads, and stamped into the heads were the numbers 76 and 77. Somewhere there were lockers with the numbers 76 and 77 painted on them, and somewhere there was someone who wanted me to take these keys and open the lockers and take a gander at what was inside. Whoever it was, he could have had the decency to tell me which lockers, and where. Even just a subtle tip-off to the city and state they were in would have narrowed things down a little.

The cuba libre and I talked it all over for a while and decided to concentrate on L.A., since we'd waste less gas that way. Union Station, Trailways, Greyhound and the Glendale Airport seemed the best batting order. It would beat warming a bench in the Cahuenga Building. I reached for the telephone and dialled the only number I ever seemed to remember right.

''allo,' the voice said.

'Hello, sweetie. How'd you like a night on the town?'

'A night where?'

'A night out. I've got a few errands to run, and I thought you could come too. Then we can get something to eat. Sound good?'

'*Sí.*'

'Well, don't fancy yourself up too much. We've got a bit of slumming to do first.'

'Slumming?'

'Never mind. I'll come by for you in about an hour, O.K.?'

'*Sí.* You make me happy.'

'Yeah, you make me happy, too.'

'I love you.'

'I love you too, *muchacha*. Now go make yourself beautiful – but not too beautiful.'

'*Sí.* I say bye-bye now.'

'Sure. Bye-bye.'

I pocketed the keys, tidied up the bills on the desk, and knocked back the last of the cuba libre. While I was locking the outside door, the peeper down the hall came staggering past with a few more yards of gauze wrapped around his head.

'Catch your head in the elevator doors again?' I asked, but I don't think he heard me. He was having more trouble with his gyroscope.

8

WE threw craps at Union Station. Locker 76 stood wide open, half broken off its hinges, and the key to 77 didn't fit. Conchita, at least, didn't mind. She seemed to think we were on some kind of treasure hunt and were going to find Coronado's cities of gold before the evening was over. I guess some of her excitement rubbed off on me, too. Even if there wasn't a pot of gold at the end of this particular little rainbow, at least I was earning the day's quarter-century. Twilight was coming on fast, and the city had a rosy blush on it, like a young girl. It made me think of the good old days, when there were still trees on Wilshire Boulevard and ice-cream sodas only cost a nickel.

I had to circle the block several times before we found a parking place near the Trailways Bus Station, and it didn't take long to tell we had wasted our time. There were sixty public lockers – four high and fifteen across and so battered up they looked like a relic from Pearl Harbor.

Third time lucky. We slid into a parking space directly across from the Greyhound Station, and I somehow knew we were on the right trail now. I jogged across the street, forgetting about Conchita until I heard the clatter of her high-heeled shoes on the pavement behind me. Her tight skirt did a lot for her, but only if she stood very, very still.

The bus station smelled of some unidentifiable fluid that might have started out as beer. A loudspeaker was announcing departures or delays or arrivals, but the information wasn't quite struggling through the static. A few soldiers and sailors were sacked out on wooden benches, others were nudging pinball machines and encouraging them with authentic Arkansas hog-calls. Nearby, an old man was watching them and playing his own game of pocket pool.

A bank of lockers ran the length of one wall, and a dozen

more stood beside the ticket window. 76 and 77 were in the longer row, in a corner where the light was thin and the cigarette butts thick. Conchita caught up with me, conquering both the Army and the Navy en route. I took a key out of my pocket, checked the number, and pushed it into the lock. Number 76 slid in with an easy, down-home feeling. There was only one thing wrong. It was a little too easy. I pulled the key out and then tried the other one. It was like slicing butter with a hot knife.

Conchita was beginning to pant a little with excitement. 'We open them now, *sí?*' she asked.

'We open them now, no,' I answered.

'But we find maybe much money inside.'

'More likely, we find much trouble inside. Therefore, we proceed with caution.'

'Now I no have any fun,' she pouted.

'Later we'll have fun. O.K.?'

'When you promise me.'

'I promise you.'

We were beginning to attract more of a crowd than I liked, and I hustled Conchita out of the waiting room. That is, I moved her along as fast as she could hobble with her knees practically tied together. We got enough whistles on the way to convince me the new act was a hit.

Conchita stood outside the telephone booth on the corner while I bought a nickel's worth of insurance. It must have been my lucky day, because O'Brien was on the night-shift, and he answered the phone himself. He made a few routine passes, and when I told him I wanted to meet him he suggested coming by my place when he got off duty.

'Not this time, O'Brien. This is strictly business.'

'Your business or mine?'

'So far, it's mine, but it may be yours, too. This afternoon I got a little gift from an anonymous admirer – a pair of keys, and I've just found they fit a couple of lockers at the Greyhound Bus Station. It's not my birthday, and it's six months until Christmas, and I've got a hunch I won't like what's in those lockers one damned bit.'

'Tell you what, gorgeous. You open up, have a look, and ring me back.'

'O'Brien, are you still employed by the Los Angeles Metropolitan Police?'

'I am.'

'Criminal Division?'

'Right-o.'

'Then shag your ass down here. I have reason to believe that whatever is in those lockers has something to do with a criminal offense, or an intended offense, and as a taxpaying citizen I want one of the boys-in-blue around.'

'Why me?'

'Because of your goddamned beautiful Irish face.'

'You convinced me.'

'Thanks, Prince Valiant. I'll be waiting in my car across from the bus terminal.'

Ten minutes later a black sedan skidded to a stop across the street and parked beside a fireplug directly in front of the station. O'Brien got out and came loping across the street. A skinny blonde kid who hardly looked old enough to be out of rompers, but who was wearing the official blue, also got out of the car, but then just stood by it doing guard duty.

O'Brien planted a size-twelve shoe on my running-board, leaned against the door of the convertible and gave me his best come-hither look. He's got the kind of leading-man good looks about him that would be much too pretty for a cop if his head didn't ride around on a line-backer's body.

He gave me that blarney smile of his and said, 'Marry me.'

'No thanks. I've been there before, and I didn't like the climate.'

'Then let's run away together,' he suggested.

'I want to, O'Brien, but I decided to give it up for Lent.'

'Well, you can't blame a guy for trying.'

'Don't be so sure, handsome.'

He'd given it up as a lost cause a long while ago, but probably thought he'd hurt my female vanity if he didn't renew his offer.

'Besides,' I said, 'we're both on duty tonight.'

He greeted Conchita with a faint leer, and asked me to run through the story again. I ran through it, omitting a few trivial details like Ann Shoemaker, Brand Brockaway and Ma Waller, and reducing it to 'I've got a missing persons case, maybe a little blackmail thrown in, just for laughs, and I've got a hunch these keys have something to do with it.'

'And did you phone the Green Feather folks to see if they could identify the sender?'

'No,' I said.

'Pretty sloppy detective work, don't you think?' He said it in a way that suggested I should be at home diapering babies.

'Not especially. If I'd phoned them, they'd have told me the envelope was sent by a middle-aged man or woman, average height, medium coloring, who paid in cash, and that I should feel free to call on them again whenever I needed assistance.'

'Do you call that female intuition?' he wise-assed.

'No, I call it good deductive reasoning. Whoever sent me those keys wanted to be anonymous. He printed my name on the envelope and put no message inside. That means he was pretty sure of not being recognized or remembered in any particular way by the Green Feather lads.'

'You could be right.'

'I am right.' Over-confidence is always my long suit.

'Maybe,' he conceded. 'But you'd be surprised how often people get recognized without knowing it. And if your friend really wanted to be anonymous, why send you the keys through a messenger service?'

'Because, my dear O'Watson, the rental period on those lockers is going to run out soon, which means somebody at the station is going to open them and hold whatever's inside until the overdue fee is paid.'

'You've got it pegged, haven't you?'

'I've got some of it pegged, and I'm trying not to be

pegged myself.'

'So you want an official witness.'

'Ah, dawn breaks over Marblehead! You may be slow, O'Brien, but you're sure.'

He didn't like it. His male vanity was as wide as his shoulders, and from the look of his shoulders you'd think he was wearing football pads under his inconspicuous regulation plainclothesman's suit with the bulging shoulder holster.

'O.K.,' he said. 'O.K., let's get this over with.'

'Ditto!'

He swung the car door open for me. Conchita started to get out too, but I held her back. 'Wait here, baby,' I said.

'I no come too?'

'You no come too. Wait here for me and be sure no one steals the tires.'

She slumped down in the seat and began to sulk.

'Look, I'd feel better if you were out of this. You'll just have to trust me. I won't be long, and afterwards we'll go to Santa Monica or Glendale, one of those roadhouses you like so well. O.K.?'

'Sí,' she said, but in a way that let me know the bottom had just dropped out of my popularity rating.

The rookie was still standing by the inconspicuous black car that matched O'Brien's inconspicuous black suit. We picked him up along the way. 'That's Harrison,' O'Brien said. From close up Harrison looked even more like a kid dressed up in his father's clothes, but the boy was certainly growing up. There was already a shadow on his lip, and in a few years he was going to have to start shaving.

The crowd inside the station shaped up pretty fast when we went in, and got very busy pretending not to notice us.

'O.K.,' O'Brien said, 'which lockers do we open up?'

'76 and 77. Be my guest.' I handed him the keys, and he passed one to Harrison. It was turning out to be the kind of game the whole family can play.

They had a nice sense of rhythm, those boys, or maybe just a good choreographer. In with the keys: click. Swing open the doors, reach in and pull. Each of them dragged out a large brown suitcase, made in the style of a trunk with brass corners and plastered over with phoney labels advertising non-existent Florida hotels, Colorado ski resorts, Hawaiian pleasure gardens. Something about the way they had to heave to get them out rather spoiled the routine, though. They set the suitcases on the floor and then looked at me as though I was supposed to give them delivery instructions or something.

'Let's get on with it,' I suggested.

The suitcases weren't locked. O'Brien and Harrison clicked them open, swung back the lids, and put me out of business. Of course, I couldn't be sure that if we reassembled all the bits and pieces we'd have Yvette LaFlamme, but it sure as hell wouldn't be Eleanor Roosevelt.

O'Brien had that bewildered look on his face they must have had at Proctor and Gamble the day the bar of Ivory Soap sank. Harrison turned away and heaved his cookies into the corner. Me? I tried to pretend it was just another clearance sale at the friendly neighborhood butcher's.

9

CONCHITA had to settle for scrambled eggs at home. Somehow, the thought of a juicy T-bone didn't appeal to me that night. I thought I'd stick around the house the next morning and do what I could to end the Mexican-American War, especially since I seemed to have lost my only case, but the telephone started having different ideas a few minutes after eight. It was O'Brien.

'Christ, are you still on the job, O'Brien? You working for a martyr's badge or something?'

'I'm double-shifting until we get a few more details nailed down, that's all.'

'Want to borrow my hammer?'

'No, I just wanted to tell you that people sometimes do remember middle-aged men.'

'You mean the Green Feather Messenger Service gets another feather in its cap?' So much for female intuition.

'Not exactly. All they could tell us was that a man came in yesterday afternoon and gave them an envelope to deliver to you. He was middle-aged, average height, and with no distinguishing features.'

'Chalk one up for me.'

'I did. But someone at Union Station recognized him.'

'At Union Station?'

'Yeah. Seems he put one of your keys into the lock and it got stuck. He panicked a bit and was about to take a crowbar to the lockers when the station manager came by and helped him get the key out. The manager recognized him as Holmes Woolcott's chauffeur.'

'Holmes Woolcott?' I gave him my best whistle. 'Then we're in the chips, right?'

'Woolcott's clean, I think, but Archie Potter looks like he's in it up to his eye teeth.'

I was awake enough now to wonder why the police force was giving away information. Maybe O'Brien was going to touch me for two tickets to the policeman's ball.

'That's your worry,' I informed him. 'My worry is whether or not I'm out of a job.'

'Not exactly.'

'What do you mean, not exactly? Is the lady who went to pieces the same lady I was looking for?'

'More or less,' he allowed.

'You mean you've lost some of the pieces?'

'No, she's all there, and her last a.k.a. was Yvette LaFlamme. Answer your question?'

'Righto. It also means I'm busted to the ranks of the unemployed again.'

'Not yet. We'd like you to keep the information to yourself for a while.'

'You mean you want me to cheat on a client? Private detectives, in case you've forgotten, get their licenses revoked in this town for a hell of a lot less than that.'

'Let's say the police would be grateful if you'd play for time. Just for a couple of days.'

A couple of days sounded like fifty bucks for the kitty, but it also made the whole case smell more and more like overripe cheese.

'O.K., O'Brien, on one condition.'

'What's that?' he asked.

'I want to be there when you interrogate this Archie Potter.'

'That's police business.'

'Exactly. And you're asking me to cooperate in police business. I, in turn, demand the right to protect myself and my client.'

'You'll keep your mouth shut?'

'I'll do my famous fresh-water clam imitation.'

'Then be here by nine o'clock,' he said.

'You're on!'

I dropped the receiver back onto the hook and reached over to touch Conchita's shoulder. She was half-awake and curled up in a no-touch position. I wanted to stay and smoke the peace-pipe, but it was clearly going to take more time than I had now.

'I've got to go, sweetie.'

Conchita shrugged my hand away.

'I'm sorry, but this case looks screwier all the time. This could be my big break. I'll go out there a nobody and come back a star! Somehow, Holmes Woolcott is mixed up in all this.'

That got a little stir out of her. Woolcott was California's richest industrialist, and the most reclusive. Conchita could recite all the facts about his marriages and his divorce settlements and his inventions and his corporate takeovers. So could most of America. But even that wasn't enough to thaw her out completely. She was still turned away from me, and as far as she could get without falling off the bed. At least she hadn't turned on the electric fence.

'If I want to find out any more,' I said, 'I've got to get

down to police headquarters, and I've got less than an hour to do it.'

My timetable didn't interest her much. Or maybe it did, because by the time I'd showered and dressed she had padded out to the kitchen, and there was fresh coffee making bubbles in the percolator. I just had time to cauterize my throat with a fast cup before I left. 'Give Lavender a call, honey, and tell him I'll be late. And I'll call you as soon as I get to the office. O.K.?'

'*Sí.*'

'And I love you, baby. You know that, don't you?'

'*Sí.*'

The kid showed real promise as a conversationalist.

10

THE interrogation room smelled vaguely like an abandoned chicken-run. O'Brien had parked me in a corner, well out of the circle formed by the thousand-watt bulb that was supposed to soften up the customers. Two uniformed men brought Potter in. He was middle-aged, alright, but definitely the far side of middle-aged. And he was of medium height, with stooped shoulders and a kind of duck-waddle when he walked. His face was round and beery, and he kept darting glances around the room as though he had misplaced something but couldn't quite remember what.

O'Brien soft-pedalled it all, whether for my benefit or not I couldn't tell. Any self-respecting sadist would have asked for his money back. O'Brien read the statement Potter had made early that morning. It gave his name as Archibald Theodore Potter. Age: 59. Height: 5' 8". Color of hair: brown. Color of eyes: brown. Address: 16 Styles Avenue, Los Angeles. Occupation: chauffeur. Employer: Holmes Woolcott. He had been with Woolcott for over ten years, he had no police record and no highschool diploma and no outstanding traffic tickets. He was a widower with one daughter, age 22, whereabouts unknown. It didn't exactly seem like the profile of a master criminal.

Whatever Potter was guilty of, it wasn't the murder of Yvette LaFlamme. After all, it wasn't in the Greyhound Bus Station that he did the two-step with the lockers, but at the train station. Still, it was obviously Potter who had sent me the keys, and that would make him an accessory of some kind.

O'Brien finished reading the statement Potter had signed earlier that morning. 'Now,' he said, 'let's run through this one more time, Archie. Why did you send those locker keys to Lamaar Ransom.'

Potter mumbled down at his knees, 'Because she's a private detective.'

'There's a lot of other private detectives in this town. Why send them to her?'

'I just saw her name in the telephone book,' he said.

'Why send them to anyone?'

'I just didn't like it. I just didn't like the whole thing because it looked like somebody was tryin' to make me like a fall-guy. I just didn't like it,' he mumbled. That made two of us.

'Was Miss Ransom employed by you?'

There was a long pause before Potter mumbled 'No.'

'Did you arrange for her to get a retainer of some kind?'

'A what?'

'Did you pay her, give her money or a check, to make this little investigation for you?'

'No, but I was gonna send her a money order or somethin'.'

I hoped like hell the stenotype girl had gotten that down. O'Brien should have asked him how much, though.

'Did you send a letter of any kind, indicating the kind of investigation you wanted, or where you could be reached once Miss Ransom had any information for you?'

'No.'

'So, you stick to your story then? If I understand it right, someone you won't name gave you two locker keys to pick something up at an unspecified location. You went to the wrong place, discovered the keys wouldn't fit, and decided you needed professional help. Is that right?'

'That's right.' Potter looked a little relieved, like a backward third-grader who's just discovered that two and two really do make four.

'So you went to the Green Feather Messenger Service and asked them to deliver the keys to Lamaar Ransom, a private investigator.'

'Yeah.'

'Who recommended Lamaar Ransom to you?'

'Nobody. I found her in the telephone book.'

Praise be to California Bell. I made a note to remember to pay the phone bill this month.

'Who gave you those keys?' O'Brien asked.

'I don't remember.' Potter was beginning to turn gray around the gills, and to suck in air in little adenoidal gulps.

'Was it Holmes Woolcott?'

'No, it wasn't. It wasn't him.'

'We can call him, you know, to confirm your statement.'

'No! Don't call him. It wasn't him. Don't call him. I'll lose my job and everything. It wasn't him,' he whined.

'Then who was it?'

'It wasn't him.' Potter was beginning to sound like a broken phonograph record.

'Woolcott will have to know. He'll have to know that you're being held on suspicion.'

'Suspicion? Suspicion of what?'

'For the moment, let's say you're being held on suspicion of being an accessory after the fact. That's enough for now. We can decide later whether to book you for first-degree murder or not.'

'I didn't kill nobody!' Potter was snuffling now, and his whole head was glazed with sweat. He looked more and more like a damp toad all the time.

'What was your connection to Yvette LaFlamme?'

'Yvette who?' He looked genuinely surprised, as though O'Brien had asked him what kind of mouthwash he used.

63

'Yvette LaFlamme. Or maybe you knew her as Blanche Framboise or Roz Landru or Marie Winslow.' LaFlamme sure got around. She was beginning to read like a page out of *The Hooker's Who's Who*.

'I don't know none of them women. I don't see any women. My wife is dead and my daughter is gone away and all I do is drive a car. I don't have nothin' to do with women. I just drive a car for Mr Woolcott and I ain't never had an accident and I ain't never had no trouble with the police.'

'Why don't you make it easy on yourself, Archie? We don't want to keep you down here, and we sure don't want to cost you your job. But somebody chopped a woman up into a few dozen pieces and put her into two suitcases and checked them at the Greyhound Bus Station. The next thing we know, you show up with the keys. What are we supposed to believe?'

'I ain't been near the Greyhound Bus Station.'

'But you've been near Union Station, and you had the keys with you then, and you sent those same keys to a private investigator named Lamaar Ransom. Why, Archie? Why?'

Archie shifted himself from one haunch to the other and blinked away the sweat that was running into his eyes. 'I was scared.'

'Scared of what?'

'I don't know.'

'Scared of the person who had given you the keys?'

'No,' he mumbled, but it didn't carry much conviction to my corner of the room.

'Scared of what, then? Scared of what would be there if you did find the right lockers?'

'I don't know. I just got scared. I thought maybe it was some kinda frame-up.'

'Who would want to frame you, Archie?'

'Nobody, I guess.'

'But maybe someone wanted to frame Holmes Woolcott. Did you think that?'

64

'I dunno.'

'Were you trying to protect him? Were you?'

Archie didn't answer this time, just snuffed up a little more air and sat there shaking his head.

'Listen, Archie, if you acted out of loyalty to your employer, then he ought to have a chance to help you. It *was* Holmes Woolcott you were trying to protect, wasn't it?'

'No!'

O'Brien lit a cigarette, took a couple of slow turns around the room, and came back to sit on the table beside Archie Potter. He put on his best big-brother manner now. 'Listen, Archie, this isn't my decision, but if you don't level with me, I'm going to book you as an accessory to murder. I don't want to do it. I don't know you, but you strike me as an honest, hard-working man who made an honest mistake. I don't want to cause you trouble, and I don't want you to lose your job, but I work for people, too, and if I don't book you after this then I'll lose my job. And somebody else will book you. How's about it?' Then, from across the room, I could practically see the little flicker of imagination penetrate his thick Irish skull. 'Archie, don't just think about yourself. Think about your daughter. Think how she'll feel when she reads this in the papers.'

Potter fell apart at the seams then. His head collapsed onto his chest and he began to wail like some huge, heavy animal in pain. The sound bounced around the concrete walls for a long while, and it stopped only when O'Brien reached forward and put his hand on Potter's shoulder.

'Who gave you those keys, Archie?'

Potter was sobbing too hard for his answer to be audible at first. Then I could just make out the name: 'Alex,' he said.

'Alex?' O'Brien asked. 'Alex who?'

'Alex Woods. Alexander Woods. Mr Holmes's secretary.'

'And where did he get them?'

'They came ... They came in ... They came in the mail,' he snuffled.

'Did Alex tell you that?'

'I seen 'em. I brought up the mail, and I seen 'em.'

'When was that?'

'Yesterday,' he sobbed. 'Yesterday. It was yesterday morning. I brought up the mail and they was in the mail. Alex ... he opened 'em.'

'And what did Alex do?'

'He asked me to find out what lockers they belonged to.'

'Why didn't he find out for himself?'

'He couldn't drive, and Mr Woolcott is out of town until tonight and he has to stay there to answer the phone.'

'So he asked you to find out where the lockers were?'

'Yeah,' Potter said.

'Did he tell you to open the lockers and bring him what you found there?'

'Yeah.'

'Then why didn't you?'

'I don't know. I got scared. And that's when I sent the keys to that detective woman.'

'Why send them to that particular detective woman?'

'Because ... because ... because Alex said if anything went wrong I wasn't supposed to call the police. He said if anything went wrong to go see like this detective woman.'

'Why didn't you?'

'Because I was *scared*! I didn't want to get mixed up in no trouble.'

'And did you tell Alex what you had done?'

'No, I didn't tell him nothin'.'

'Why not?'

''Cause when I got back he wasn't there.'

'Where is he?'

'I don't know.'

'You mean Alex Woods gave you those keys, sent you off to find out what was in the lockers, and then went away himself?'

'I guess so.'

'Doesn't that seem strange to you? Especially when he was Mr Woolcott's private secretary and had to be on duty that day?'

'Yeah, it's all strange,' he agreed. 'But I didn't do nothin'. I just took them keys and got one stuck, and this guy knew who I was, and I got scared.'

'Why would Alex Woods send you off that way? Why didn't he wait until Mr Woolcott came back? Or telephone him to ask what he should do?'

'I don't know. I don't know nothin'.'

O'Brien gave Archie the benefit of his Irish grin. 'But you knew more than you were telling, didn't you?'

'Yeah, I guess.'

'O.K., Archie, one more question and then I'll let you go. How did Alex seem to you when he gave you the keys? Was he angry or nervous or excited? Did he seem frightened?'

'Maybe a little nervous.'

'Do you know why?'

'No, he just seemed kinda nervous.'

'Can you guess why?'

'I don't know,' Potter answered. 'Maybe he was trying to save Mr Woolcott some trouble. He's always doin' somethin' to save the boss trouble.'

Me, I didn't like the way he said 'boss'. It was like he was spitting out a poison mushroom he'd found roaming around in a bowl of fruit salad.

'O.K., Archie, I'm going to let you go now – on your own recognizance. Do you know what that means?'

'What?'

'It means I trust you, Archie, even though you lied to me. It means I trust you not to leave town and not to talk to anyone about what's happened. Am I right? Can I trust you?'

'Yeah, sure. I didn't *do* nothin'.'

'Maybe not. But you're our only witness so far, so take care of yourself. And if you think of anything you forgot to tell me, or if you see anything or hear anything that might help me solve this case, give me a call.'

Potter's face began to turn the color of old putty when O'Brien told him to take care of himself. Obviously he was thinking about those suitcases. So was I, and neither one of us wanted the next set of keys to have our numbers on them.

11

ON his way out, O'Brien highsigned me to stay put. I wondered if he was planning an encore – not that what he'd just accomplished was Academy Award material, but it wasn't bad for routine police work. There was only one problem. I still didn't know where that left me, taking twenty-five bucks a day to find a broad who'd already been sent to the hamburger factory.

'Thanks for the performance,' I said when O'Brien came back.

'Always happy to oblige a lady.' He rolled his eyes enough to show their bloodshot suburbs.

'Let's cut the malarkey, O'Brien. I want to know what this is all about.'

'It's all about murder.'

'Sure it is. That's what worries me.'

'No need to worry. I'd like you to keep the whole thing under your hat for a while, that's all.'

'I don't wear hats, O'Brien, and I happen not to be on the payroll of the Metropolitan Police.'

'Do you want to be?' he asked.

For a minute I wondered if it was an offer, but I didn't think they were in the market for square pegs these days. 'Hell, no,' I said. 'I don't want to have to jump every time somebody with a couple of stripes happens to let a fart.'

'If you'd clean up your language, Lamaar, I could take you home to mother.'

'I don't go for older women, O'Brien. Even you should know that. And I don't particularly go for cheating on a client, even when I don't happen to like the client very much. So level me.'

He was beginning to sag a bit after his night on the town, and he eased himself into a chair with that little-boy awkwardness big men often have. He looked down to check what was left of the creases in his undertaker's trousers. There wasn't much. 'We think,' he began, 'we think we've got a chance of cracking this one pretty fast, if we've got a few days to play with. At this point, the more people who know about the murder, the less time we've got.'

'And what do I do when my client starts to put the heat on?'

'Say you think you're onto a good lead,' he suggested.

'Maybe I should say Yvette's just gone off someplace to try to pull herself together.'

He groaned a little and massaged his face with one of his huge, freckled paws. Then he said, 'I think you can do better than that. Just get on with the case as though you didn't know anything about what happened last night.'

'Give me one good reason.'

'Alright. I've done you a few favors, yes? And in your business it helps to have a sweet, lovable cop like me on your side, right?'

'Occasionally. V-e-r-y occasionally, O'Brien. Every now and then, about once every leap year, you let me wrestle a piece of information out of you five minutes before you announce it to the press. That's what I want right now. Information.'

'I can't give it to you,' he admitted, giving his head a bulldog shake.

'You're protecting somebody, then. Somebody upstairs has put the old thumb screws to you boys. Who is it? Holmes Woolcott?'

He didn't say anything, but he shifted on his chair like he badly needed to take a pee.

'Well,' I said, 'is it Mr Aviation or isn't it?'

'No,' he said finally. 'It isn't Woolcott.' Then he amended it a little. 'It isn't anybody. Let's just say that in the interests of justice – '

'Wait a minute, buster. Save those lines for the

newspaper boys, O.K.? My client wouldn't be interested in paying me to find somebody who isn't lost anymore.'

'She can afford it.' He knew he shouldn't have said it, but by the time the message got to his tongue it was too late for an interception play.

'Well, well, well. And how do we know it's a she?'

He turned the color of a travel-poster sunset. 'We know a lot of things,' he muttered.

'And you're not telling much, right? O.K., so I proceed with the investigation then. For how long?'

'For a few days,' he hedged.

'How many days am I supposed to stay dummied up.'

'Until I let you know. Two or three. Maybe more. A week at the most.'

'Alright, O'Brien, I'll play tiddly winks with you, but I'm not going to get played for a sucker. I'll investigate this case, and I'll see to it that my client gets value for money. I'm going to leave no stone unturned, as they say in the comic books, and if something slimy comes crawling out from under, that's alright too. But I'm not going to protect you or any of the other boys in blue. And I won't protect fat cats like Holmes Woolcott. Savvy?'

'You do your job,' he sighed. 'I'll do mine.'

'Swell, but do me one favor.'

'What is it?'

'If you find me in a couple of suitcases, do what you can to take care of Conchita.' I didn't like the neon lights that turned on in his eyes then. 'On second thoughts, do me a favor and don't take care of her. O.K.?'

'O.K.'

He made it sound as though we'd made our way through the agenda then, and the meeting was about to adjourn. When he stood up he seemed to be reminding me that he was one very tired guy, and I was all that stood between him and forty winks. Well, he'd have to get by with thirty-nine. I let him pilot me to the door as though I was going to toddle off like a good girl and put up a few more quarts of strawberry jam or knit another square for the afghan.

When I asked him the question it caught him off stroke. In fact, he damned near capsized the whole rowboat.

'Tell me what you know about a Hollywood creep named Brand Brockaway.'

He reassembled his face and said, 'Who?' But it didn't convince either one of us, and he knew it.

'You don't have to give me his life history. Boil it down to the important things.'

'He's just another two-bit actor,' O'Brien said. That didn't tell me anything I couldn't figure out for myself, but what came next made me feel a lot better about the knee I'd planted in Brockaway's crotch. 'He was picked up a few years back in San Francisco and charged with roughing up a prostitute.'

'How badly was she roughed up?'

'She never regained consciousness.'

'And Brockaway?'

'The D.A. didn't have enough for a conviction. But don't jump to any conclusions. He'd been seen with her the night she was beaten, that's all. And they'd had a bit of a rumpus. There was no evidence that it amounted to anything more.'

'The guy's puss is all I'd need as evidence – that and his reptillian manner.'

'The courts couldn't do much with that kind of evidence.'

'But I could, baby. In fact, I did. And how does Mr B. make his do-re-mi?'

'He used to get occasional bit parts in pictures, walk-on stuff. Now he works mainly for a place called the Fairfield Academy.' I didn't give him so much as a raised eyebrow on that one. 'And he still does a little, well, film work. Lately he's been working for the porno trade, mostly.'

'So even eroticism has fallen on hard times.'

'It's the draft, you know.'

'Yeah, sure. It's even hard to get a loaf of bread these days. But it's never hard to find a heel like Brockaway. Thanks for the tip, *amigo*.'

'It's not a tip. We can check Brockaway out for

ourselves,' he said.

'You do that. And ask him about the stainless-steel truss he's wearing.'

'The what?' O'Brien asked. He was cute when he didn't understand something. Little gullies came between his eyebrows that looked like an advertisement for soil conservation.

'So long, handsome. Don't take any wooden shamrocks.'

12

THE air in the bull-pen must have been even more fetid than I thought, because the exhaust fumes outside smelled pretty sweet by comparison. As I drove I sorted things through a bit and however I sorted them, Brockaway and the Fairfield Academy and Holmes Woolcott seemed to come out on top. Well, there wasn't much I could do about Woolcott. It would take something longer than a putting iron to touch him with, but it shouldn't be hard to find out something about old fish-eyes, and I thought I knew just the way to get the low-down on the Academy, if Conchita was willing.

Given the break-down in diplomatic relations, though, it would take some *cojones* to ask her, so I decided to stop and buy some at a joint called Victor's. They were just opening up for the lunch-time crowd, and I had the place to myself. It had that cool, clean look I like. The bar was polished to a high gloss and the glasses were lined up waiting, like soldiers on parade, and you didn't have to chisel a hole in the cigarette smoke to breathe. The regular bar-tender wasn't on duty yet, but a neanderthal with a smashed-in boxer's pug asked me what I wanted. The Chamber of Commerce probably didn't list him as a tourist attraction.

'Give me a cuba libre,' I said.

'Give ya what?'

'I'll have a cuba libre.'

'We got scotch, we got bourbon, we got gin or vodka.'

'Got any rum?'

'I guess so,' he grumbled. 'Ya want some rum?'

'I want a cuba libre. In case you've lost the recipe, here's how it goes. You put a couple of fingers of rum in a glass, then some ice, some coke, and a twist of lemon. If you don't have the lemon, forget it. If you don't have the ice, just give me a rum and coke. If you don't have the coke, give me two fingers of rum, preferably in a clean glass. If you don't have the rum, shag your ass out and get some. And while you're out, pick up some ice, a lemon, and some cokes.'

His face gave a twitch or two that could have meant something was happening inside his noodle. Finally he said, 'You want a rum and coke?'

'My, how nice of you to offer. Yes, please, and with a twist of lemon.'

'We ain't got no lemons yet.'

'Then let me have a rum and coke, O.K.?'

While he tried to read the labels, I took a gander at an *L.A. Chronicle* someone had left on the counter. If Walt Disney was looking for new plots, he wasn't going to find them there. An old lady had died in Seattle and the neighbors had found her six weeks later. Probably just sort of nosed her out. Another kid had drowned off the beach at LaJolla while his mother brushed up her suntan. The D.A. in Marin County was going to prove 'beyond the shadow of a doubt' that Dickerson and Halberman were guilty of industrial espionage, and he was demanding the death penalty. He was heaving around a lot of rhetoric about the Nazi menace, and I wondered if he wore a red-white-and-blue necktie in court.

The gorilla brought me a rum and coke, managing to slop only a couple of tablespoons onto the newspaper. The drink felt good going down, and for a little while I could forget the screwy job I had to do. Forget and cheer myself up with the mounting casualties in the Pacific, the stockmarket quotations, and tips on twelve ways to change the look of your basic black dress. Maybe I'd clip that one out for Lavender. There was a long report that didn't make sense, on the collapse of the office building in Santa Monica. It had something or other to do with metal fatigue, with the steel girders getting hardening of the arteries. But it was a new building. Nobody had even moved in yet. Maybe they were using old steel, though, that they hadn't wanted to bend into aircraft carriers.

I had another rum and coke before I left, and I guess it did the trick, because I was able to persuade Conchita. In fact, it didn't take much persuading. Maybe the kid's got show-business in her blood. She called the Academy and the secretary gave her an appointment for that afternoon at four o'clock. She also found out that the deposit on tuition, if she was accepted, would be $200. Then I telephoned Ann Shoemaker and told her I was making real progress and expected to have a full report for her within a week. I also said I needed $300 for some unexpected expenses, though, and she agreed to send it by messenger. So now O'Brien had me taking money under false pretenses. Maybe that's show business, too.

By the time I got to the office, Lavender was looking a little stir-crazy. Either his sex life had to improve or business had to pick up. Otherwise, a few nuts and bolts were going to start coming loose.

I pulled a chair up and sat down facing him. 'How's life, black beauty?'

'Zilch,' he said, and held up a thumb and forefinger crooked into a circle.

'How's your soldier boy?'

'Still on guard duty.' I was afraid he was going to start crying all over the new desk blotter.

'Cheer up, I've got some very sexy business for you.'

'I ain't goin' on no motel patrol,' he sulked.

'You don't have to. What do you know about porno films?'

He perked up and then did his best to look outraged. 'Do you mean blue movies?' He managed to sound like a Salvation Army matron who's just been propositioned over

74

her tambourine. 'I don't know *nothin'* 'bout blue movies, Miss Scarlett.'

'Well, I want you to find out. Within the next few minutes a messenger is going to deliver an envelope with $300 in it.'

He whistled appreciatively.

'I want you to take $100 and rent us the hottest stuff you can find, and the most recent. Tomorrow night I'll take you to the movies. I'll even spring for the popcorn.'

'You are not, by any chance, contemplating an orgy, are you?'

'No, just a little routine detective work. Now I'm going to put my feet up and rest my brains for a while. Buzz me if J. Paul Getty comes in to get out of the rain.'

'We ain't got a buzzer,' he reminded me.

'It's not raining, either.'

The look he was giving me as I started to close the door let me know he was at least off the critical list for a while.

'There's an invitation for you. It's on your desk,' he called after me. Sure enough, it was, lying there like a pretty little rectangle of freshly fallen snow. Obviously my reputation as a connoisseur was spreading. It was an invitation to a show of paintings by Alexander Woods, at a place called the Tower Gallery in Beverly Hills.

13

I PACKED Conchita into a taxi at nine o'clock the next morning. She was so excited anybody would have thought DeMille had sent his private limousine purring up to collect her.

'Listen,' I said. 'This isn't a picnic, it's an assignment. I want to know everything that goes on at the Academy. I want to know who works there and who studies there. I want names, ages, descriptions. And I want you out of there like greased lightning if anybody starts trying to find out too much about you. O.K.?'

'*Sí*,' she said, but the old milky way was still lit up in her eyes.

'And I want to hear from you at least twice a day – morning and night,' I insisted.

'*Sí*, I call you.'

'But only when you're sure no one can overhear you, alright?'

'*Sí*.'

'Take care of yourself, sweetheart. *Hasta la vista*.'

'*Hasta la vista*,' she answered, and as the cab pulled away from the curb I had the feeling she hadn't listened to a single word I'd said.

I went back inside and called the office, but there was no answer. Thirty minutes and two cups of coffee later, I tried again, and a velvety voice told me, 'This is Lamaar Ransom's office. Mr Trevelyan speaking. May I help you?'

'Yes, you can. I've just lost my virginity. Can you help me find it?'

'Did you look under the bed?' he asked.

'No, I'm afraid I might find a *man* under there.'

'I'll be right over, m'am.'

'No, stay where you are. I'll come to you. But I'll be a little late. I'm going to stop by a place in Beverly Hills called the Tower Art Gallery.'

'You want to buy a picture?'

'No, I just want to *get* the picture. And maybe my cultural horizons could use some broadening. Speaking of which, what luck did you have with the films?'

'I rented three. One of them's called *Forbidden Fruit*.'

'Does it star Carmen Miranda?'

'No, J. Edgar Hoover, I think.'

'The idea doesn't do much for me,' I confessed.

'It doesn't even do much for *me*.'

'O.K., I'll see you about noon. Try to hold off the Apaches until I get there with the cavalry.'

What was the arty set wearing these days, I wondered? The types that talked about brushwork and color harmonies and transcendental values? I didn't know, so I settled for standard-issue gaberdine slacks and a plain camel-colored shirt, but I left a few extra buttons open just to confuse the opposition.

Probably the owner hadn't lost too many nights' sleep trying to decide what to call his gallery. It was in a stone tower that might have been salvaged from an old Errol Flynn movie. It even had a moat around it, with a few albino goldfish making ripples in the water. At first I thought I was too late, because it sounded as though a demolition crew was going to work on the inside. But it was only Sebastian Trope making with a little creativity.

'Sebastian Trope!' he shouted when I put my head in the door. 'Sebastian Trope!' he repeated, and I thought it was probably Lithuanian for 'the ceiling is caving in'. He was a little man, just too tall to be officially classified as a dwarf, and he was wearing a dirty smock with a silk foulard scarf tied round his neck. He had a beret on his head, and his feet peeked out of a pair of sandals that once, a long while ago, had seen better days. 'Sebastian Trope!' he shouted again, and thrust first his bushy eyebrows, then his hand up at me. It was the first clue I had that Sebastian Trope was his name.

'Hello. I'm Lamaar Ransom.'

'Wonderful, wonderful!' he bubbled. Stanley couldn't have been any more enthused when Livingston popped out from behind a rubber tree. 'This is wonderful!' he said. 'Lamaar Ransom. Wonderful, wonderful. You have come to see the exhibition?'

'I think you're showing some pictures by an acquaintance of mine. Alex Woods.'

'Alex Woods? Alexander Woods? A wonderful painter. A genius. He has vision. His palette is superb, superb. Let me finish my piece, and then I will show you Alex's wonderful pictures. You must, however, stand back, just there. This will only take a minute. Wonderful, wonderful.'

He parked me in a corner and finished loading up a wheel-barrow with Salvation Army crockery, glasses, old tin cans and milk bottles. A walled ramp curled around the inside of the tower, ending near a skylight at the top. Pictures were hung along the ramp, but only the tops of them peeked down at me. Sebastian Trope began to hustle the wheelbarrow up the ramp, panting, whistling, and every now and then shouting 'Wonderful, wonderful!' Halfway up he looked down at me. He was just tall enough to get his head over the ramp. 'Stand back now,' he shouted. 'You are most fortunate to be here for this wonderful moment. I shall *create*!'

And I shall probably throw up, I thought.

Trope rattled and banged his way up the ramp, and then there was a moment of sweet quiet, the kind that's supposed to come at the eye of the hurricane. Suddenly it all came raining down onto the floor of the tower – bottles and glasses, dimestore silverware and scrap iron. Through the din I could hear a tiny voice shouting 'Wonderful, wonderful!' Not wanting to seem too gauche, I shouted too. 'Wonderful! Bravo!'

A few minutes later, Sebastian Trope came trundling his wheelbarrow down the ramp. His bushy brows were dancing with excitement, and his breathing was a little like a bull-moose in heat. 'How was it?' he asked.

'In a word, it was wonderful,' I said.

He liked that a lot. In fact, he lit up like a synagogue on Friday night.

'So few people understand,' he groaned.

'How true, how true.'

'The act of creation,' he said, 'is always an act of destruction as well. We destroy to create, to make new.' He was really warming up now. 'Michelangelo, to make his David, had first to destroy a block of snowiest marble, to hammer it away. The old masters who ground their colors, they too were destroying in order to create. We must get back to the essentials! Only by destroying can we make a truly new art.'

It was just a shame it wasn't Christmas. The guy could have stood in for the fruitcake.

'That's the reason I live in this tower,' he confided.

It was said in a whisper, damply close to my ear, as though that answered any questions I had, including the riddle of the Sphinx. 'Everyone should live in towers,' he insisted. 'Everyone! Towers are wonderful, wonderful, they conduct all the energy upwards, into the zone of pure Platonic forms where everything is continuously destroyed and created again. Do you understand me?'

'Completely,' I lied.

'Do you, by any chance, live in a tower?'

'No, but I'm looking for one.'

His eyebrows semiphored his appreciation. 'That is truly wonderful. Now I comprehend why this piece is so good.' He gestured to the garbage heap that covered the floor. 'Your energies have joined with mine. The tower has released them!'

I wondered who had released Sebastian Trope, but I didn't let on.

'Would it be alright if I sort of wandered around? I'd like to see the pictures by Alex Woods. I know I'm a little early, but I've got a meeting of the Board of Directors at the museum tonight, so I can't come to your opening.'

'Ah, dear Alex, he is a wonderful painter,' Trope bubbled. 'Yes, yes, let me show you.'

He skipped ahead of me up the ramp and made me feel like Snow White hi-hoing off behind her dwarfs. Woods definitely worked with oils, but I wasn't too sure about that wonderful palette. His technique seemed to be to smear layers of sludge-colored paint over other layers of sludge-colored paint. He favored a kind of circular motion, and at the center of each circle there was an almost-recognizable image. In one there was either a bouquet of flowers or a helicopter. In another there seemed to be a toilet bowl. Several showed what could have been hands clawing up out of the muck. I thought I'd better sign up for an art appreciation course.

Every few feet up the ramp, Trope would lean over to study his own masterpiece. From the little squeals he gave, it seemed to get better and better all the time. He liked it best of all at the very top, where the wall stopped and he could dump his garbage over.

'You do understand, don't you? You do understand about *destroying?*' His eyes began to glaze over with the sheer rapture of it all. A hundred feet up in the air with a lunatic like Trope, I'd confess to understanding Einstein's theory. He was edging closer than I liked, and there was a lot of air between me and the floor.

'I do, I do.' I tried to make it as breathy and aesthetic as possible, then ducked around him and trotted down the ramp with the midget Michelangelo doing his wonderfuls behind me the whole way.

I picked my way through the bomb site and got within sprinting distance of the door. Next time I'd have to remember to wear my track shoes.

'Thank you for your invitation, Mr Trope.'

'But of course, of course. You must come often, and we will create together!' His eyebrows were pumping away again.

'By the way, Mr Trope, how did you happen to get my name?'

'We get names from many sources, my dear. Art lovers recommend fellow art lovers. Artists give us names. We take some from the society columns. We get names from everywhere, my dear, everywhere. Simply everywhere. I am so happy that we got yours, Miss Transom.'

'Ransom,' I corrected him.

'Wonderful, wonderful!'

Walking back to the car, I thought I'd have to send him a couple of new adjectives for his birthday.

14

LAVENDER and I were just closing up shop when Conchita telephoned. The kid didn't have much to report, but it was clear the Fairfield Academy was good therapy for her. From the excitement in her voice anybody would have thought she'd just been elected homecoming queen, or at least sweetheart of I Felta Thi. She'd been photographed from every angle, she said, which didn't do much for my blood-pressure, and she had a *muy hermosa* room-mate named Ingrid Seagram, which did even less. But what really got Conchita purring was that her bedroom had blue satin bedspreads and a matching skirt on the vanity table – vintage Hollywood, it sounded, and obviously just the thing to set her heart a-flutter. Well, I'd have to call in the decorators before she came home, get them to do something about the abandoned hunting-lodge decor I always seem to favor.

We picked up the films and a projector, and stopped off for some salami and rye and a few beers. Then we made for Loma Drive. It's in the old residential section of Los Angeles that stretches for a mile or two west and northwest of Pershing Square. The area is just starting to slide from middle-class to seedy, but it's somehow got a kind of homey, well-fed air about it that I like. The streets are lined with palms, and single or double houses are set back from the sidewalks with little aprons of lawn in front of them. Half the palms are rotting, and the lawns are already fried crisp by this time of the year, but it still seems a retreat from the concrete checkerboard of downtown L.A. Every now and then there's a touch of local color – bungalow courts in authentic Spanish-modern, with red tiled roofs and stucco walls. Mine's the one with the jungle of hibiscus bushes out front.

I made sandwiches while Lavender threaded the film into

the projector. He managed to get it in ass-backwards, so we treated ourselves to a few numbers flashing by in a roar of static. After that he figured out a way to drape the whole living room with the film, and I thought about calling in a few friends for a Halloween party, but by the time he got it rewound I was wondering if it was worth the trouble. The first little number was called *Family Games*, and I guess it was supposed to be the answer to everybody's incest fantasies. The opening scene was shot in a rancid-looking kitchen with mother serving dinner to the family. She moved very slowly around the table, pausing at each corner so the camera could get a good shot of the bruises on her thighs. Daddy got a slice of meatloaf on his plate and a side-order of cleavage in the face. The daughter – who miraculously looked about two years younger than Mommie – got the same. Junior got a slice of meatloaf in his lap, which it took Mommie a long, long time to clean up. Then they all settled down to eat meatloaf. From the way they were licking their lips, though, they were thinking about other kinds of meat. Probably Mommie was a lousy cook anyhow, and she must have forgotten to turn the oven off, because everybody was getting mighty warm, and beginning to undo a button here and a zipper there. Then the film cut to the kids' room. You could tell it was their room because of the football pennants all over the walls. Mommie tucked son in very carefully, and Daddy tucked daughter in very carefully – real Louisa Mae Alcott stuff. Then Mommie and Daddy went tiptoeing out, which wasn't easy with Daddy's hand up Mommie's skirt and Mommie's hand in Daddy's fly, but they managed it. A couple of real acrobats they were.

'Want another beer?' I asked Lavender.

'Later,' he said. 'We don't want to miss the punch line.'

The punch line turned out to be a kind of sexual alphabet soup. Daughter was frightened to sleep alone, so she got in bed with son, and they made a lot of racket with the bedsprings, and that must have kept Daddy awake, because he came in and gave them a lecture, and then got under the sheets to follow it up with a live demonstration, and that got Mommie up, and the whole thing started looking like a pretzel factory. You could tell Mommie by her bruises, though, and Daddy and son both wore black socks, so the one left was daughter. That's called detective work.

'My, oh my,' said Lavender, 'now I know how *deprived* I was as a child.'

'Did you say depraved?' I asked him.

'I said de-*prived*. All we did after supper was listen to *Green Hornet* on the radio. And if I'd even looked at my sister crosswise my momma'd been after me with a rollin' pin.'

'Smart momma. Is this really the last word in blue movies, or have you just brought me some of the rejects?'

'The man say it the hottest stuff in town.'

'What man?'

'*The* man. I talked to lots of 'em, and this one is supposed to be like the porno king.'

'Maybe he'll put you on his mailing list,' I suggested.

'Not me! I done give him *your* name.'

'Thanks a lot. At least I'll get a few obscene phone calls now. What's this little sex feast costing me?'

'Eighty-two dollars and fifty cents, with the projector. Is it helping you solve the case?'

'It's doing about as much for my case as it's doing for my libido. O.K., let's roll the next one.'

Cheap-thrill number two was called *Hitchhikers*, and it starred two men and two women who looked suspiciously like Mommie and Daddy and son and daughter. The men were hitchhiking and the women picked them up, but from there on the finale was a lot like *Family Fun*, but with trees instead of football pennants in the background.

'Are you as bored as I am?' I asked Lavender.

'However bored you is, I is *border*,' he answered.

We yawned our way through *Forbidden Fruits* then. It was the same old scenario, but everybody ate grapes the whole time. Any of the films would have been good vehicles for Brockaway, but he didn't show up in them. I wasn't surprised, because they'd been kicking around a long time.

Either that or somebody kept them packed in barbed-wire. And O'Brien suggested Brockaway had only gotten into the business recently. I should have spent the eighty-two fifty for a valve job on the Plymouth; it even sounded sexier.

We killed two more beers, and I filled Lavender in as best I could on the case. Talking about it like that, I realized just how little I did know. But it was enough to make him worried about Conchita, and visions of suitcases were still dancing in my wee little head when the telephone rang.

I was definitely on the prime sucker list now. Somebody else wanted to rent me films – 'dese films' he called them. 'It's real classy stuff,' he assured me.

'How classy?'

'Great lookin' dames, good lookin' guys, real classy. They's special made for private customers.'

'They sound expensive.'

'Maybe we make a deal. They ain't on the market,' he assured me.

'How old are they?'

'I got a couple what was just made last week.'

'One of them's not called *More Family Fun*, is it?'

'They ain't got no names, but they ain't nothin' like that old schlock. Dis stuff's the real McCoy.'

'How do I see them?'

'Well,' he said, 'we gotta be real careful. You got a car?'

'Most of one.'

'Dat's a joke, huh? Most of one. Dat's real good. You near Pershing Square, ain't you?'

'Near enough,' I conceded.

'You come to Pershing Square at eleven o'clock, we can maybe talk about it. You come by yourself.'

'I'm afraid I'll have to bring my business associate. He advises me on my film collection, and he's practically like my shadow anyhow.'

He wasn't too happy about it, but I wasn't too happy about the kind of rendezvouz he suggested either. 'I dunno,' he said. 'I dunno. Dis has gotta be real private-like.'

'Well, thanks for the call. I really enjoyed our little chat.'

'Hold it,' he answered. 'Wait a minute now. Is dis friend of yours the guy what was askin' about films?'

'The same.'

'He's O.K., I guess. But don't try to bring nobody else.'

'Girl Scout honor, I won't.'

'I'll be on the south side of the square at eleven o'clock, O.K.? With a newspaper under my arm.' Christ, the guy must have teethed on *Black Cat* magazine.

'And what's your name?' I asked.

'Just call me Max.'

'Hello there, Max. Now be sure you fold your paper so the used-car ads are showing.'

'The what?'

'The used-car ads. Just in case somebody else is walking around Pershing Square in the middle of the night with a newspaper under his arm.'

'I get it. Sure!' He liked that little touch. It was what he would have called 'classy', I think. Some days the fruit cake seems to come down like manna from heaven. This was one of those days, I guess.

15

MAX was standing just outside the cone of light made by one of the lamps in the park, looking about as inconspicuous as a turd in a punchbowl. Unless he was concealing a couple of airplane tires, he weighed in at about 250 pounds. His brahma bull neck was being slowly strangled by a grimy-looking shirt collar, and he was sausaged into a navy blue suit with a dandruff shawl draped over the shoulders. It wasn't hard to believe he was a little cog somewhere in the porno industry. He flashed the used-car ads at us.

'Evening, Max. How's it hanging?'

'Shhh, not so loud,' he said.

'Do you think we're being followed?'

'Ya never know. Dis is real hot stuff.' He meant it, or at least he thought he meant it. The guy was so scared that if somebody stepped on a twig, he'd start climbing the nearest lamppost. I could see him as the fat kid with his hand caught in the cookie-jar.

'You picked an awfully public place for such a private chat, Max. But why don't you ditch that paper, since it tends to glow in the dark, and let's take a little stroll.'

He threw the paper into the bushes as though it had gotten too hot to hold, and waddled along between Lavender and me. 'How much ya pay?' he asked.

'That depends on what you've got,' I said.

'Ya wanna see some good porno films, right?'

'Maybe, if they're new ones, and if I like the casts.'

'Great lookin' dames. Great lookin' dames,' he said. He was having trouble breathing and walking at the same time. It wasn't so much the physical energy it took as it was all that coordination, all those synapses having to plug into the right connections.

'And what about the guys?'

'Great lookin' guys, too. Real movie-star types, ya know? Real great lookin' guys.'

'I'm looking for one particular gent, my favorite actor. He's got a greasy pompadour and the kind of cute little moustache that tickles a lady's fancy. His name's Brand Brockaway.'

Max stopped dead still on that line. He didn't say anything, and I couldn't see his face, but he had other ways to let me know I'd scored a bull's-eye. He farted. It was a nice, polite, *sotto-voce* kind of fart – nothing brassy or showy, but I felt sorry for anybody downwind of us.

'The name seems to ring a bell,' I said to Lavender.

'It do indeed,' Lavender answered.

'Well, Max, can you deliver?' I asked.

'Yeah, I think so. Yeah, I think maybe I've got somethin' wid him in it.' Max was learning to walk again now.

'When can I see it?'

'I bring it to ya tomorrow night,' he said.

'How much?'

'Fifty clams,' he answered.

'That's a pretty high rental fee, isn't it?'

'Naw, dat's cheap. This ain't the kind of film ya can rent. Dis is real private,' he assured me.

'Twenty-five,' I said.

'Twenty-five?' he moaned back. He sounded like a kid who's just dropped his popsicle in the sand.

'You've got real good ears, Max. I said twenty-five.'

'Thoity,' he countered, but it was more a question than an answer, and he gave out with a lot of whine when he said it.

'Look, I'm a working girl. Do you know how many cans of Spam I could buy with twenty-five dollars?'

'O.K., twenty-five. But dat's cheap,' he whined.

So are you, I thought. You're so cheap you're wholesale, but I'll take the gamble.

We arranged for him to deliver the film tomorrow night at ten o'clock. Max waddled away like a pregnant rabbit, and I drove Lavender home. Then I went home to do a few rounds with the pillow. It kept reminding me the other side of the bed was empty. I punched it a couple of times but it wouldn't shut up. In fact, it was still yammering away when the alarm clock screamed seven-thirty.

16

I COULD hear Lavender singing as soon as the elevator doors opened. That meant it was Saturday, and his big night at the U.S.O. Of course, it could also have meant it was payday, but since I couldn't hear him doing a buck-and-wing on the desk, it must be just a standard-issue Saturday.

'Morning, brown eyes, what's the cause for rejoicing?'

He showed me all his pearlies and said, 'Tonight's the night!'

'Got your cookies all packed?' I asked.

'Packed and tied up with a red satin ribbon! He's got a weekend pass.'

'Want to come to the movies tonight?'

'No, m'am!' he said. 'We're gonna make our own. Leastwise, I sure am gonna *try*.'

'Well, just remember that penetration – '

' – however slight – ' he took it up.

' – constitutes – '

' – an offense!' he shouted. 'My, do I love the *offense*.'

He was flashing a klieg-light smile in my direction.

'Did you read the paper this morning?' he asked.

'Only my horoscope.'

'How was it?'

'Lousy – and accurate as usual.'

'Then allow me,' he said, and bent over the desk to turn through the paper that was lying there. His bottom did a jazz routine while he ran a finger down the columns. 'Here it is!' he said.

There it was alright, with a Santa Monica dateline. 'The body of Alexander Woods, the twenty-three year-old abstract painter whose exhibition opened yesterday evening with a gala reception at the Tower Gallery in Beverly Hills, was found yesterday in the wreckage of the Hillmann Building. Firemen, searching for possible gas leaks in the building which collapsed without warning on Tuesday, discovered Woods' body late last night in the cellar, pinned beneath a concrete slab. The painter had been dead for more than twenty-four hours, officials reported. As scientists and engineers continue to probe the causes of the building's collapse, Police Captain Arthur Hare assured newsmen that Woods' death would also be fully investigated.' There was another paragraph, to the effect that Woods worked as secretary to Holmes Woolcott, who had recognized the young man's gifts as a painter and supported him during his years at art school. He left no surviving relatives and would be buried at Forest Lawn on Monday. Then the reporter tried to say something about

Woods' paintings, and the loss to the art world, but he made about as much sense as I could have made.

'You should get a raise for this,' I said to Lavender. 'Or at least the afternoon off. I'll give you the afternoon off.'

'I always have Saturday afternoon off,' he reminded me.

'That's alright,' I assured him. 'Take it off anyhow.'

He gave me a deep music-hall bow. 'How can I ever express my gratitude?' he asked.

'You'll think of something. That's what I pay you for.'

'Does it help solve the case?' he asked, pointing to the paper.

'Not quite. What it means is that I not only have a missing person who isn't missing, but we've now got a prime murder suspect who's not going to be able to talk.'

'Do you think Woods did it?'

'No. If he wanted to hide Yvette's body, why would he have sent someone to find it?'

'Maybe he wanted to frame the chauffeur, this Porter person.'

'It's this Potter person,' I corrected him, 'and if it was a frame-up it was pretty clumsy.'

'Who does that leave?' he asked.

'It could leave Brand Brockaway.'

'The porno heart-throb himself?'

'Yeah, King Slime. But chopping the lady up would have taken more guts than he's got. Hell, he probably has to have a shot of novacaine just to get his nails trimmed.'

'Maybe he paid somebody to do it,' Lavender suggested.

'I wouldn't put it past him, but a real pro wouldn't have done it that way. He'd have put LaFlamme in a concrete corset and taken her for a swim.'

'So maybe it was Woods after all.'

'Maybe it was,' I said. 'Or maybe someone wants it to look that way. I don't know. I can't think straight, and none of the pieces of this thing *look* straight, and I didn't sleep last night. To make it worse, there's a gang of riveters working overtime in my skull.'

'You want a drink?' he asked. Something in the way he

asked let me know he understood the sort of mean reds I was having, and it helped more than a drink would have helped.

'No thanks, if I keep that up I'll lose my looks. What else does a girl have going for her in this lousy town? No, I'll skip the drink, but I'd like to have a little chat with Madame Shoemaker.'

'Your very own confidential secretary will attempt to connect you with that number right *now*,' he beamed.

'Thanks, pal.'

I got a couple of other secretaries first, and then the bouncer, but finally Shoemaker came on the wire. She didn't waste any time with pleasantries.

'I had been expecting your report,' she said.

'There's not much to report.'

'I dislike paying for merchandise that isn't delivered,' she shot back at me. Next time I'd call her from a bullet-proof telephone.

'Let me try to make this clear, then. I'm not used to playing with an incomplete deck. You've held back the aces on me,' I said. Never mind. I was holding back a pair of jokers, but she'd have to figure that out for herself.

'I do not follow your gambling allusions,' she said. Her diction.was freshly starched this morning. She must have stayed up half the night just ironing it.

'You've asked me to find one of your girls. She was last seen at your Academy – ' Last seen in one piece, at least. 'I need to know something about her activities, her friends, her interests. I've got some good leads. In fact, I think I got the key to the whole thing a couple of days ago.' I said that for Lavender's benefit, to make it worth his while to bend over like that with his ear to the door. It could put a fellow's back out of joint.

'Then I suggest you proceed with what you know,' Shoemaker instructed me.

'That's the trouble. I don't know anything. I only have a few miscellaneous leads and some unsorted hunches. They won't fit together into any kind of pattern unless I can come to the Academy and ask a few questions. I'll pretend to be a reporter doing a piece on the school, or a new girl interested in enrolling.'

'We aren't accepting new girls,' she snapped back. Really? My information was different.

'Then say I'm a reporter,' I suggested.

'It would interfere with the work here. It would unduly excite the girls.'

'Since when don't publicity and show-business go together?'

'This is not show-business, Miss Ransom. This is a respected academy for training in the thespian arts. We need no publicity and we want no publicity. My students all know that,' she assured me.

'Then say I'm your long-lost daughter. Say I'm a former pupil. Say I came to read the gas meter. But either I make you a visit, and soon, or you can solve your own case.'

'I like your spirit,' she said. Coming from a piece of old steer hide like her, I guess that meant something.

'Thanks. When do I come?'

'Come tomorrow afternoon at three o'clock. It's rather quiet here on Sundays, but some of the girls will be rehearsing their scenes.'

'And who am I supposed to be?'

'Let us say you are a former pupil of mine.'

'I couldn't have made a better suggestion myself.'

That was that. For now all I could do was bite my nails and work crossword puzzles. Then maybe I could go home and wash my hair all afternoon, buy a twenty-five-dollar ticket to the movies, and wash my hair again. I wondered if they needed any more help at the U.S.O.

Nothing happened for the rest of the morning except that the minutes piled up in one corner of the office and then in another. They piled up slowly and they didn't get very high before they came tumbling down again. It was like a spastic trying to make a wall out of building blocks.

Around noon the telephone went off and gave me a mild case of cardiac arrest. It was Conchita, sounding a lot less

91

chipper than she had sounded the day before. She'd spent all morning waiting to do a screen-test and the cameraman hadn't shown up. It seems he got a snoot full during the night and managed to fall down a couple of flights of stairs. The kid was really all broken up about it, but she was looking forward to her walking lesson.

'Your what?'

'My walking lesson,' she repeated. 'They make us to walk very sexy.'

It was strictly coals to Newcastle. Conchita already had a walk that could torpedo the whole Seventh Fleet.

'That sounds nice,' I said.

'*Sí*, very nice. And maybe tomorrow I have a screen-test.'

'Great. Maybe I can see it tomorrow.'

'You come here?'

'Yes, I come there. And you must be a very good actress and not show that we know each other. *Comprende*?'

'*Comprende.*'

'Nothing else to tell me?'

No, nothing else, except that Ingrid Seagram had warned her she must be 'careful', whatever that meant. Now I had two reasons for wanting to meet Ingrid Seagram. One reason would have been enough.

17

THE afternoon came and went about as fast as molasses in January. The evening went a lot slower. I tanked up with enough ninety-proof to anaesthetize me against fat Max, but I needn't have bothered. Ten o'clock finally arrived, but he didn't. Obviously he'd decided not to do business with the peanut gallery after all. I was rethinking the whole idea of joining the Women's Army Corps when Conchita phoned with another of her information bulletins. She'd been advised to change lipstick colors. The new shade was called 'Coral Seas' or something. I went to bed then and did another ten stiff rounds with the pillow. The pillow won – but only on points.

The next day, not wanting to make a bad impression on my employer, I got to the Academy two hours early and took a hike around the neighborhood, leaving the car parked at the foot of the drive, where it couldn't be seen from the house. The area had a modest five-figure respectability about it and sprinklers going on all the lawns. It all looked stockbrokerish and plumply self-assured; you could hear the mahjong tiles clicking all the way down the street.

I got a little trigger-happy, I guess, because it was a full half-minute before three when I rang the bell at the Academy. It answered me with a carillon that would have put Westminster to shame. The house had obviously been here a generation or so before the stockbrokers began building their fieldstone ranch houses. It stretched several wooden stories into the air, and towers and turrets shot up even higher. Every available angle had been decorated with scrollwork and gingerbread, stained glass windows were scattered here and there across the façade, and balconies jutted out from several of the windows. It was the kind of Victorian nightmare that would have made Emily Brontë feel right at home.

Ann Shoemaker herself opened the door, obviously determined that not a moment of my visit would be unchaperoned. She gave me what I think was supposed to be a won't-you-come-in nod, but the look in her eyes told me I was as welcome as a polio epidemic.

'You are very punctual,' she observed.

'I try to be.'

'It is a quality I admire, but which seems no longer so fashionable as it was in other times. Come in, please. I have informed the students of your visit.'

I stepped into the hallway. Outside the thermometers were all percolating, but inside the house it was as chilly as Grant's Tomb. I squinted along behind Shoemaker, trying to take my bearings in the dark oak maze of the hallway.

Here and there, set back in recesses, were either suits of armor or ancestors of the lady of the house. There was, at any rate, a metallic kind of family resemblance.

First I was shown into the parlor, where the girls apparently took their tea-breaks. It was all surprisingly chintzy and Great Aunt Maude in style, with flowered slipcovers on the sofas and chairs, stacks of fashion magazines, a phonograph and records, and a cabinet-style radio inspired by the Lincoln Memorial. At the back of the room were large windows that opened onto a tiled patio and gave a clear view of the family of cast-iron deer grazing on the lawn. Over the stone fireplace was a gray smear that I might have mistaken for mildew if it hadn't been surrounded by a fancy gold frame.

'Alexander Woods?' I asked.

My keeper shot me the sort of look that suggested she might have made a few mistakes in sizing up the opposition. 'Yes,' she grunted, and cancelled the lesson in art appreciation.

'This,' said Shoemaker, 'is a kind of recreation room for our students, though it is sometimes used as a rehearsal room as well. We are, you know, terribly pressed for space.'

I cluck-clucked my sympathy with the problem. After all, I had it at home myself, every time I wanted to swing a cat.

'On the other side of the hall are a reception room and office,' Shoemaker said, continuing her little Cook's tour, 'and behind them the dining room and conservatory. The kitchen, served by a dumb-waiter, is in the basement, as it so often was in these Victorian houses.' Maybe she thought I'd signed up for the new course on architecture. 'There are also cloak rooms and storage rooms which I think would not interest you.'

At that moment the sound of rapid machine-gun fire came from upstairs, with a nice jazzy musical accompaniment.

'That,' Shoemaker enlightened me, 'is one of our dancing classes. The sound, of course, carries terribly in such old houses.'

'Me, I'd say it carried very well.'

'Another of your needling remarks, I presume. It is a pity that a young woman of your intelligence and female attractiveness feels the necessity of employing such obvious defense mechanisms.'

'It's just my way of reminding you that I haven't been sent here by *House and Gardens*. I'm less interested in the physical appointments than the human ones.'

'As my former student, you would, however, be interested to see such things, would you not?' You could have etched crystal with the acid in her tone.

'O.K., O.K., it's a marvelous little set-up you've got, and I'm thrilled for you, but I'm positively dying with curiosity to see the rest.' To prove my sincerity, I fluttered my eyelashes for her.

'Very well, if you insist,' she said, with a warning hiss on the s's.

She led me back into the dungeon of a hall and up a staircase that couldn't quite make its mind up about the best route to the next floor and seemed to change directions a half-dozen times along the way. The higher we got the more the dancing class sounded like a firing squad.

From the noise level I'd expected something like the Rockettes' chorus line, but there were only three girls hoofing away in the ballroom that ran across the front of the house. They were teaching the crystal chandeliers how to do the shimmy. The three looked enough alike to be triplets, but maybe it was just the rehearsal shorts and the blonde hair that did it. The shorts were real enough, but the hair was as artificial as a nightclub lobby. So was their dancing ability. Ginger Rogers could definitely stop worrying. But if the tap-dancing looked like a farmer cleaning his shoes after a stroll through the barnyard, it wasn't from lack of good coaching. Rigsby Riley was out in front doing his damndest to inspire them, and there were girls all over America whose taps would melt just at the thought of working with the man who invented the dance spectacular.

95

Riley looked as tweedy as he always looked in his newspaper photographs, even though he wasn't wearing tweeds. He wore white linen trousers, a white silk shirt and the black-and-white oxfords that were his trademark. Hedda Hopper assured her panting readers that he had forty identical pairs, all custom jobs from London. He had first made his mark on Hollywood with the shoes and a wardrobe of Saville Row suits; everybody wanted to invite one to a party. From those modest beginnings, Riley had become the local Mr English, the last outpost of empire. He played polo with Douglas Fairbanks, had the Duke and Duchess of Windsor to tea when they visited Hollywood, and tooled around town in a custom-made Rolls Royce. But he probably wouldn't have made it on sartorial style and weak tea alone. Somewhere along the line, shortly after his arrival from points unknown, he persuaded one of the top studio execs to give him a modest budget of a quarter-million to shoot a three-minute film sequence. It required building a scale model of the Eiffel Tower, spraying it silver, and sprinkling about 10,000 would-be starlets all over it. They did a cute little dance routine, with split-second timing, while a two-hundred-piece studio orchestra played a jazzed-up version of the *Marseillaise* in the background. It was a sensation, and from those modest beginnings, Riley had skyrocketed into the Hollywood empyrean. He was, it was said, a technical genius as well as a whiz-kid choreographer. He had, in any event, a famous eye for legs. It formed a kind of bond between us.

If Riley was working there, teaching these peroxided cows how to lift their feet, then the Academy stood higher in the local stock-market than I'd thought. And he was giving it the real trooper's special, too. In the corner of the ballroom somebody was hammering out 'We're in the Money' with a rhythm obvious enough for the lame, the halt and the blind to follow, but Riley was underscoring it with ONE-TWO-THREE-FOURS that should have cleared up any doubt their might have been in the matter. It didn't, though – probably because the three floosies couldn't count that high.

Just to see Riley hoofing away like that, his two-tones twinkling, was worth the price of admission. The guy's energy was diabolical, and not a lock of carrot-colored hair was out of place. The girls' little platinum pates, meanwhile, were looking more and more like old Brillo pads. It was all strictly pearls before swine.

We sat down to wait for the travesty to end. When the reprieve finally came, the ugly sisters stumbled off to the locker room. Riley draped a towel around his neck while he sauntered over to us, but it was really just another costuming trick; he looked like the most strenuous thing he'd done lately was ease the top off a soft-boiled egg.

When Shoemaker introduced me he bowed over my hand like it was a certified holy relic and made me worry about whether I'd cleaned my nails properly that morning. 'Delighted,' he said, and with just a little imagination I could believe him. I could also believe he'd sized me up, right down to the price of my drawers, the minute we'd walked into the room.

'Miss Ransom is a former pupil of mine,' Ann Shoemaker announced.

'But she is surely not in show-business,' said Riley. 'I would certainly have seen her. And I could not have forgotten,' he twinkled.

'No,' said Shoemaker, 'she is in public relations.'

Actually, I preferred my relations in private, but I didn't let on.

'Are you planning to work for the Academy?' Riley asked.

'No,' I said. 'I was just passing by, and thought I'd drop in for old-time's sake,' I said. Chew the fat, you know, and have a giggle or two with the iron maiden here.

'A pity. Yours, I think, is a highly valuable profession, both a science and an art when properly practised. And you no doubt have great success.'

Would you mind telling that to the gas company, I thought.

Riley's tape-measure eyes were re-checking his first impressions, and they seemed to like the results. 'What agency do you work with?' he asked.

'None,' I answered. That much, at least, was the truth. 'I prefer to free-lance. That way I can pick my own clients.'

Shoemaker obviously thought that was enough tête-à-tête, because she started issuing her marching orders then. 'Please don't let us keep you from your work, Mr Riley. I know you have another group now, and Miss Ransom wanted to meet some of our students.'

'I am really most happy we met,' Riley purred. 'Perhaps I might consult with you at some point. Have you a business card?'

'No, I'm sorry, but I left them in my other purse. The working-girl purse, you know. But I'm in the book.' Both numbers, too – home and office, and they've both got 'Private Investigator' written there in the fine print.

'I hope that I shall again have the pleasure,' Riley said, and something about the way he said it, the way he slanted another stock-taking glance in my direction, suggested the old horizontal confrontation. Or maybe those jade eyes were sending a different kind of message. Riley wasn't the typical Hollywood skirt-hound, and whatever went on behind his crumpets-and-tea routine was probably about as straight as a bobby-pin.

'Thank you,' I told him. 'It was marvelous to watch you work.'

'Cheerie-bye, then!' he chirped.

Riley tapdanced over to the piano and went into consultation. The type who had been making with the heavy-footed musical accompaniment looked like a failed missionary, but she was wonderfully color-coordinated; her hair and skin and dress were all dove-gray.

We eventually met a few of the girls. They all seemed to be named Constance or Grace, and they all had something to hide. With one it was pimples, with another buck-teeth, and somebody named Renate was doing her best to shovel enough upper-class syllables to bury a West Virginia

accent. Most of the staff, Ann Shoemaker explained, were
free on Sundays, but we would probably find a few more of
the girls in the conservatory downstairs, scattered around
under the palms. One of them, Adrianna DeForrest, was
stretched out on a wicker chaise spearing chocolates with
long, pointed nails painted the color of fresh chicken blood.
Another, Rosemarie Somethingorother, was hidden behind
a movie magazine and never came out. In the far corner
Conchita was reading aloud from a script, and a long, lean
lady with honey-colored hair seemed to be coaching her.
Shoemaker piloted me round the room, making sure I
didn't fall into a tub of orchids, and ground out the
introductions. When we got to Conchita, the kid gave a real
drama school performance that left me wondering if I ever
had met her before. The girl with her was Ingrid Seagram,
and she had eyes of pure cornflower blue. It's my favorite
color.

I had coffee with the girls, served by an ancient,
distracted-looking maid, and shot the breeze for a while. If
I'd expected some ominous signs of criminal activity, of
white-slavery and opium dens, I was disappointed. It was
all a little like a group of sorority girls waiting for their
dates to come and take them to the big home game, except
that there was a lot more Max Factor around than you'd
find in any self-respecting sorority house. The exceptions
were Conchita and Ingrid, who could get by on their own
chemistries. The one dark and well rounded, the other pale
and angular, they couldn't have been more different.
Conchita thought as little about being beautiful as a rose
must think, and she was just as generous about it. Ingrid,
though, showed with her every movement that she had
thought a good deal about it, come to all the right
conclusions, and accepted it as a kind of birthright. Singly
or as a pair, they were equally easy on the eye, though.

It struck me that a girl could get used to this, but a girl
could also cease to see the forest for the trees. I made my
goodbyes, and I meant it when I said I hated to have to go.
Conchita, I thought, ignored me a little too convincingly,

but after all, it was the role I'd given her. Ingrid, on the other hand, gave me a nice flash of cornflower blue and said she hoped we'd meet again very soon. So did I.

Shoemaker shooed me out of the front door with one of her cobra hisses, and I might have written the visit off as a loss to the detective business, whatever it did for my general muscle tone, if I hadn't nearly collided with Big Max, the Prince of Pershing Park. He didn't have a newspaper under his arm this time, but he did have a lovely purple mouse on one cheek and the world's largest bandage on his nose. He treated me like The Invisible Woman, and I pretended not to mind.

18

OBVIOUSLY word about my new, improved mousetrap had gotten around town, because the world began to beat a path to my door on Monday morning. When I walked into the office Lavender was sitting behind his desk doing his damndest to look businesslike and efficient, which wasn't that easy with the rose and purple window-pane checks he was wearing. On the opposite side of the office Big Max had wedged himself into a wooden armchair. He was wearing the familiar greasy blue suit, a fresh dandruff shawl, and yesterday's bandages. His face was as humpy as a boarding-house mattress.

'Good morning, Mr Trevelyan,' I said, hooking my shoulder-bag onto the corner of the desk. 'Any appointments for me?'

Lavender ran a careful finger along the blank page in the calendar. 'Starting at nine-thirty, you're booked up solid for the rest of the day,' he mused.

'It looks as though we're going to have to expand the staff after all.'

'It do, it do,' agreed Lavender.

Then I waved a hand at Max. 'Is this the first appointment?'

'No,' Lavender said. He clicked a pencil against his teeth and contemplated the calendar again. 'No, as a matter of fact, Miss Ransom, I was trying to find some way to squeeze the gentleman in between your nine-thirty and ten o'clock appointments. But you know the duchess always takes so much time – '

'Not the duchess again! Did someone steal her tiara?'

'No. It's her poodle's diamond choker this time.'

'What is the world *coming* to, Mr Trevelyan?'

There was a rumble from the other side of the room. Max was trying to heave himself out of the chair. 'Just a minute,' he protested. 'I got here foist.'

'Excuse me,' I said. Then I took a long, careful look at him. 'I say, I do believe we've met before.'

'Aw, hell,' he muttered, 'you knows who I am.'

'But of course! How silly of me. See here, Mr Trevelyan, isn't this our very own Max Pershing?'

'Why, Miss Ransom, I do believe it is one and the same. How is it that I too failed to recognize him?'

'Perhaps,' I said, 'because he has been so terribly disfigured.'

Max was still thrashing around in his chair. Then he decided to give it up for now. 'Ya know who I am,' he pouted.

'But of course, Mr Pershing. It's just that it's so early in the day, and you do seem, somehow, altered.'

'My name ain't Poishing,' he corrected me. 'It's Leone. Massimo Leone.'

'Silly me! Now wherever did I get the idea your name was Pershing?'

'Dat's where I met youse,' he sulked. He wasn't sure whether to play the game or not, but he didn't seem to feel he had much choice. He was right. It was nice to see the little rat squirm for a while.

'To be sure. I have such happy memories of that brief encounter. Now, if you'd like to see me on business, my secretary would be happy to make an appointment for you.'

'Naw,' he squirmed. 'I gotta talk to ya now.'

'You've come, I'm afraid, on our busiest day. This *is* difficult. I'd so much like to oblige an old acquaintance.'

'Ya can give me five minutes. Dat's all I need.' He was really beginning to squirm now, and I wasn't sure how much more hip action the chair could take.

'Well, perhaps – '

'But Miss Ransom,' Lavender interrupted. 'Whatever shall I tell your nine-thirty appointment?'

'Say that I'm in a conference with an old friend, and that I'll be free as quickly as possible.'

'She is too generous for her own good,' Lavender shot at Max. 'And she will be the *death* of me.' He gave his eyebrows a long-suffering hitch before he began furiously crossing out imaginary appointments and re-arranging my calendar for the day.

'So, Mr Baloney,' I said, 'if you'd like to step this way?'

I held the door to my inner sanctum open for Max, who brought the chair with him halfway across the office. 'Leone,' he mumbled. 'Leoneleoneleone.' He and the chair finally got their divorce, and Max came waddling in without it.

My visit to the Academy had hit pay-dirt after all. Just how much, I didn't know, but things were getting off to a nice start, at least.

'Now,' I said, tidying up the bills on the desk, 'what can we do for you, Mr Leone?'

He didn't answer. He was too busy checking out the terrain and wondering whether he could risk sitting down again.

'Go ahead,' I said. 'Sit down and rest your brain.'

He lowered himself onto the edge of the chair and balanced his elbows on the desk.

'Comfy?' I asked.

He mumbled something that sounded vaguely positive.

'Well, then, what can I do for you?'

'Nothin',' he said.

'Nothing at all? Well, I'm pleased to have been able to help you, and perhaps you'll pay us a call again when you're in the neighborhood.'

'Just don't do nothin',' he said. 'Like I'm in enough dutch already.'

'How did that deplorable state of affairs come about?'

'Huh?'

'How did you get in dutch? And with whom?' I asked. Then I translated it for him. 'With who?'

'It don't matter. I dunno. Ya workin' for Shoemaker?'

'Whatever makes you think that?'

'I dunno. What was you doin' there yesterday?'

'At the Academy? Why, it was simply a social call.'

He snorted. Even Max couldn't quite buy that one.

'I'll tell you what, Max, why don't we talk about you for a while? For instance, where'd you get that lovely purple mouse?'

He touched his cheek and winced. 'I fell down stairs.'

'Leone, you're too stupid to fall down stairs. If you'd told me you'd fallen *up* the stairs, I might almost have believed you. Almost. Who worked you over?'

I could tell I was getting through to him, because he answered me with another of his slow, rattling farts.

'Who did it, Max?'

'I dunno,' he answered. 'I dunno.' He was sweating all over his side of the desk now. I edged the electricity bill in my direction to keep it dry.

'Where did it happen?'

'In the park.' At least his memory functioned, even if most of the other departments upstairs were closed for the duration.

'After you left us?' I asked.

'Yeah.'

'Who did it?'

'I dunno. It was too dark.'

'Is that the reason you didn't keep your appointment on Saturday night?'

'Yeah. Ya workin' for Shoemaker?'

It wasn't hard to figure out what the creep wanted to know.

'And if I am?'

'Don't say nothin' 'bout them films,' he said.

'What films, Mr Leone?'

'Dem films youse guys was gonna rent.'

'I seem to remember, just vaguely of course, that we *did* discuss films on Friday night, and in fact that I was going to rent one from you.'

'Dat's what you gotta not say,' he whined.

'Why not, Max?'

'Listen, how much ya take?'

'Take? For what?'

'Not to talk ta Shoemaker 'bout what we said. What'll it cost?'

That old familiar feeling was coming back to me. It was called slime. I leaned across the desk so Max wouldn't miss any of the important syllables. 'Listen, grease-ball, I'm not for sale – not at any price, and least of all to you.' He farted again, and I tried to ignore it. 'If you want to discuss your little problem with me, fine. But that means you've got to level with me. Just because we happen to wear the same school tie doesn't mean I feel any obligation to save your fat ass.'

He was sweating so hard now I thought he might float out of the room, and I wanted a few questions answered first.

'What's your connection with the Fairfield Academy? What do you do there?'

He hesitated for a minute, then gave a great heaving sigh like a cornered elephant and surrendered to the easy way out. 'I'm the cameraman,' he said. 'I do the screen tests and like films kinda.'

'Like blue movies, kinda?'

'Sorta.'

'Wonderful. We're making great progress. And what happens to these little blue movies? Do you always handle the rentals yourself?'

'Naw,' he answered. 'I dunno. They're like for real special customers.'

'Whose customers?'

'I dunno. Shoemaker's, I guess. She keeps 'em all. She keeps 'em in a big safe in her office.'

'And you don't know who sees them?'

'I dunno. I dunno nothin' about it. I just make 'em, dat's all.'

'And this little goodie you were going to rent me? How did you plan to get it out of Shoemaker's vault?'

'It wadn't there. I was workin' on it. I was gonna give it to her later.'

It was a shame the plan had backfired on him. It was probably the first original idea he'd ever had. But meanwhile, the picture of the Academy was getting clearer and dirtier by the minute.

'Now, Max,' I said, 'I'd like you to put your famous brain to work for me. Show me your best Quiz Kid stuff. I want you to think far, far back – to about ten days ago, and a little sex epic you were making with Brand Brockaway and Yvette LaFlamme.'

'LaFlamme?' he asked. He had the sort of dazed look he would have had if a waiter had asked him whether he wanted his steak *signé* or *au point*.

'Don't you know the lady?'

'Sure. But we wadn't makin' no film with her.'

'Why, was she too shy?'

'Naw, we made some with her, but not no ten days ago. Maybe a month ago, when she first come.'

'My information is that she and Brockaway were rehearsing a scene for a film and had a quarrel over his performance in it.'

'Sure, they had a fight.' He brightened up then, wanting to show off his famous powers of recall. 'But it was like a poisonal thing. It wadn't no film.'

'What kind of personal thing?'

'Well, I dunno.' I thought I could actually see a blush rising around the edges of his bandage, like a kind of strangled sunset. 'It was kinda poisonal,' he repeated.

'Had they, perhaps, been intimate?' I suggested.

105

'Huh?'

'Was there, shall we say, something between them?'

'Naw. It was real poisonal.'

It was a little like trying to tunnel through Mount Rushmore with an ice-pick. 'Mr Leone, would you, in your considered opinion, venture to suggest that Mr Brockaway had been screwing Miss LaFlamme?'

The blush was beginning to melt his bandage now. For a porno filmmaker, Leone was a real Boy Scout.

'Naw,' he finally answered. 'Naw, he wadn't doin' nothin'. I guess he couldn't, and Yvette made fun of him or somethin'.'

So that was what Brockaway had meant when he said Yvette LaFlamme had objected to his 'performance'.

'Thanks, Max. You can spare me the painful details. But the impotent king of the sex epic was in the little film you were going to bring me Saturday, right?'

'Yeah.'

'And who else?'

'DeForrest,' he said. 'Adrianna de Forrest. And somebody named Renate.'

'Sounds pretty tame,' I ventured.

'Well, the girls, ya know, they kinda made it interestin'.'

Yes, so I could imagine. Maybe it would have been worth twenty-five bucks after all.

'Dat's all I know!' said Max. He seemed a little too eager to get the idea across, and yet it wasn't that hard to believe him. Some two-bit cameraman who couldn't get a job with the studios, he'd been picked up by Shoemaker for the old what-the-butler-saw routine. And when he decided to try a bit of moonlighting, somebody gave him the sap.

'I told ya everythin' I know,' Max insisted. His voice was needling up to the full-whine level again.

'I believe you,' I assured him.

'Den tell me if ya works for Shoemaker.'

'That, Max, seems to be the question everybody's asking these days. The answer is that I don't know myself.'

'Then why was ya there?' he persisted.

'Let's just say I like the décor.'

The cash-register rang up No Sale again. 'The what?' he asked.

'Skip it. Your secret is safe with me.'

'Yeah?' He rearranged the lower half of his face into a slow, neanderthal grin. 'Yeah?'

'Mum's the word.' After all, whoever objected to his free-lance activities knew about them already. Even Max might realize that if he took a long look at himself in the mirror. But maybe he didn't have the stomach for it.

'T'anks,' he said. 'Dat's swell.'

'Don't mention it. Always happy to oblige an old friend.'

Max took a good grip on the desk and heaved himself upright. Then he started backing out of the room, saying 'T'anks' every few feet. He had his ass halfway through the door when O'Brien called, and I let the Criminal Division wait until he got the rest of himself through.

'O'Brien? Sorry to keep you waiting. I had a friend here shooting the breeze. Or do I mean passing wind? Never mind, now I can give you my undivided attention.'

'How's it going?'

'Splendidly, splendidly. Wonderful, wonderful. Business, in fact, has never been better. Word's getting around about my integrity, my complete honesty with my clients.'

'Thanks for the favor,' he said.

'Favor?'

'Sure. Thanks for keeping quiet about that business last week.'

'Business? Oh, you mean the little mix-up at the slaughter house. Tut-tut, it's the least I can do. Besides, I hear we're both back to square one. I've lost my missing person, and you've lost your prime murder suspect.'

O'Brien sounded like he had had another hard night. 'He didn't do it,' O'Brien said. 'Woods didn't do it.'

'What makes you think that? Did he revive just long enough to give you a statement? I thought that only happened in B movies.'

'The time was wrong. He was dead before the building

107

collapsed. Somebody sapped him and brought him there later, and then the building collapsed.'

'Spectacular timing, don't you think?'

'Lousy, if you ask me.'

'Well, thanks for the inside information. As an admirer of Wood's superb palette, I am of course eager to know all I can about his tragic death. But what makes you so damned sure he didn't do the little hatchet job and then get bumped off?'

O'Brien was trying hard to be patient, and trying even harder not to tell me more than he wanted me to know. 'I think,' he said, 'that Woods may have had some idea who sent those keys. I think he was trying to protect Holmes Woolcott, and that somebody knew it and was afraid he'd do too good a job of it. That's all.'

'Is that what you call male intuition?'

'No, just a calculated guess,' he admitted. 'Maybe Woods killed LaFlamme, but I don't think so, and I'm telling you that because it means we're still working on her case. I was afraid you'd think it was closed after reading about Woods.'

'From my point of view, it damned near is,' I admitted.

'What's that supposed to mean?'

'It means my client isn't too happy with my non-progress reports, and that I'm probably about to get laid off. She's going to start leaning on me. Yesterday, in fact, she already had that Tower of Pisa look about her. And then it's going to be hard not to tell her the truth. After all, that's what she paid me for.'

O'Brien said, 'Play for time.'

'I don't think your killer's playing, O'Brien. I think he's taking all this very seriously.'

'Stall for another couple of days, if you can.'

'If I can. You wouldn't be trying to put my ass in a sling, would you?'

'No.'

'I'd like to be looking into those Irish eyes of yours when you say that. Don't shit me, O'Brien.'

'I'm *not*,' he insisted.

'Don't. And may the fleas of a thousand camels nest in your crotch if you ever try.'

There was a click then, and O'Brien was gone. It wasn't like a boy from a good Catholic home to hang up that way. Maybe he'd gone rushing off to the john to check out his crotch. I laid the phone back in its cradle just long enough for it to start ringing again. The voice that answered when I picked it up did a lot more for me than O'Brien's could ever do. It was Ingrid Seagram – she of the cornflower eyes – giving me the message that Conchita was busy and wouldn't be able to telephone that morning. My little tamale was not, I thought, doing a very good job of keeping our relationship out of the public domain.

'Thanks for the message,' I said.

'It's alright,' Ingrid answered. Her voice made soft music against my ear. 'I'd like to talk to you myself.'

'Your place or mine?'

'Do you know a restaurant called Ricardo's Steak House?'

'Yes, it's over in Glendale, isn't it.'

'That's right. Could you meet me there around noon?'

'Of course.' I'd have swum the Hellispont, too, if that were part of the arrangement.

19

I COULD remember when Ricardo's really was a steak house. In the good old days of the Depression it took up the first floor of a decaying frame house, and Papa Ricardo, Mama Ricardo, and a baker's dozen of assorted little Ricardos all lived upstairs. You could get a steak two inches thick, baked potato and salad for $2.00, plus free advice from Mama Ricardo on cures for arthritis or for broken hearts. Then one day Ricardo's more prosperous fellow-immigrants discovered the place and adopted it as a worthy cause. The parking lot filled up with black Cadillacs and the coatracks inside filled up with camel and vicuna, and plastic blondes started coming out of the woodwork. These days the steaks were tougher, but the atmosphere was all soft plush. The building was a long, powder-blue box, with narrow archer's slits instead of windows, so that the shadows stayed long inside even at high noon. The lamp on each table, shaded with rose-colored silk, didn't give them much competition, and a rippling fountain in the lobby only added to the feeling that you were entering some seaside grotto. Faint music oozed through the velvet-covered walls as though it weren't quite sure it would be welcome.

At twelve o'clock there were a half-dozen couples in the place. The men all looked on the down-hill side of fifty, the women a couple of decades younger. Maybe they'd decided to celebrate Father's Day a few weeks early this year. The *maitre d'* twitched his waxed moustache at me and asked if I was meeting a friend. I said yes, and he suggested we might like a quiet table. It wasn't a hard order to fill, since Ricardo's always had the subdued air of a classy funeral parlor on a slack day. There were even great burial bouquets of flowers peeking out of the shadows here and there.

Two cuba libres later, the place was beginning to fill up, and I was playing mumbletypeg with the bread knife. I wondered if I could put the tab on expenses, but that depended on whether or not Ingrid Seagram had in mind a business lunch or just a we-girls social chat. Above all, it depended on whether she showed up or not. I was just starting a little dialogue on the subject with the third cuba libre when I spotted her talking to the head moustache. He nodded her in my direction, and she came floating toward my table. She was wearing a simple yellow cotton dress, but the way it rippled when she walked suggested a real maestro of the scissors had contributed to the general effect. A golden tan, honey-colored hair and those cornflower-blue eyes helped, of course. It seemed a long time before she reached the table, as though she were walking through depths of space the rest of us didn't understand anything about. It was worth the price of admission, alright.

She apologized for being late. I would have waited a couple of weeks, but I didn't tell her that. I did tell her she looked more beautiful today than she had looked yesterday, and she brushed the compliment away with a little throaty laugh that implied most days were that way. Then she suggested we order.

'I'm famished,' she said.

'So am I,' I answered, and I wasn't really thinking about steak and baked-potato.

It looked like a social lunch after all, just a couple of girls out on the town. Ingrid talked a little about herself, the Academy and the girls who worked there, and what an iron horse Ann Shoemaker was. She could have been reading from the telephone book for all I cared. Her deep voice, with the slight break in it, was like a cool breeze in summer, and I had absolutely no complaints about the weather.

She kept up the Lorelei routine until coffee arrived, and then let me know it was strictly expense-account stuff after all.

'Are you,' she asked, 'satisfied with the way the case is going?'

'The case? Which case is that?'

She smiled then, as though we had just shared some very private joke, and gave her coffee another stir.

'Conchita suggested you weren't really satisfied with the progress you were making.'

'Conchita?' I asked. 'Of course, the girl you were working with yesterday.' It sounded as flat as a boardinghouse pancake, and we both knew it.

'Don't worry,' Ingrid reassured me. 'She hasn't been indiscrete. She is, however, somewhat transparent. It's hopeless to try to keep secrets from a roommate, you know.'

A girl might have fun trying, though.

'I've been rather worried myself about Yvette's sudden disappearance,' she told me.

111

'Was she a personal friend?'

'No, only a classmate, but if her disappearance has anything to do with the Academy, it of course concerns me as well.'

Apparently Conchita had kept at least one secret from her roommate, since Ingrid seemed to think we were still dealing with a missing persons case.

'What can you tell me about Yvette?'

Ingrid brushed back a stray lock of hair and dabbed at her broad, full mouth with a napkin. 'Not much, I'm afraid. And probably nothing you don't already know for yourself.'

'Try me,' I suggested.

'She was vulgar.'

'Check.'

'She was aggressive.'

'Check.'

'She was not very subtle.'

'Ditto.'

'She was working for someone.'

'She was what?'

'She was working for someone,' Ingrid repeated. 'Someone outside the Academy.'

'What makes you think that?'

'I'm not quite sure – something about the way she looked at people, the kinds of personal questions she asked.'

'And what do you think she was trying to learn?'

'I can't imagine. Certainly there are things to be found out, things that might be, well, used against the Academy, but it didn't seem that simple.'

'Was she the blackmailing type?'

Ingrid didn't hesitate. 'Of course,' she said. 'But whom would she blackmail?'

'Ann Shoemaker, maybe.'

She paused as if weighing the suggestion and brushed a strand of hair away from her cheek. 'No,' she finally answered, 'I think that was a little out of her class.'

You're right, I thought. It would be like Mickey Rooney taking on the Brown Bomber.

'No,' Ingrid continued, 'I think it's more likely that whatever information she was looking for she was passing on to someone else.'

'And you've no guess, then, what the information might have been?'

Ingrid hesitated. 'Perhaps,' she said, 'it had something to do with extracurricular activities at the school.'

'You mean the sex epics?'

'Yes,' she said, 'the films. And the occasional favors the girls were able to provide,' she added.

'You mean the Shoemaker allows gentlemen callers?'

'Oh, no,' Ingrid corrected me. 'Nothing like that. Or perhaps something like that, but not quite the way you mean it. At times Miss Shoemaker asks one of the girls to be a kind of companion to one of her wealthy friends. One of her backers, I think. Someone's investing a lot of money in the Academy, because it certainly doesn't get by on tuition fees.'

'Maybe film sales are good,' I suggested.

'They could be,' she said. 'I suppose they are. I've got no idea what sort of price such products command.'

'I have,' I told her. 'They're not cheap, and your headmistress obviously has a rather select lot of clients who prefer to remain anonymous. Some people are willing to pay a lot of money for the privilege. They'd probably offer good wages for the right sort of companion, too.'

'I may be able to find out just how much.'

'You've got a plan?'

'I've got a date,' she said. 'Tonight I'm attending an informal dinner party, given by what Ann Shoemaker describes as one of her oldest, dearest, most intimate friends.'

'That could be either a skunk or a rat.'

She flashed a brief, tolerant smile at me. 'Whichever it is, I'll find out.'

Somehow it didn't add up. The lady across the table from me was just that – a lady. She had an authentic finishing-school accent and a personal style that suggested

113

she had eaten pablum from a silver spoon and graduated from that to finer, fancier things. If she'd told me she was having dinner with the Rockefellers, I wouldn't have been surprised, but I just didn't see her as the *plat du jour* on Ann Shoemaker's dating menu.

'Why did you accept?' I asked.

She took a while to formulate her answer, and while she paused her face suddenly had a drawn, haunted look that made her beauty seem fragile and threatened. 'It's difficult to explain,' she began. 'Let us say, for now, that I have personal reasons, reasons of my own for wanting to know something more about Ann Shoemaker and her friends.' She leaned across the table and laid one cool, tapered hand across mine. 'I think,' she said, 'that I could tell you, that you would understand, but the time isn't right for that.' She drew her hand away.

'You aren't, perhaps, a little afraid of what you may find out?'

'Should I be?' she asked.

'I was only remembering you had warned Conchita to be careful.'

'Oh, that!' She laughed, but the laugh was brittle, and she seemed to tremble slightly. 'Yvette had disappeared a few days before. And Conchita, like Yvette, was asking rather personal questions. That's all.'

'You were right to be concerned,' I said. I owed her at least that much of the truth, if not more. 'The danger is real enough. In fact, it may be much worse than you think. My guess is you're safe enough at the Academy, but anywhere else you'd be advised to keep one eye on the nearest exit.'

Ingrid raised the faint, delicately arched lines of her brows. 'Is that a warning?' she asked.

'It is,' I said, 'and a damned good piece of free advice.'

'But you can't fill in any details for me?'

'No, at this point I'm not at liberty to do so, as the law boys would say.'

'When you are?' she wondered.

'When I am, I'll tell you the whole messy story.' And all

the rest, too, I thought. I'll tell you anything you want to know – my vital statistics, my medical record and how scared I was of my first-grade teacher, Miss McGeeney. I'll tell you about wrecking my father's car when I was sixteen, and how I fell in love with my gym teacher, and the way I break out in hives when I eat strawberries and how much I gave last year to the March of Dimes.

Ingrid interrupted my pipe-dreams to signal the waiter for our check. He brought it crisply folded on a silver tray, and she reached for it, but my reflexes were just that much faster.

'This is on me,' I said. 'I'll charge it to my client as a business expense.'

'Wouldn't she be surprised if she knew?' Ingrid said.

'She'd blow a gasket, and you know what?'

'What?'

'It couldn't happen to a nicer dame.'

20

'... and Sunday afternoon we went to the movies,' Lavender said.

'What did you see?' I asked.

'I don't *know*. We saw it twice, and I didn't know both times.'

'Who was in it?'

Lavender pushed a pensive finger against his right temple. 'I think,' he said. 'I think maybe it was Sonia Heinie or Johnny Weismuller because there was a lot of snow around, or maybe it was a lot of *trees*.'

'Love is blind.'

'That is a mighty catchy phrase, Miss Ransom.'

'Thanks. Remember to give me credit if you use it. Did you hold hands with him in the movies?'

'Not exactly.'

'How do you not exactly hold hands?'

'Well, you sorta edge up onto the arm of the seat and *graze* a little.'

'It sounds very subtle.'

'That's it! That's the word! You gotta be real subtle. He's real young, you know, and come from a kinda sheltered home. But he send out *real* nice vibrations.'

'Next time you two have a date I'll have to switch on my seismograph.'

Lavender frowned and said, 'You don't think I'm serious.'

'I know you're serious, sweetheart, but I don't want you to get roughed up – inside or outside. Remember that Marine sergeant.'

'He was a *animal*. This one's different, and he come from a real good family.'

'Mine, too,' I said.

'Your what?'

'My lunch date. She comes from a good family, too – but I mean the grade-A certified kind that get their names in the blue books.'

'What name would that be?'

'Seagram.'

'Like the whiskey?'

'Yes, like the whiskey. That's what she says, at least.'

'And you think her name's really Old Granddad?'

'I think maybe it's not Seagram. She says she's from Portland, that her parents are dead, but the voice is pure New England.'

'Maybe she been taking elocutionary lessons,' Lavender suggested.

'Funnily enough, that's what she said. That she'd been coached to play debutante roles – *Philadelphia Story* stuff. But it's not just that. It's the way she moves, the way she thinks, the way she wears clothes.'

Lavender pushed himself back from the desk, stood up, and did a fashion-model stroll around the office, showing off his zoot suit. 'Some of us,' he said, 'just know how to dress. We born with it, the way some of you white folks

116

born with natural rhythm.'

'You're right, you're right. She hasn't got the kind of style you've got, of course. But everything about her suggests money, and I just don't see her in that scabby Academy.'

He stopped in front of me and shot his shirt-cuffs down to show off his rhinestone cufflinks. 'You interested for professional reasons?'

'Partly,' I said. 'At least, it's not *all* personal. She knows a lot about the Academy. She seems to have made it a point to find out, and I'd like to know what her interest is.'

'Maybe Conchita knows,' he hinted, raising an eyebrow in a way that made the point better than words could do.

'Conchita, I think, is too carried away by the starlet role to pay that much attention. And if she showed her hand with Ingrid, someone else may realize what she's really there for. I don't like it. I don't like the whole set-up. I'll give her another day or two, but that's the limit.'

'Meanwhile?'

'Meanwhile, I don't know. I think I'll try to get a line on Ingrid Seagram. What do you know about coming-out parties, Mr Trevelyan?'

'Coming-*out* parties?' He made a pair of startled eyes for me. 'I don't know nothin' 'bout how other folks do it, but my uncle brought me out when I was only twelve-years-old, and I been out ever *since*.'

'That wasn't quite what I had in mind.'

'No?' He tried his best to look hurt, but managed to look as though he was about to wet his baggy pants.

'I think,' I said, 'that I'll go down to the library and do some research. If Ingrid Seagram is twenty-two or twenty-three, and if she did make a debut, I've only got a couple of years to check on. The papers from Boston or New York or Philadelphia ought to have something.'

'Am I just supposed to mind the shop, then?'

'No. I want you to put your magic fingers to work.'

'Oh, no,' he protested. 'Don't you know you can go *blind* if you do that kinda stuff? Or crazy? You can end up in a

117

wheel chair!'

'I had in mind a little telephoning.'

'Dat *is* a relief, but he on duty today.'

'Well, then, haul out the yellow pages and see what you can learn about the Academy. Who holds the title to the property, whether there's a mortgage on it, and in whose name. And while you're at it, you might try to find out something about Woolcott International.

'What you think I am, Dow Jones?'

'No, just my trusty, resourceful assistant, my confidante, and my second best friend.'

'You win! I will dial my fingers *raw* for you. I'm gonna leave no number unbuzzed.'

I was, I thought, sending us both off on wild goose-chases, but it beat sitting around and waiting for the Green Feather people to deliver another of their grisly little presents.

21

ONLY her hair was different. It was shorter then, and it hadn't yet been gilded by a California sun, but it was Ingrid's delicately modelled features that stared up at me from the front page of the *New York Times* society section. The name was Ingrid Leslie, not Ingrid Seagram, and the background was all Eastern bluestocking, not Portland proletarian. But even that might not have been enough for the *Times* to give her such star billing. What put the thumb on the scale was that her father, Alfred Leslie, had recently won the Nobel Prize for physics. He was a widower, a Princeton professor, and Ingrid was his only child. The article put Ingrid in sharper focus, but it made her association with the Fairfield Academy even fuzzier than before. I re-read the *Times'* twittering prose, and it only confirmed the first impression – that Ingrid was as out of place in Shoemaker's sex factory as Amy Vanderbilt in the Brooklyn Dodgers' locker room.

I heaved the volume shut and carried it back to the reference librarian. From the way she watched my approach across her oiled wooden floor, I thought I must have left on my golf cleats, but she was only suspicious that I'd ask for another volume. She jabbed her hornrims back onto her witch's nose and rasped, 'Have you finished?'

'Yes,' I whispered. 'There aren't any funnies in the *Times*.'

She snorted and gave me what I think was supposed to be a contemptuous look, but through the bottle-thick glass her eyes looked like a pair of anemic moons.

'By the way,' I said, 'you wouldn't know where I could find any information on somebody named Alfred Leslie, would you? He won the Nobel Prize for physics three years ago.'

Obviously she wasn't used to such flattering appeals to her intelligence. She pushed out her bony chest and actually tried to smile, but gravity was working too hard against her.

'*Who's Who*,' she advised. Her owl imitations must be the life of the party.

'I know who,' I answered. 'I want to know what he's doing now.'

She jabbed a finger in the air in a way that suggested he was right there in the building, snuggled away in an airless little office on the second floor. I glanced up at the ceiling, which looked like the inverted hull of an abandoned three-master.

'Up there?' I asked.

'Dead,' she gurgled. Then she made a swift little tour with the finger, jabbing her glasses into place, checking her brooch, adjusting her shoulder pads. Or maybe she was crossing herself. 'Dead,' she repeated. 'Mortal sin.'

'Suicide?'

She raised her finger, buried it in the frizz at her right temple, and let off an imaginary shot. If her veins weren't full of library paste, I think she'd have bled a little for me.

I tried to look suitably stunned by her performance.

'Tragic,' she pronounced in a graveyard whisper.

'Tragic,' I echoed. 'When did it happen?'

'Last year. December. Tragic.'

I thanked her, and to show my gratitude tried extra hard not to make one of the floorboards squeak on my way out.

On the way back to the office I imagined a half-dozen possible scenarios that could have brought Ingrid to L.A. She was ashamed of her father's suicide and wanted to bury her past. She had seen too many Shirley Temple movies and had an old-fashioned case of starletitis. Her father hadn't left her a penny, and she hoped to use her good-looks to turn a semi-honest buck. Or maybe her Bryn Mawr years had given her literary ambitions, and she was actually snooping out a sensational exposé of Hollywood flesh-trading. Or she could, of course, be into it all deeper than I thought. Maybe it was the Leslie fortune that was bankrolling the academy, watering the potted palms and gilding the stags on the lawn and keeping Leone's cameras grinding. None of the explanations fit, though. It was like trying to put together an elaborate picture puzzle with all the important pieces missing – you know, the ones where you see both the blue of the sky and the tops of the trees.

I was idling at a traffic light, still arranging and rearranging the pieces I did have, when Brand Brockaway came slithering out of the Pink Lady Bar on the other side of the intersection. He had a snoot full, but by the time he lurched to the curb thoughts of his adoring public must have started dancing through his wee pointed head because he seemed to make a conscious effort not to lean too far to starboard. His hand shot up and a phony diamond flashed in the sun as he signaled a taxi. If I'd never seen his manicured face again it would have been too soon, but maybe it wouldn't hurt to know a little more about Shoemaker's leading man. When the light changed I drove halfway down the next block and pulled over to the curb. In the rear-view mirror I saw a canary-yellow taxi nudge out of the traffic and pull to a stop. Brockaway eased himself in as though he had a lapful of fresh eggs, and when the taxi passed me, I swung in behind.

Since Brockaway's head wasn't visible through the rear window of the cab, I presumed he was catching a few bloodshot winks. They must have done the trick, because when he stepped out at the main gate of Pantheon Pictures a half hour later, he was strutting his stuff for the chorus of star-gazers that always gathered there. He glittered over to the gate-keeper, said something to him, and sauntered off along the palm-lined private road that's been called everything from the main street of Hollywood to the ass-hole of Hollywood. With Brockaway on the scene the debate seemed settled.

I parked the car and wandered over to join the girls making cow-eyes in front of the gate and fingering their Brownies. They were radiating enough collective electricity to put the Hoover Dam out of business. The big flutter of the day seemed to be that Preston Sturges was having lunch in the studio commissary with Fred MacMurray, and one or both might appear at any moment.

'Isn't it just dreamy?' someone oozed.

'Dee-vine,' came the answer in 98 proof bottled-in-bond Mississipian.

A sour-sweet smell of sweat was coming off them, and it had its virtues, but by late afternoon it would be a lot less alluring, and their rayons would be bagged out at the knees, and their artificial gardenias would have all gone limp. Still, you had to give them credit for that pioneer-mother, westward-the-wagons kind of stamina. They'd stand there all day in hopes of mistaking an unemployed grip for Edward G. Robinson.

I edged around them and made what I hoped was an appropriately fluttery approach to the Tudor-style gate house.

To the fat jowls hiding inside I said, 'Excuse me, sir, but didn't I just see you talking to Brand Brockaway? In person?'

'Yeah,' grumbled the public relations department. 'Yeah. Brockaway, said his name was.'

121

'Is he making a picture here?'

'Don't ask me. Had an appointment with casting.'

'How *thrilling*,' I lied, and wondered if there really was a chance of Brockaway going legit. Horror movies weren't so big anymore, but they were probably due for a revival. I gave the jowls a couple of parting giggles and went back to the car. The upholstery was as hot as a short-order griddle, and I didn't feel like frying there for the rest of the afternoon waiting for Brockaway, but then I didn't have to wait that long. A half-hour later he staggered out of the gate again, looking even farther gone than when he'd made his loopy exit from the Pink Lady, but without the drunk's rubber joints. He seemed dazed, and he even forgot to preen his tail-feathers for the autograph-hunters. He just stood in the middle of the sidewalk, wiping his face with a white handkerchief the size of a tablecloth, and occasionally shooting glances over his shoulder down Asshole Drive. Then, robotlike, he started walking toward the bus-stop on the corner. I watched him for a while, propping himself against a lamppost, but when his bus came I decided not to follow. I didn't feel like puttering along behind in the diesel's exhaust just to collect a few more intimate secrets about Brockaway's scabby life. I could imagine them well enough, and it gave the day a certain luster just to know that whatever had happened inside the golden gates of Pantheon Pictures seemed to have unravelled his yo-yo string.

22

LAVENDER ticked off what he'd been able to learn while I was out playing Nick of the Woods.

'There's no mortgage on the Academy,' he said. 'The title's held by the Franklin Real Estate Company, which bought the place two years ago from the estate of Estelle Perkins, the old-maid daughter of the man who built the house.' He checked his notes again and clucked a little as he surveyed the terrain. The notes sprawled across three sheets of paper. 'The Franklin Real Estate Company is part of a con–, con– .' He squinted one eye and tried to decipher his own handwriting.

'Conglomerate?' I suggested.

'How you know that?'

'Lucky guess,' I said.

' – is part of a conglomerate with real estate all over California. Mostly office buildings, but also some apartment houses, a few restaurants, and a big hunk of beach south of Malibu. Oops, almost forgot. Also a couple of airports for private planes.'

'And who owns the Franklin Real Estate Company? Benjamin Franklin?'

'Don't *rush* me,' he said, really warming to his performance now. 'Dat is *some* bucket of worms. This Franklin Company is owned ninety per-cent by a company in Texas that makes tractors and bulldozers and stuff, and *it's* owned by a company in New York that is just strictly for investments and is owned by about a dozen banks. And them banks,' he said triumphantly, building up to the punch-line, 'is owned by Woolcott Industrials!' He flashed some porcelain at me and said, 'How's *that* for detective work?'

'Superb,' I told him, and I meant it. 'And you mean you did all that with those magic fingers of yours?'

'I did it all,' he beamed, 'with one phone call.'

'Who'd you call, Holmes Woolcott?'

'Nope, called somebody I know at the First National, in the investments department. The director.' He leaned back to let that one impress me. I was impressed.

'Mr Trevelyan, I had no idea you moved in such elite financial circles.'

'A fella got to have *some* secrets,' he insisted, riding back in the chair with his hands clasped behind his head, elbows out in a V-for-Victory sign.

'And what else did you learn for me?'

He sprang back to his notes, shuffled the pages noisily,

and cleared his throat. 'Woolcott's 49, married three times, studied a year in Heidelberg, graduated from Cal Tech, and is rumored to be worth about ten billion dollars. Most of his money's in Woolcott Industrials. Woolcott Industrials owns in some kinda crazy way this Franklin Real Estate Company, and they own an airplane factory, which everybody knows – ' He raised an eyebrow to check that one out with me.

'O.K.,' I said, 'that's Woolcott's pet project.'

' – and a few munitions factories,' he added, 'and some radio stations besides those other ones I talked about, and some hotels in Hawaii that ain't too popular now, and a steamship company and a whole lot of newspapers and a railroad or two and some oil wells and a big chemical company and a whole lotta companies that don't do nothin' but just own other companies.'

'Go to the head of the class, Mr Trevelyan. You've really done your homework this time.'

'It's not what you know, it's *who* you know,' he underscored.

'This financial wizard at the First National wouldn't by any chance be an old flame, would he?' I guessed.

Lavender sighed, 'You is too *sharp* for me.' Then, recovering, he said, 'Not really an old flame. More like a kinda middle-aged one. And he's got this real cute little bald spot that he try to cover up with anything that grows around the edges. Look a little like he use a egg-beater on it,' he laughed.

'You're incorrigible,' I said.

'Ain't *done* it,' he snapped. 'I changes my underwear every day and takes a bath every Saturday night whether I needs it or not. I ain't none o' your riff-raf.'

'Obviously not. Not with the kind of connections you've got.'

He gave me a withering look along the length of his nose, so concentrated that his eyes started to cross, when the corridor door banged open and Ann Shoemaker shot through like a Marine sergeant leading his troops over the top. Lavender was suddenly very busy filling his fountain pen.

'I demand an explanation!' Shoemaker barked, spraying frostbite across the room.

'Have you an appointment?' I asked in my most clipped, businesswoman-around-town kind of voice. 'It's five o'clock, and we normally don't see clients this late.'

She ignored me and stomped ahead into my inner sanctum. I shrugged at Lavender and he shrugged back, and I followed Shoemaker's track. It was about as hard as tracking a wounded rhinoceros through a rose garden. She let me get seated at least, and used the time to marshal her inimitable glacial control.

'One week ago today,' she said, 'we made a business agreement. Your services were employed to locate one of my students, Yvette LaFlamme.' She paused to let that sink in and then continued to read the riot act. 'Yvette LaFlamme has been dead for a week. Her body was found by the police and an investigation is already in progress. How is it that you knew – or pretended to know – nothing of these events?'

I showed her the palms of my hands. They were lily-white. 'I don't have free access to police information, and a missing persons case is normally a job for the police, not for a private investigator. That was made quite clear to you,' I reminded her.

'Murder is hardly a matter of state secrecy,' she hissed.

'Maybe not, but my teletype's broken, and I'm not getting the regular police bulletins these days.'

'It is inconceivable to me that a detective would not have access to even such basic information.' She might have been spelling out the words in mid-air with a bull-whip.

'Perhaps,' I suggested, 'I was too busy cutting through the smokescreen you put up around this case. You gave me as little information as you could, and then you expected me to proceed with complete discretion, without casting any shadows on your precious academy. If you ask me, the place has about as many shadows in it as the whole L.A.

sewer system.' So, of course, did my position in the case. 'I told you,' I said, choosing the words as carefully as possible, 'as much as I could. I could, in a few days, have told you a good deal more.'

'That,' the iron mask clanged, 'will not be necessary. You may consider our business relationship terminated.'

'Then you have no interest in finding out who murdered Yvette?'

'My interest is in protecting the reputation of the Academy. Yvette's disappearance could have meant embarrassment to us, and therefore I wished to know her whereabouts. The sordid details of her death do not interest me.'

'You're really all heart and a mile wide, aren't you?'

'My emotional life is hardly your concern, liebling.'

'Sorry, but in biology class I became especially interested in cold-blooded animals. You know, fish and reptiles and various things that crawl.'

Looking into her eyes was like staring down the barrels of a sawed-off shot-gun, but I was damned if I'd be the first to waver. I won. She did a swift little ballet with the facial muscles and rearranged her mug into its usual smug, superior lines.

'I am scarcely surprised at such impertinence,' she said, and then plunged a hand into the mouth of her overgrown purse. She brought out a small leather-bound book, flipped open the pages, and barked out the weekly financial report. 'According to our original agreement, you would be entitled to a fee of $200 for your eight days of so-called work on this case. That, as it happens, is precisely the amount which was given you as a retainer. You have, however, also received the sum of $300 for expenses. I shall expect full and complete itemization of those expenses before the week is out, and a refund of any amounts not satisfactorily accounted for.'

She flipped the book closed. 'Is that perfectly clear?' she growled.

'Aye-aye, sir,' I answered, and gave her a brisk salute.

'And if my expenses are more than $300, I'll expect your check for the balance. You may, of course, wish to indicate that a portion should be dedicated to your favorite charity.' I had in mind something like the Transylvania Society for the Prevention of Cruelty to Vampires, but I didn't let on.

'Your impertinence can be very tiresome,' she spit out.

'And so can your superior, holier-than-thou, boarding-school-mistress attitude. What I've learned about your very professional, very respectable acting academy is the sort of stuff *Police Gazette* readers eat for breakfast. Or before breakfast. I don't know who's running offense for your fancy little operation, but he's obviously a well-heeled kind of heel, and I've got more than a vague idea who it is. You didn't want me to find Yvette LaFlamme. You never cared what happened to Yvette LaFlamme, you were only afraid she'd somehow let the lid off your private sewer and the smell would get around town. That's the reason you didn't want the police involved, and so you picked me as patsy of the week, but it didn't quite work out the way you wanted it to. That's tough shit, but it doesn't give you grounds for storming in here like Grant taking Richmond.'

She studied me for a moment, her mouth a fresh seam waiting for the riveter. Then professionalism got the better of her. 'You have,' she pronounced, 'quite attractive coloring when you are angry. I find you, otherwise, a trifle pale.'

'Remind me not to audition for a part in one of your film spectaculars.'

She didn't flinch, but I knew she'd chalked that one up on a mental blackboard of accounts collectable.

'We can, I think, terminate this discussion,' she announced. 'I will expect a statement of expenses.'

'Don't hold your breath,' I warned her. 'On second thought, please do.'

As she stood up she said, 'What a pity. You could have been a useful ally.' With one hand she fumbled at the bun screwed to the back of her neck; it was the only time I'd seen her make a gesture that wasn't purposeful and perfectly controlled. Then she turned and walked out, her back as straight and rigid as an oil-derrick.

A few minutes later Lavender drummed his knuckles against the door. 'Not now, sweet chips,' I answered. 'I'm going to put on my thinking cap for a while.' The trouble was, I couldn't find one my size, so I settled for a drink instead.

A half-hour later, after muttering a few incantations against Shoemaker and Brockaway and Leone and a certain musclebound Irish cop, I decided to telephone Ingrid. She was the only one I knew who just might make sense out of the fun-house I'd been wandering through. At any rate, I thought her voice might be soothing for the nerves. It was.

'I hadn't expected to hear from you so soon,' she said.

'It would have been sooner, but I couldn't borrow a nickel. I just wanted to say – if you're interested – that I'm a little more at liberty now to talk about the case you asked me about at lunch today.'

'Does that mean you're no longer employed?'

'It means I'm thinking of trying to sell apples at Hollywood and Vine.'

'Would you work for me?' she asked. I hoped she wasn't a stickler about not mixing business and pleasure.

'The "For Rent" sign's on the door.'

'I'll pay you your customary fee,' she said. 'Whatever you think is fair under the circumstances – ' Her voice was a cool mountain stream and I wanted to bathe in it.

'Are you still there?' she asked.

'Yes,' I said. The rusty green filing cabinet reminded me where I was. That and the bands of late-afternoon sunshine that were busy sucking up dust from the floor. 'But if it's the old missing-persons routine,' I added, 'you should know that she's no longer missing.'

'It's not that,' she insisted. 'Or not just that. I really can't talk now,' she said, lowering her voice to a throaty whisper. 'Can I see you tonight?'

'I'm home all evening,' I suggested, and told her the

128

address.

She picked it up. 'Good. I'll come by whenever things quiet down a little here. Probably around ten or ten-thirty. And I'll bring you a check.'

'But you've got a big date tonight,' I remembered.

'It's off,' she said. 'I've suddenly become *persona non grata*.'

'Join the crowd.'

'Until tonight, then,' she murmured, and the line went dead.

As I craned back in the chair the battle fatigue was still there, but it no longer seemed like the guys in black hats were running the whole show.

23

WHEREVER I spun the dial that night, Sinatra was mooing for the girls. I couldn't figure out exactly what effect The Voice was supposed to have on the female libido, but I guess it put me in a distinct minority. Even the spaniel eyes and the twenty pounds of shoulder padding were reported to do their magical bit for the eternal urge. So I settled for listening to my own footsteps as I walked the linoleum and waited for Ingrid. It was nearly eleven when the buzzer sounded and sliced off the last wooden minute.

A misty summer rain was falling outside, and Ingrid was dressed for it. She wore a tan poplin trench coat, the collar turned up around the slender column of her neck, and her hair was tucked up inside a matching fedora whose wide brim was sloped down over her forehead. For a moment I thought I might have invented her, but when she stepped inside, took off her hat, and shook loose the pale curtains of her hair, I had to admit that genes and money and brains and Bryn Mawr had accomplished more than my Vargas-girl fantasy life could ever have done. Her faint, spicy perfume hung on the air, and when she smiled it was like being presented with a bouquet of Baccarat roses. Doing

129

business with her was definitely going to strain a few paragraphs in the code of professional ethics.

And it was clearly a business call, despite the way she coiled, like a sleek cat, with her legs tucked beneath her at one end of the sofa while I mixed drinks. Hoyle couldn't have spelled out the rules any more precisely, and he would have needed words to do it. Ingrid did it all with muted gestures, with a slight toss of her gleaming hair, with a sudden deepening of the intense blue of her eyes. It was enough. Romance, she made it clearly known, was of no interest to her now, but she couldn't deny spectators whatever pleasure they might get by observing her from a polite distance. That way she could share her beauty and still keep it for herself – like the landed gentry opening their parks and gardens to rubbernecking Sunday tourists.

We clinked our glasses in a toast, and I was proud of the way my hand kept from trembling. Then the preliminaries were over.

'You'll accept my offer?' she asked.

'In principle, yes. But I'll need to know more about the assignment you had in mind.'

She moistened her lips and stared down at her glass, rattling the ice-cubes a little as though they might help with her answer. The faintly puckered lines appeared again between her eyes. 'Frankly,' she said, 'I don't really know myself. I only know you were hired by Ann Shoemaker to undertake some kind of investigation.' She hesitated, took a sip of her drink, and added, 'Something to do with Yvette's disappearance.'

'Yes,' I agreed, 'that was the assignment.'

'And you've been relieved of the assignment?'

'Right. I got the sack shortly after five o'clock this afternoon, and it didn't exactly produce an attack of hysterical weeping.'

With one finger she slowly traced a circle round the rim of her glass, then raised her eyes to mine. 'I'm not,' she confessed, 'in the least interested in a career in pictures.'

'It's a loss to the box office, but I didn't really think you

130

were.'

'I had other reasons for enrolling at the Academy. They wouldn't seem like very good reasons to most people – '

'Try me,' I suggested.

It was all turning into a blind alley, and the Academy seemed the only way I might find out what I wanted to know.

'And what was that?'

She ignored the question. That, she seemed to say, would come in its own time, in her own way. 'My name,' she said, 'isn't Ingrid Seagram.'

'I know,' I helped her. 'Your name is Ingrid Leslie. You're twenty-three years old, you graduated from Bryn Mawr a year ago, and your father was a professor of physics at Princeton.'

She laughed softly. 'I'm obviously hiring a good detective,' she replied.

'It was luck.'

'And a lucky one, too. That's even more than I'd hoped for. I thought – ' she faltered. 'I thought at one time I could figure things out for myself, but it isn't that easy, and I guess I need help.' She clearly didn't like admitting it any more than she liked needing it.

'We all do once in a while,' I said, trying to muster my best motherly expression.

'You probably also know how my father died,' she said, her voice making a faint but unmistakable break at the end of the sentence.

'I don't know any details,' I hedged.

'He shot himself with a target pistol. Through the right temple.' Each careful, precisely articulated word was paid for with a tearing of fresh wounds deep inside her. But she went on, 'It was December 2nd of last year. That morning, at breakfast, we'd planned a trip to California. Father was going to attend a scientific convention in San Francisco, just after Christmas, and he thought I'd enjoy the trip.'

'How did he seem then? Was he depressed or anxious about anything?'

This time her laugh was brittle, bitter, angry. 'Depressed? I never knew my father depressed, and I'd never known him happier than he was then. Once I'd graduated he seemed to feel he'd got over the worst hurdles. My mother died when I was three years old, and he did everything for me. He couldn't do enough, in fact, but he was always concerned that he might do something wrong, that I wouldn't get the right kind of affection or attention or something. In the last few months of his life he seemed to feel he'd been successful after all.'

'I don't think anyone could quarrel with that.'

'Not with anything he had done,' she said. 'Even Father began to realize that, and he seemed suddenly so much younger and freer.'

'He wasn't ill?'

'Absolutely not,' she insisted.

'Maybe he wanted to spare you.'

'It occured to me at first. It seemed the only explanation, but his doctor assured me Father was in the best of health. He wouldn't have lied to me,' she added.

No, I thought, that wouldn't be easy.

As if anticipating my next question, she said, 'There was no problem with his work, either. He used to joke that he'd spend the rest of his life in the shadow of his own success. The Nobel Prize, he meant, but he was going to San Francisco to read a paper on his latest research, and he thought it was more important than anything he'd ever done before. He had a chair at Princeton, and he wasn't in any financial difficulties. He had a large private income of his own, and my mother had had even more. Her money was all left in trust for me.'

'So you think, then, that he didn't commit suicide after all?'

She took a quick, deep breath that trembled in her throat. 'I wanted to think that,' she said. 'God, how I wanted to think that. But he was alone in his study. I'd been out all afternoon,' she remembered, 'and when I came back I looked in, but he was at his desk, and I didn't want to bother him. A few minutes later I heard the shot.' She shuddered as it exploded again in her memory, and tears glistened in her eyes. 'I ran in,' she said. 'I ran in and found him, and he was alone, still sitting at his desk. No one could have come in or gone out without my knowing it,' she asserted, calmer now and more assured.

'Was there any letter or note for you?'

'Nothing.'

'And were the police satisfied it was suicide?'

'They never doubted it. But since I seemed to, they made some kind of test to be sure he'd fired the gun.'

'The Lund test?'

'Yes,' she nodded, 'that's the one.'

I couldn't guess where this was all leading, what goal she had in mind as she guided me, gently but firmly, through this twisting maze. I only knew it was important to her to get me there in her own way, to reveal the destination only when the right moment had arrived.

She seemed to sense what I was thinking, because she said, 'I guess it still seems a long way from Princeton, New Jersey, to the Fairfield Academy.'

'Yes, even as the crow flies.'

'It was important to me to know why my father killed himself. At first it was a kind of crazy obsession. It was all I knew that I could do then, and for a while it was all I seemed to have to live for. Now – ,' she faltered. 'Now, it's not so much an obsession as it was then, in the days after I found him. But it's still there – a kind of cause, maybe. He was a great scientist and a good father and a good *man*,' she stressed, 'and I have to know. There was only one thing to go on, a note in his calendar. It said "Woolcott – 2 p.m." '

'Woolcott,' I observed, 'has a knack for cropping up in all the most unlikely places.'

'Money works that way,' she knowingly informed me. 'Still, I don't know if he really turned up. I was out for the afternoon, and the note could have meant Father was simply expecting a phone call. He once did some consulting work for Woolcott Industrials. Or it could have meant someone from Woolcott Industrials was coming to see him, but not necessarily Holmes Woolcott himself. He doesn't get around much, does he?'

'Not in public, at least. A photographer could bankroll himself for quite a while with even a snapshot of Mr Aviation.'

'Exactly. So I don't see him strolling across the Princeton campus and knocking on Father's study door. But the name was all I had to go on, so I came to L.A., hoping to learn more about him, to pick up a clue somehow or other. I got nowhere,' she admitted. 'I thought about trying to get a job at Woolcott Industrials, but I didn't want to use my real name, and without it I couldn't claim much by way of education. Even if I could, I'm not quite sure what a degree in English literature would get me in that kind of company. Then I played a long-shot, and asked Father's broker to do a little snooping for me. He's the one who came up with the information that Woolcott owns the Academy. It was hard to see a man like him being involved in that kind of operation, and it certainly couldn't be interesting to him as a tax write-off. And just because it *didn't* make sense, I decided to enroll and see what I could find out.'

'And what was that?' I led her on.

She thought about it for a moment, biting gently at her lower lip. Finally she said, 'Not much, really. Not much more than I told you at lunch – the films, the blind dates. I'd about made up my mind that Woolcott used it ocasionally for his own private amusement, the way some people like to raise their own vegetables. Then Yvette didn't show up one morning, and Ann Shoemaker began to panic. It wouldn't have passed for panic with anyone of more mortal flesh, of course.'

'Did her rivets begin to corrode a little?'

'They did,' she laughed. 'And then Conchita turned up, and then you turned up, and here I am.' She set down her glass and folded her arms, folded them high so that her tapered fingers embraced her own shoulders, and tilted her lovely head to one side, as though to signal that the next move was mine. The rain outside had increased to a faint drum-beat against the windows. My heart was echoing it.

'Your intuition is in good health,' I said. 'Shoemaker was fit to be tied when Yvette disappeared, and she was willing to unwrinkle a lot of the folding green to find out where she was. Frankly, I think she was afraid Yvette was going to talk a little too loudly about the Academy's extracurricular activities. Today she found out Yvette was dead, and that terminated our business arrangement.'

'Dead?' Ingrid whispered. She shuddered and hugged herself tighter with her arms. 'Was she – '

'Yes, she was murdered, and I don't think you want to know too many of the details. From the beginning, Holmes Woolcott has cropped up in this case like the famous bad penny. He's too big to be involved in any direct way, and he's too rich to have to be. But his empire is involved somehow.'

'I want you,' she said in a crisp, firm voice, 'to find out how.'

'That's a big assignment,' I answered. 'It's probably too big for me. My business is bush-league stuff. You need one of the big agencies.'

'I don't think so,' she said pensively. 'I think you're just what I need. You don't have to concentrate on Woolcott. Concentrate on Yvette's murder, and maybe the next step will be clear then. Meanwhile, I'll find out all I can from inside the Academy, if my credibility isn't too badly damaged.'

'Should it be?'

'No, I don't think so. At least, I think I've done a pretty good job of acting like a would-be movie-star. But Ann Shoemaker was pretty brusque when she cancelled my date for tonight.'

'No explanation?'

'Nothing.'

'Maybe,' I suggested, 'Yvette's death has them running for cover. It could be they've decided to go legit for a while.'

'Wrong!' she countered. 'Conchita's booked for

tomorrow night.'

'I knew I should have jerked the kid out of there last week,' I muttered.

'But maybe she'll find out something,' Ingrid said.

'More likely,' I answered, 'she'll be found out herself. She's about as transparent as a soap-bubble.'

'Not quite so fragile as that.'

'No,' I agreed, but then neither was Yvette LaFlamme. 'Listen,' I said, 'I don't like it. Whoever silenced Yvette is more than just a killer. He's a maniac with a very perverse sense of humor. No, I think Conchita's going to have to start playing hookey. I'm not too thrilled about your going back to that chamber of horrors either, but at least it was your decision to go there in the first place. I didn't send you there ...' I thought a minute, but the wheels weren't revolving too swiftly tonight. It had, after all, been a long day, and the hands on my watch were arranging a rendezvous at the number twelve.

'Listen,' I said finally, 'I want to talk to Conchita, but away from that place. Could you cover for her if she takes a little stroll tomorrow morning – say, right after breakfast?'

'I think so,' Ingrid nodded.

'Fine. Have her take a walk. If you turn left when you leave the driveway you soon come to an unpaved sideroad. I forget the name, but it seems to lead back to another housing estate. It must be the back way in or something, because there was no traffic there on Sunday. I'll pull into that road, just far enough not to be visible from the main street. Tell Conchita to meet me there as close to nine o'clock in the morning as she can make it.'

'I'll tell her,' Ingrid assured me. 'You're pretty crazy about her, aren't you?'

'Sure I am,' I said. 'Or maybe I'm just doing my bit for Mexican-American relations.' I was lying, and Ingrid's eyes told me she knew it. A half-hour later, when the door had closed behind her, the faint trace of her perfume lingered on the air, but it was Conchita's face I saw in my dreams that night.

24

THE rain had started again, lazy and warm, but not so lazy that I wasn't soaked through by the time I could hoist the top of the car. The difference it made was debatable, since the canvas was as full of holes as a slice of delicatessen Swiss, but it made things seem a little cozier. The windows fogged over, the air grew so thick you could spoon it up, and I felt the start of that long, slow, easy slide into sleep. I didn't fight it, because I'd made the ship just as the gangplank was being cranked up, and the rest of them were left standing on the pier. Their faces grew smaller and smaller, and one by one they vanished – Shoemaker, Brockaway, Leone, even Ingrid. Soon you couldn't see the twin suitcases sitting at their feet, only the green-foamed rise and fall of the ocean swell.

The latch on the car door clicked me awake. A fire-alarm bell couldn't have done the trick any better. Conchita slid onto the seat beside me, and at first it seemed like a re-play of the night before. She wore Ingrid's trench coat and the wide-brimmed hat dipped over her eyes, and it all sent a faint shiver racing down my spine. I didn't stop to wonder why, but pulled her toward me and held her without saying anything until I was convinced she hadn't just wandered in out of my dream. Somewhere, so far away it might have been across the state line, a dog was barking. Otherwise, the only sounds were the rustle of rain against the canvas roof, the faint whisper of Conchita's breath against my ear.

'I miss you,' she murmured.

'I miss you, too,' I told her. 'I didn't know how much I *could* miss you. But it won't be long now.'

'I come home?' she wondered.

'You come home,' I said. 'You come home very, very soon.'

'Not today?' she asked in a voice embroidered with

protest.

'No,' I said. 'Probably tomorrow.'

'*Bueno.*' She pulled away from me, but only to give me the gift of a smile. 'Because today in the *tarde* I have screen-test,' she explained, looking as if she'd just strolled through stardust instead of rain. 'And tonight,' she remembered, 'I meet someone *muy importante* in Hollywood.'

'That's what we've got to talk about. I can't let you go tonight,' I said.

'Not go?' Her petals began to droop.

'This way,' I suggested, 'you can concentrate everything on your screen-test. And what's happening tonight could be ...' I wasn't sure myself what I thought it could be, but I settled for saying, 'It could be dangerous.'

'But I promise to go,' she pouted.

'Don't worry,' I said. 'I'll be going in your place.'

'You,' she wondered. 'Why you go too if it dangerous?'

'Why? Because I'm working on a case, and this may help me solve it. Besides, I'm being paid to take risks. You're not.' I didn't add that if the chips got called in, I wanted them to be mine and not hers.

She didn't like it, but at least she had her screen-test as a consolation prize. It was all written in her dark, bright eyes as obvious as a tabloid headline. She weighed things up, a piece at a time, and decided the total was still in her favor.

'*Sí,*' she said. 'And what I do?'

'Go ahead with it,' I answered, 'just as though the plan hadn't changed. Get yourself dolled up for your date and pretend to be all excited about it. Ask Shoemaker's advice on what you should wear – that sort of thing, and if anything goes wrong, tell Ingrid. She knows what I've got in mind.'

'She knows?' Conchita asked in a voice that seemed to call for explanations.

'Yes,' I said. 'I'll explain it all later. Now what's the game-plan for tonight?'

'The game?'

'The plan. What's the set-up?'

It was the same game-plan Ingrid had before she got
scrubbed at the last minute. At nine-thirty she would leave
the house, walk to the foot of the drive, and be picked up by
a black chauffeur-driven limousine. And she was not to
mention the date to any of the other girls.

'Good. I'd hoped they wouldn't change the m.o. on us.
Now here's what you do. You leave the house just as
planned, but do your best to keep in the shadows of the
trees beside the driveway, and when you're out of sight of
the house, wait there until you hear someone get into the
car and the door slam. That'll be me. When the car leaves,
come back here. I'll park the Plymouth in this same spot
and leave the spare key under the floor-mat. Drive yourself
home and wait there for me. Don't answer the telephone,
and in case anyone buzzes, don't go to the door. I'll pick
you up later and bring you back to the Academy, unless
I've decided you shouldn't come back at all. But it's
probably not a good idea for you to drop out too soon after
tonight's little rendezvous.'

As Conchita listened to me, she began to work up a little
enthusiasm for the part she was to play. I did what I could
to fan the spark by saying it all depended on her now, on
how good an actress she was. Then I made her repeat the
evening's program for me, step by step. It seemed a little
too easy, too neatly wrapped in cellophane when she played
it back, and that bothered me, but it had the virtue of
getting her off the firing line. Or so I thought as I held her
again and felt the roof daintily sieving water onto us.

25

'WHAT have you got,' I asked Lavender, 'that's kind of sexy
without being too sexy?'

'What's too sexy?'

'That red taffeta number of yours, for example.'

'Honey, that is a *designer* dress.'

'Well, it's not quite designed for me. I want to show a little cleavage, but my navel I prefer to keep a military secret. And remember that Queen Shoemaker prides herself on running a high-class establishment.'

Lavender began to scrawl a fresh doodle on the desk blotter while he thought that one over. Finally he said, a little doubtfully, 'I got a white chiffon. It's like this Roman-lookin' style, with a big gold belt.'

'Somehow that doesn't sound like what the well-dressed Mexican-American is wearing these days.'

'You *right*,' he agreed, with a dramatic sigh of relief. 'Also, it's real new, and I haven't worn it myself – 'cept just around the house.'

'Then that one's definitely out of the question. Things could get rough, and I wouldn't want to pucker the chiffon. I think I really need fatigues and combat boots.'

'Now *that* sound sexy,' he beamed.

'But not quite right for the part.'

'No? Well, then …' He tapped a melody against his teeth with the pencil. 'I know,' he said suddenly, 'why don't you wear something of Conchita's?'

'Because she's shorter than I am, and a little broader in the stern.'

'Oh … But you sure you not a *tiny* bit bigger in the waist than I am?' he asked, sizing me up with a skeptical eye.

'I'll wear my whale-bone corset,' I said.

'My, oh my, you *does* got a problem, Miss Scarlett.' He ran through his wardrobe for me. 'The black one a little green on the seams now. The red taffeta's too sexy and the white chiffon too Roman, and I *know* you ain't gonna like that old flamenco skirt.' The slope in his shoulders told me he was beginning to give it up as a lost cause.

'And those are the only choices?'

'Time's *hard*,' he informed me with a sigh. 'Couldn't you whip somethin' up out of the dining-room curtains?' he wondered.

'They're Venetian blinds,' I said, 'and tend to scrape in the crotch.'

'Then it's gotta be that red taffeta thing.'

'I'll catch pneumonia.'

'It ain't that low-cut. Besides, you can pin a corsage in there or a lace hanky or something.'

'I suppose I *could* wear a flannel shirt under it.'

'You a real trend-setter.'

'I know. It all started when I did that advertisement for Fruit of the Loom.'

'So you gonna wear the red taffeta?'

'So I'm gonna wear the red taffeta, I guess. Can you loan me those earrings, too – the big gold hoops?'

'They my momma's, but I reckon she don't care.'

We closed up shop early that day, and on the way to Lavender's place I stopped at a drugstore to buy some black rinse for my hair. The label said it was guaranteed to wash out. If not, I'd reverse the local pattern and be the only girl in town with black hair and blonde roots. I waited in front of Lavender's apartment house while he assembled the rest of my Mardi Gras costume. He came skipping down the walk after a few minutes, holding a brown paper grocery bag out in front of him and whistling 'Mexicallie Rose'. I didn't know until I got home that it contained not only the dress and the earrings but also a patented Munsingwear hold-down foundation girdle. It looked like something that had been shot out of season.

The hair tint worked wonders. It dyed not only my hair and my eyebrows but the bathroom sink, part of the floor, a couple of towels, my fingernails and my forehead. A gallon of Chlorox solved the problem, though, and the results weren't really so bad. I could, I thought, pass at least by candlelight for a Mexican-American whose mother had had very fair skin, but as I was leaving the bathroom I caught another angle in the full-length mirror on the door and realized there was a certain curious inconsistency in the picture. So I dug around until I found an old tooth-brush and used it to add the finishing touches. I wasn't planning for anyone to make the old comparison test, but I couldn't be quite sure what the evening might bring. After all, it's just those little touches that make the difference between the amateur and the pro.

I needed a shoe-horn later, when I wedged into Lavender's red taffeta strangulator, and it didn't leave much to the imagination. I could even see a mole on my right hip that I'd never noticed there. Before I left I had a double-strength cuba libre to loosen the joints and afterwards chewed a couple of peppermints to make sure my breath was kissing-sweet. Then I bundled up in an old Macintosh so I wouldn't get arrested for indecent exposure on the way to the car, but I still felt like something that had been very snugly wrapped in shiny paper by one of the over-priced gift shops in Beverly Hills. That didn't bother me so much, though, as thoughts about the creep who might be trying to unwrap me in another hour or two.

Night was beginning to pull her curtains when I left the apartment, and the job was finished by the time I got the Plymouth parked on the side-road, shucked off my raincoat and hooked Conchita's white silk shawl around my shoulders. I tucked the key under the floormat and reorganized my beaded evening bag, so the Mauser 7.65 didn't make quite such a conspicuous bulge in the side. Then I stepped out, eased the door of the car shut as quietly as I could, and hiked back down the main street, feeling the heels of my shoes sink a couple of inches into the rain-softened road with each step. Overhead, there were already a few stars nailed to the sky. I got to the driveway of the Academy less than five minutes before the big limousine pulled up with diamond-flashes of chrome and a throaty purr that was a lot quieter than the neighborhood crickets. The chauffeur got out without saying anything and opened the door for me, but as I stepped in I caught enough of his profile to recognize Archie Potter, the mug O'Brien had worked over the week before. The leather seat was as soft as a baby's bottom, and as I settled back against it I thought of Cinderella going off to the ball. But then I remembered Mr Aviation's famous appetite for beauty, and hoped he hadn't ordered me as the entrée of the evening.

26

I WAS beginning to feel like the baton in a relay race. Potter turned me over to a butler who was wearing bouncer's shoulders under his cutaway and a prize-fighter's scrambled nose in the middle of his face. He wanted to take my shawl, but I kept a hammerlock on it while he led me across the pink marble hall and passed me on to a lady's maid who showed me into what she called the powder room. There was powder there alright – a dozen different shades in crystal boxes, as well as a whole arsenal of lipsticks in all the shades mother nature forgot, and a few quart bottles of Chanel. The lady's maid wanted to help me fix my hair, but I assured her it wasn't broken. She also wanted to take my shawl, but I clung to it as if it were the Golden Fleece, and she finally gave up. Just to humor her a little I made a few passes at my hair with a tortoise-shell comb, dabbed on some lipstick, and dribbled a teaspoon of Chanel down my cleavage. Then she led me out of the powder-room, back across the pink amphitheater, and through another gold-leafed doorway, where she turned me over to a quality-control expert who was obviously supposed to spot any rotten apples before they got into the barrel.

She was sitting behind a lacquered desk that seemed to have the whole history of China painted on it, but she stood up briskly when we came in. 'I am Alma Nugent,' she said, and paused to let the announcement sink in. She had a trim, youthful figure draped in brocaded silk, but her face seemed held together by a fine mesh of wrinkles, and her white hair gleamed like a Rinso ad. The cool, washed-out gray of her eyes was set off by glittering red lips. When she pursed them, as she did now, they looked like a bisected cherry.

'Won't you sit down?' she invited.

I sat down. Then she took to the needlepoint herself and reached a gold cigarette case across the desk to me. 'Would you care to smoke?' she asked.

'No thanks, I don't smoke.'

'Very good. Mr Woolcott cannot bear cigarette smoke anywhere in his presence.' She paused to make another cherry for me. 'He also cannot bear the odor of cheap perfume,' she continued. 'It irritates his sinus membranes.'

I made what I hoped was a sympathetic murmur.

'May I ask if you have recently had any communicable diseases?'

Only cholera and advanced neuro-syphilis, I wanted to answer, but instead I gave her a wide-eyed 'No'.

'Marvelous,' she said. 'And have you recently had a chest x-ray?'

'Last month,' I lied, 'and the results were negative.'

'You have not had a cough, fever, or any aching in the joints?'

'No,' I answered, and it was true if you discounted the pain in the ass I was having at that moment.

'You are not, I hope, disturbed by such questions. You see, we must exercise certain precautions.'

'Of course.'

'And now, if I may venture to become rather more intimate ...' She paused for a discrete little dip of the eyes, as rehearsed as the rest of her stale routine. 'You are not, I presume, currently having your menstrual period?'

I shuddered a little, as though the very thought was almost more than my well-bred nature could tolerate, and shook my head. No, I was mercifully free of the curse.

'Very good. It is, once more, a question of odors,' Alma Nugent patiently explained. 'Indeed, all of Mr Woolcott's ... ah, sensory organs ... are somewhat ... They are, shall we say, rather sensitive, and require special attention. It is, for example, necessary to avoid bright lights and sudden loud noises.' I thought I knew a cozy corner in Forest Lawn where he'd feel right at home.

'Have you any questions, my dear?' she asked in a crisp,

census-taking voice.

No, I didn't – none, at least, that she was likely to answer.

She gave me a final once-over with her eyes, and I thought she was about to ask if she could count my teeth, but then she seemed satisfied enough, and jabbed a buzzer on her desk. A slender young man with wavy hair crowning his sultry, Latin good looks waltzed through a door in the back of the room, nodded to old cherry-lips, and ushered me out, but not before she'd asked if I didn't want to leave my stole on her hat-rack.

Swivel-hips led me upstairs, and I should have counted the steps on the way, just to be sure there really were as many as in the Empire State Building. At the top we started confusing anyone who might have put a tail on us. We made a couple of lefts, I remember, then a right, walked a half-mile along a corridor whose carpeting was so thick I was afraid I'd lose a heel in it, and after that there were a couple of more subtle manoeuvres – up one staircase, then down another. I thought we might bump into the architect who built the place, stumbling on his Rip Van Winkle beard and looking for the way out. Instead, what we finally saw was the goon brigade – half-a-dozen muscle-bound types lined up along a corridor and trying to blend in with the tapestries. Obviously we weren't far from the throne room. Even without the royal guard, it would have been hard to miss, since the doors were two-stories high and covered with bronze reliefs inspired by the Kama Sutra. There was even a resident Punjab to open them. My guide made me a brisk garden-party bow and said, 'This is where I leave you,' finishing off with a cute little wave of the wrist that suggested I was to go into the lion's den without him.

The room was so dark it took me a while to readjust the retinas. The only light there was came from pierced brass lanterns that hung from the ceiling and sent an occasional half-hearted flicker into the shadows. Oriental carpets were strewn about the floor, and here and there blood-red cushions were piled on them next to low brass tables. There

145

was a sickeningly sweet odor of incense in the air, and from somewhere far away came the sound of a flute, tirelessly repeating the same few notes over and over again. It was like walking onto a set for *The Fall of the House of Usher*, and if Lavender's dress hadn't been so tight, I'd probably have jumped out of my skin when the voice floated across the room.

'Come to me, my dear.'

I took my bearings as best I could without a guide dog and stumbled my way through the pillows.

'Over here,' the voice helped me.

Over here turned out to be a platform raised slightly above the floor but blending cunningly with the rest of the room. It was a neat camouflage job, alright. Half-sitting, half-reclining against a gross of silk pillows was the legendary Holmes Woolcott, wearing a black kimono. You could still recognize him, even if the famous profile was as much a thing of the past as a good five-cent Havana. His cheeks were collapsed to show the death's-head beneath, and his eyes were hooded as if he were either half-asleep or had a snoot full of junk. No wonder he wasn't too keen on smiling for the birdie. He held a hand out – a kind of claw, really, with long, twisted yellow fingernails – and beckoned to me. I eased a little closer and sat on the edge of the platform, reminding myself how good I used to be at the hundred-yard dash.

'Please remove that absurd drapery,' he sighed. The whole family seemed obsessed with unveiling ceremonies tonight.

'Ah, yes,' he whispered, when I'd folded the shawl and laid it beside me. Then he sank back on his pillows with a little gurgle, as though the effort had been too much for him, but he was still keeping the cleavage I'd revealed well within his bomb-sight. Apparently he liked the view, because he gave a contented moan every now and then, blowing an occasional spit-bubble through his beefy lips. This was going to be a lot easier than I'd thought. When he hooked one of those claws down between his legs, I wondered if he'd had a tetanus shot lately, but since he could always buy himself the Mayo Clinic, I didn't worry too much.

After a few minutes of wrist action under the kimono, he grunted, 'Give me … Give me … Give me your shoe.' I slipped off the right one and handed it to him, hoping he wouldn't notice the sole was coming unglued. It didn't seem to matter, though. He got his tongue down inside it and obviously liked what he found there. To each his own, as they say in the song, but one of these days the guy was going to strangle to death on a Blue Jay corn pad.

I spent the next few minutes pretending to study the landscape, and then Woolcott gradually came down off the mountain top. The exertion had put strawberry blotches on his putty-colored skin and a kind of death rattle in his throat. He really fell asleep for a while, and I hung around waiting to see what he'd do for an encore. I couldn't leave anyhow until my shoe dried out. After a few minutes his eyelids snapped open like a pair of overwound window shades, and Woolcott was his old frisky self again.

'Come closer, my dear.' I inched one haunch and then the other in his general direction.

'No, no,' he protested. 'Come here, beside me,' and then, 'Ah, yes, *that's* better,' when I'd got within arm's reach. He put a claw on my thigh and started checking the thread-count in the taffeta.

'Do you,' he asked, 'like Dom Perignon?'

I was about to say I hadn't met the gent when something in the shadows went pop and paralyzed my vocal chords for a minute. A pair of hands came between us holding a silver tray with two glasses of bubbly on it. Whoever owned the hands must have been standing in the wings all the time, just waiting for his cue.

Woolcott swished the champagne around in his mouth like it was Listerine, and then slurped it down. It seemed to charge his batteries a little.

'How old are you?' he asked.

'Twenty-four,' I answered, shaving off a few birthdays

that I hadn't enjoyed anyhow.

'And you are part Mexican, I believe.'

'On my father's side,' I told him. My own father wouldn't have known the difference between a taco and a tango, and he probably would have thought a tortilla was a very small whore.

'Physically, such racial combinations make for quite interesting results,' he nodded, 'even if they do disturb the natural order of things.' The observation rang a few political bells, each one a little more cracked than the one before. 'But never mind,' he waved it away. 'Are you happy with your work at the Academy?'

I flapped my eyelashes for him and did my best to gush an answer. 'Oh, *sí*, it's wonderful! We have such good training, and show business is very exciting.'

'Perhaps,' he ventured, 'I could help you with your career.'

'Oh, *señor* ...' I fumbled, trying to seem at a loss for words. 'Oh, *señor* ...'

'I have many friends in the movie industry,' he declared, gulping down another dose of Dom Perignon. 'Producers, directors, and very important businessmen, of course. Would you like to meet some of them?'

'*Sí*,' I cooed.

'It could be arranged. It is necessary from time to time for me to entertain such friends ...' He paused, and I knew we were about to get to the fine print at the bottom of the contract. 'Naturally, it is more pleasant when there are beautiful women here.'

I smiled understandingly and glanced down to see the claw inching up my thigh again.

'I would, of course, expect to pay you for the time you would take away from your ... studies.' He belched and held his glass up for a refill. The magic hands appeared and did their trick again. 'Any contractual arrangements you might make for further services to my friends would be up to you.' I was beginning to think we might both sink in the quicksand of his soft-sell, but then he nailed me with his eyes and asked, 'Do I make myself clear?'

'*Sí,*' I answered, trying to make it sound as if it rose up from my groin.

He relaxed again. 'You are very beautiful,' he repeated, and his hand crabbed its way a little higher. I thought about offering him my other shoe.

'Would you tie me up?' he asked suddenly.

'Tie you up?'

'Yes,' he grunted. 'Tie me very tightly.' For once I wished I hadn't skipped the chapter on knots in the Girl Scout Handbook.

'I wouldn't want to *hurt* you,' I protested.

'But I like it, my dear,' he answered slowly, stressing each word for me and studying my face from beneath his drooping lids.

'Well, if it make you happy ...'

He laughed deep in his chest. It sounded like someone rapping on a coffin lid.

Hands materialized again, holding two lengths of coarse hemp rope. It wasn't exactly my cup of tea, but it would stop the advance of the crab people. Besides, I had the reputation of the Academy to think of, and I wanted to be a credit to Lady Shoemaker's upbringing.

I trussed him up like the Thanksgiving turkey, but I didn't get very high marks. Home economics was never my best subject. 'Tighter!' Woolcott ordered, his blubbery lips drawn back to reveal mauve-colored gums with tiny baby teeth sprouting from them. 'Tighter!' I did my best to oblige, and he struggled against the ropes until they were tinted with his own blood.

While Woolcott lay crooning to himself and working up a sweat, I couldn't help thinking about the good old days of motel entrapments, when the air was as fresh and as sweet as the first hyacinth of spring, and a girl could still turn an honest buck. Something black and sour was coiled in my stomach, threatening to make a sudden bolt for freedom. I sat down and kept watch on it, holding Conchita's shawl in one hand and my beaded Mauser-holster in the other.

149

Woolcott finally came out of his trance, grunting orders to the hands. They levitated the ropes away and sponged him off and then set a jade bowl down in front of him with a doll-sized jade spoon in it. He ladled a little mound of white powder onto the back of one hand and snorted it up. Ferris wheels started revolving in his eyes. At first I was afraid he might insist on a co-pilot for his space flight, but he seemed happy enough making a solo. While he was up there counting stars, I tried to put together what the newspapers said about the reclusive tycoon and what this cosy hair-down evening at home had shown me. The only thing that made sense of it, that patched the two halves together, was Woolcott's notorious sense of ego. He was in his recreation room now, and he was giving it everything he had, but I suspected there would be quite another Holmes Woolcott to be seen in the boardroom. He might not look any less like a discarded mummy, but my guess was he'd give himself up as completely to the titillations of economics as he did to his more private fantasies. But he was burning himself out in the process. He looked closer to seventy than to fifty, and the wisps of hair matted against his skull were battleship gray. Still, I couldn't get over the feeling that even when he was floating somewhere in the stratosphere, he was sizing everything up, totaling accounts, making the little brain cells dance for him.

Maybe he was tuned in to my radio waves, because he stirred a little on his pillows and said, 'You will do.' The slurred voice seemed to echo out of some distant cavern, but it got to the point. 'We will notify you when your services are required, when the right party comes along.' Obviously I'd passed my test with flying colors, but who was Mr Right? And what did Woolcott get out of the little soirées he arranged for his influential friends? I was sure he got his money's worth, and with compounded interest, but I didn't know how. I was still feeding what I knew through the hopper when a hand took hold of my elbow and started guiding me out of Woolcott's dusky chamber of horrors. My right shoe made a squishing sound when I walked.

27

As I rounded the last turning in the stairs, I caught a glimpse of Alma Nugent's ermine head. She was waiting in the center of the hall, under a crystal chandelier that sparkled like a pre-war Fourth of July fireworks display. At first I thought Snow White would want a report on the evening's party games, but she was really there just to follow through as chairman of the aloha committee.

'We shall no doubt see you again,' she purred, 'and next time you needn't trouble about your hair or your wardrobe. Everything will be provided for you here.' She was a cool cookie, alright, and had obviously made herself indispensible to the Woolcott menagerie. She was the kind of jewel of a secretary who'd do anything for her boss – type, take dictation, walk the dog, feed the lions, butter his toast, stroll across an occasional bed of burning coals – as long as the price was right.

I was being nudged along south by south-west, in the general direction of the front door, while the briefing continued. 'It is, of course, strictly forbidden to discuss your visits here. Mr Woolcott is determined to maintain his privacy, and you can assist him in that. When he is pleased, Mr Woolcott can be very generous ...' And when he isn't pleased, I thought, he'd probably find a way to get the message across without involving Western Union.

The bouncer opened the door for me, and Alma Nugent pressed a small, thin package into my hand. 'This is only a little token of Mr Woolcott's generosity,' she said, creasing her cherry lips into a lousy imitation of a smile.

'*Muchas gracias,*' I replied, and then walked damply down the steps to the limousine, where Archie Potter was waiting for me. As he held the door open, there was a question in his eye that I hadn't seen there before, but if he was thinking of trying to cut in on the boss's territory, he quickly changed his mind.

The leather seat gloved me, and I sank back in it to have a look at Woolcott's farewell present. It was an oval gold compact with an etched sunburst on the lid. Just what I didn't need – and he probably ordered them by the gross. I clicked on the reading light to have a better look; it was only plated after all, but inside, folded into a crisp rectangle, was something I could use better than a compact. It was a fifty-dollar bill. He probably ordered those by the gross as well, just to light his cigars. Whatever else this screwy case was or wasn't, it could keep a girl in pin-money alright, and there was clearly more where this came from if I didn't mind paddling around in the sewers to find it. I minded. Besides, the case was all backwards, and it wasn't even really mine. It had started with the phoney French frill, and that was O'Brien's case now. What Ingrid wanted was something else again, but I had a feeling I couldn't help her learn to live with her father's death, and if Woolcott had any idea what that one-liner in Alfred Leslie's calendar meant, he wasn't going to blab it to his playmate of the evening.

Usually a private investigator gets a jumpy client who wants a lot of information for very little do-re-mi and wants it fast. You get it or you don't, depending on the circumstances. But every now and then you start finding out more than you want to know, sometimes more than it's safe to know. At that point common sense says to cash in whatever chips you've got left and go home. That's what common sense started telling me the night we found LaFlamme salted away at the Greyhound Bus Station, and I should have listened to it then instead of O'Brien's warmed-over blarney. Next it was a pair of eyes in my favorite color and a set of legs in my favorite shape that started running the show. So I ended up playing cowboys and Indians with one of the world's most well-heeled chiefs, who probably had even more exciting indoor sports in mind for the next visit. Woolcott himself seemed content to let most of it happen in the playground he'd built inside his own head. That's why he needed the coke. But his so-called friends might be a little more active and expect more group participation. It all kept circling back to the question of what Woolcott got out of it. Was he just showing his famous hospitality – fresh towels in the guest bathroom, fresh flowers on the desk and a fresh tart between the sheets? Or was he using the girls somehow to get the goods on the opposition? I had a strong hunch the whole operation was strictly business. It explained Woolcott's investment in the Academy, it explained the exclusive film-showings, and it explained LaFlamme's being put through the grinder when she started asking too many questions, the way she had at Ma Waller's. But the real answer was that I didn't give a damn what the answer was. I was going to go home and do some washing. First I was going to wash my hair, and then I was going to wash my hands of the whole lousy case.

By now the Cadillac had floated down out of the hills, easy as a feather in the breeze, and we were back in the real Los Angeles, where most people spend most of their lives trying to make a couple of frayed ends meet. Also, down here you remembered there was a war going on. The car hummed past an occasional tavern or an all-night drugstore, and in the pools of light they laid down on the sidewalk, you almost always caught a glimpse of somebody in uniform. And even behind the darkened windows of apartment houses there were guys turning over in bed, scratching themselves, and catching another fast forty winks before the alarm jerked them awake for jobs at aircraft factories and munitions plants. When you added all that up, it made Woolcott and the Academy and the whole lousy mess seem like pretty small and pretty mealy potatoes.

I leaned forward and hammered my knuckles against the plate-glass window that separated the driver from his cargo. Potter glanced around and eyed me through the fishbowl, while my mouth made motions to suggest it wanted to talk to him. He played with a few dials, there was a blur of static, and his voice growled through a loudspeaker, 'You want somethin'?'

'Yes,' I answered. 'Can you hear me?'

'Yeah.'

'I've got some things to pick up at home. Drop me there instead of at the Academy, O.K.? It's closer, and I've got my car there. I can drive back.'

'What's the address?'

I gave it to him and then sank back to enjoy the last few minutes of upholstery. The moon got higher and the houses got lower and farther apart, and we were tooling along familiar palm-lined streets now. Potter spun the car to the right at the next intersection, and up ahead I saw the trusty Plymouth parked at the curb. I hammered on the glass again and this time used sign language to bring him in for a landing. It was a perfect threepointer. The moon was so bright it seemed like second-hand daylight, and it was weird to be the only person walking around in it. The rest of the world must have overslept. There was no sound except the clicking of my own heels against the concrete walk, and then the light rasping noise as my key fitted into the lock. I twisted the key and reached down to turn the knob. The metal was there, worn and smooth and familiar to the touch. I'd turned it before, in all kinds of weather and all kinds of moods. I'd turned it to walk in and find an emptiness hollower than the one inside me, and I'd turned it and opened it and found something even better than what I dreamed on my way home. This time the doorknob fitted just as familiarly into my palm as it had a thousand nights before, but between the polished metal and my hand there was a new sensation – something fibrous, shifting. I froze then, for how long I don't know, but whatever was draped over the doorknob refused to go away. Finally I stepped back and lifted it up. It gleamed glossy black in the moonlight, like a slender hank of silk, except for the end that had been ripped out of the scalp and was matted together with a dull crust of blood.

28

AT headquarters they said O'Brien was at home, but it took nearly five minutes for the telephone to wake him, and by then I'd almost given up. 'Be at home, you bastard. Be at home,' I kept growling at the receiver. There were still cobwebs in his head when he answered, but I didn't have time to wait while he called in the chimney-sweeps. The way I told it probably didn't make much sense anyhow, but he seemed to get the message.

'Sit tight,' he said. 'I'll send a print-man out, and I'll get there myself as soon as I can. Probably in half an hour.'

Telling me to sit tight was like telling a hungry dog to sort of keep an eye on the pot-roast. I prowled the apartment again, and it kept repeating the same story. Nobody had been there since I'd left. I crawled around the floor looking under chairs and tables and sofas, and I'd probably have started climbing the walls next if I hadn't caught a glimpse of myself in the mirror. What looked back was a clown face, a face pretending to be the soft, gentle brown girl I knew as Conchita, and succeeding in looking like a bloodless witch. The eyes were puffy and frightened, the skin pasty white, and the chaos of black hair that framed it seemed brittle and ugly. But at least it took some of the cutting edge off hysteria, and I decided to leave it to the cops to search for needles in haystacks. I settled for peeling off the second skin Lavender had loaned me, and washing out the worst of the black rinse I'd used for my clever little impersonation. The suds I churned up looked like dirty snow.

I was knocking back the second dose of Ron Rico when O'Brien arrived, his print man trotting up the walk behind him. The two smeared graphite all over the apartment and succeeded in getting only one clear print, from the inside frame of a closet door, and I was pretty sure it was either

mine or Conchita's. In the movies a fingerprint expert can
turn up more than that on a broken potato chip. Then the
boys in blue started combing over the rugs and the
upholstery, looking for blood flecks or messages written in
braille. All they found were a couple of dimes and a broken
comb behind the cushions on the divan. Every now and
then O'Brien gave me a look that I think was supposed to
bolster my confidence, but instead resembled the early
stages of glaucoma.

Finally, even O'Brien seemed to realize he was warming
up in the wrong ball park, and sent his Man Friday back to
headquarters. 'Can you fix me some java?' he asked.

'Sure,' I answered. 'One spoon of strychnine or two?'

'I'll take it black,' he said, as I wandered through the
archway into the kitchenette.

Everything seemed to take a long time. My hands went
out in slow motion to get the can of Maxwell House, and I
watched them very carefully twist off the lid, lay it aside, lift
the spoon and measure out the grounds. Water came from
the faucet like a lazy ribbon and crept up the sides of the
pot so slowly that a couple of lifetimes went by before it was
full. I was watching the flames drift a bright blue collar
around the bottom of the pot when O'Brien came in. He
didn't say anything. Instead, he put a hand on my
shoulder, and everything went back to the right speed
again, so suddenly I was dizzy, and had to turn to lean
against him for support. I felt my own hair damp against
his shirt, and through it I could hear the steady, powerful
drumming of his heart. He hooked an arm around my
waist, cradling me against his hard body, and it was nice
not to have to worry about unimportant things like
breathing, standing up, and keeping the valves shut down
at the water works. After a few minutes the music of the
coffee percolating brought me back to the world again, and
I remembered who it was I'd been using as a wailing wall. I
leaned back so I could look O'Brien in his Irish eye and
said, 'You son of a bitch.'

'What?' He was playing the wounded suitor, the knight

who's just discovered a spot of rust on his armor.

'You heard me, you son of a bitch.' I slammed two mugs down on the counter and shot coffee at them, while O'Brien turned and dragged his weary ass back into the living-room.

He was making notes in a stenographer's pad and pretending not to notice I was breathing the same air when I sat down facing him. 'O.K., O'Brien, drink your coffee. Maybe it'll help rev up the little grey cells.'

He grinned lopsidedly then and raised the cup in a kind of salute. 'Do we smoke the peace-pipe?' he asked.

'Hell, no, copper. It was playing footsies with you that started this horror movie in the first place.'

'Wait a minute,' he said, his face flushing like a desert sunset. 'Get off that high horse of yours. I asked you to keep LaFlamme's murder to yourself for a while, and I asked you to pretend to be working on the case. But you lost the case Monday morning, right?'

'Score one for City Hall.'

'Am I right or am I wrong, Lamaar?'

'You're right, O'Brien. Don't rub it in. But the point is, if I'd leveled with my client a week ago, when I should have, this one would have gone straight into the out-basket and Shoemaker's face would already have faded into the heavenly host of satisfied customers. You're the one who dangled the bait, and I'm the jerk who went for it.'

O'Brien massaged his face with his beefy palms and then pretended to be looking at the notes he'd made. 'Alright,' he said, 'I had an idea you'd do more than pretend, and I had an idea you might turn up something useful for us. But I'm not the one who brought Conchita into it.'

'Score another point for City Hall.' It went to the quick, that one, and quivered there like an arrow that's just thudded into the target.

'Besides,' he added, 'none of this is helping us find her.'

'Probably the keys will be here any minute,' I suggested, 'if you can just be patient.'

'Stop wise-assing and use your noodle for something,' he

barked. 'Whoever left that hair is telling you to lay off, that he's got Conchita and she's in danger unless you stop snooping around. She's alive, though. Otherwise, none of it makes any sense. If she's dead, he doesn't have a hold on you.'

When I looked at him again, his face seemed to go a little out of focus. I got a good grip on my bottom lip, and when it promised to stay still I answered him. 'You could be right, you stupid, flatfooted Irish cop. You just might be right – for once.'

'Of course I'm right,' he boasted. 'It doesn't figure any other way. Blow your nose and start at the beginning.'

I started at the beginning, and this time I didn't leave out any of the sub-plots. I told him about Shoemaker's first visit, about the way Ma Waller ruptured a blood-vessel when she saw that photograph, about playing knees-up with Brand Brockaway, about the phantom farter of Pershing Square. I sketched in as much as I knew about Ingrid Seagram, a.k.a. Ingrid Leslie, and about Woolcott's little soirée.

He heard me out, making an occasional note for himself, and when I'd finished he asked, 'You're sure you didn't mention tonight's arrangements to anyone but Conchita and Lavender?'

'Sure I'm sure,' I said wearily.

'Then either somebody intercepted her on the way here, before she even got in the door, or somebody showed up later.'

'She wouldn't have opened the door,' I said.

'She wouldn't have opened the door,' O'Brien corrected me, 'unless she knew the person on the other side.'

'Nix, O'Brien. She never got this far. If she had, there'd be some trace, something to show she'd been here.'

'Are you sure?' He didn't give me time to answer. 'What would she have been carrying with her?'

'An evening bag,' I said.

'That would be easier to carry off than a hundred-and-ten-pound female.'

'Hundred-and-twenty,' I corrected him. 'But I still don't think she was ever here. It's hard to describe, but if you know someone well ... If you know someone the way I know Conchita, somehow you can tell.'

'Maybe you're right,' he admitted. 'And if you're right, it means somebody intercepted her. Maybe it happened as soon as you'd pulled the switcheroo at the Academy.'

'Then how did the car get here?' I asked.

'Somebody else brought it. Or somebody followed Conchita and nabbed her before she could get in the front door. But I still think it was someone she knew ...'

'Why?'

'Because otherwise there would have been a scuffle. Probably some of the neighbors would have heard something.'

'Maybe they did,' I suggested hopefully.

'No,' he said, 'they didn't. Harrison, the kid you met last week, has been ringing some doorbells. I told him to let me know if he learned anything, and otherwise just to keep an ear on the radio.'

I walked over to the window and bent down one of the slats of the blinds. The squad car was nosed up behind the Plymouth, and somebody was sitting in it with the door open and one leg propped on the curb.

'Alright, O'Brien. You've got it all pegged. Now how about a motive?'

'Somebody wants to shut you up. You've come too near the real pay dirt.'

'Like Yvette LaFlamme?' I guessed.

'Yeah,' he grunted, 'like Yvette.'

'Who was she, O'Brien?' He pretended to be checking his notes. 'For Christ's sake, copper, this is no time to play tiddlywinks.'

'She was a police informer,' O'Brien said. 'She was working for us.'

'Beautiful. So you knew how dangerous this case was.'

'No,' he said. 'It could have been a lot of different things. She was a tramp, she'd been in trouble before. In fact, that's how she first started with us, because of some deal the D.A. made with her.'

'What was her assignment?'

'It's hard to say exactly. First the Narcotics Squad put her onto something, and along the way she got wind of a blackmail operation. It may have been tied up with the drug racket. Maybe not. Pressure was being put on people, and it had to do with ... with their sex lives and stuff.' He blushed like a kid pronouncing his first dirty word.

'So she went to Ma Waller's,' I helped him out.

'Yeah,' he sighed, 'but she was barkin' up the wrong tree. We knew that all along.'

'And who suggested she enroll in finishing school?'

'The Academy was her idea. She thought she was onto something.'

'Obviously she was right.'

'That's why we wanted to play for time.'

'And that's how I got put on your sucker list. Thanks a lot, O'Brien.' He let that one ride. 'O.K.,' I admitted, 'so we both got a little too enthusiastic about our work. The question is, what happens now?'

'We give it to the missing persons bureau,' he said, 'and let them work it over. Meanwhile, we run back through everything Yvette ever told us about the Academy, anything else we've got on file, in hopes of finding out who fingered Conchita.'

'The same procedure you used with LaFlamme, right?'

He paused a minute, trying to wish away the question. 'Yeah,' he confessed.

'And where did it get you? Not even half-way to first base. If it had, you wouldn't have needed me nosing around in dark corners for you.'

He shrugged surrender with the palms of his hands. 'It's all I can do,' he said.

'Well it's not all I can do!'

'Don't be crazy,' he said. 'The whole point is for you to lay off.'

'Lay off? Sure, I lay off and then the hatchet-man brings

Conchita home tied up in pink silk ribbons and we all live happily ever after, right? Wrong, copper. You're pretty sure Conchita knew whoever kidnapped her. Even if she didn't, she does now, and he's not going to send her home just because I've been a good girl. Besides, you're not dealing with a nice, healthy, high-spirited Boy Scout kind of kidnapper, O'Brien. This guy chopped up your informer and packed her away in a couple of suitcases. He probably killed Alexander Woods, the Rembrandt of Beverly Hills. My guess is the same little ghoul is the fellow who rearranged Massimo Leone's ugly puss, or paid somebody to do it for him. Now he's kidnapped Conchita and left me a personalised calling card.' We both glanced down at the same moment, at the anonymous-looking manilla envelope O'Brien had shoved the hair into. It gave off the wet chill of an open grave. 'Add it all up, copper, and what do you get? You get murder and mayhem, blackmail maybe, and throw in some dope just to sweeten the broth a little. More than that, you get a guy who likes to play games, somebody who enjoys the old-fashioned sport of the thing. So don't tell me to be a good girl and stay home picking the lice off the African violets. It's not that simple.'

He didn't have a reply, and the silence was a lot worse than telling me I was right in the way I read the case.

'In short, O'Brien, you'd better come up with a little more imaginative approach.'

'And if we move in too close?' he asked. 'If we move in too close, Conchita's dead. If we can work from a distance, maybe she'll stay alive a while longer ...'

'Sure,' I snarled, 'what's the kid got to lose but a little hair? I can always get a wig to bury her in.' It was the wrong thing to say. It made it too real for both of us. O'Brien flinched, like he'd taken a brass-knuckled left in his gut and was trying not to show how much it hurt.

'O.K.,' I half-apologized. 'O.K., O'Brien, do it your way, and I'm going to do it mine. But if I'm supposed to be keeping my snoot out of this case, it's not good public relations to have a cop car sitting out front.'

He stood up then, unbending like a man who's just realized how tired he is, and then realized there were still a lot of miles between him and bed. 'I'll do everything I can,' he promised, keeping his eyes on his oversized brogues.

'Sure you will. So will I. Now move your ass out of here before you start giving the neighborhood a bad name.'

29

BY the time the sun poked the first orange fingers into the living room, I'd worked out a dozen plans of attack, and they all had the stink of Corregidor on them. Also, they all kept revolving around the Academy, and it was still too early to start ringing doorbells in that part of town, unless I really wanted to advertise that I was on the prowl. Then it clicked. In the bottom of my purse I found the envelope I'd used to scribble a few lines while O'Brien was grilling Archie Potter, and the address was there alright. I didn't know what I expected to find out from Woolcott's chauffeur, but it beat all hell out of sitting there and twiddling my thumbs.

I took the Mauser out of the evening bag and slipped it into the inside pocket of my windbreaker. Then I loaded the outside pockets with billfold, keys, a pad of paper, a couple of pencils, and a penlight. That way I wouldn't have to worry with carrying a purse. I turned off all but one light in the apartment, flicked on the radio, and took the phone off the hook. Then I pushed open the bathroom window, tossed the windbreaker out onto the ground, and squeezed through the narrow opening. It wasn't quite such a tight fit as Lavender's red taffeta number, but it ran a close second. I'd have to loan it to him for his next big date. I got into the jacket and pulled myself up with one hand on the window ledge, high enough to grab the bottom of the window and haul it down again. The disappearing act wouldn't fool anyone for long, but maybe it would buy me a couple of hours – enough time to get to Potter's place and back.

I cut through to the next block commando-style, over a fieldstone fence and through somebody's Victory garden, trying not to bruise too many salads on the way. It was a ten-minute walk then until I got within hailing distance of a taxi. When I gave the cabbie the address, he looked at me like I'd just escaped from the local booby-hatch. Then he made that kind of shoulders-up shrug that means a buck is a buck.

Styles Avenue runs for a quick two blocks through the old section of Bunker Hill. On the corner where it starts, there's a gas station that folded during the Depression and across from it the kind of fly-specked cafe that should have been condemned a long time ago by the department of public health. The street ends against a cyclone fence covered in signs that announce DANGER: HIGH VOLTAGE. Behind the fence there's nothing to see but a vacant lot with a few pits in it that might have been foxholes. I told the cabbie to let me out at the corner, and he pulled into the gas station to turn around. Pasted against the inside of the plate-glass window was an advertisement for Country Cottage Dinner Ware – only ten cents a place-setting if you bought ten gallons or more. Next to it was a poster showing a scarlet mouth with a finger raised in front of it and the motto 'Loose lips sink ships'.

I walked the length of the street and back again, looking at broken orange crates, soggy pasteboard cartons, rusty oil drums, and occasional fragments of heavy-duty machinery that probably even the boys at Cal Tech couldn't identify anymore. Potter's house was near the end of the second block. It was like all the rest – a tiny frame cottage that still showed a few traces of paint on its weathered front, but to the left of it, where its twin should have been standing, was a garage made of concrete blocks, sealed with heavy-duty steel doors. Obviously that was where Woolcott's Cadillac spent the night. Old money bags was really all heart; he couldn't bear to think of his limo getting a case of the sniffles. Potter, of course, could take care of himself.

The cottage had a wooden porch with a broken railing running around it. The steps sighed down a couple of rotten inches when I stepped on them. The lightbulb that burned beside the door needed hosing off, and the door wanted a couple of hinges for Christmas. There was no bell, so I knocked. When nobody answered, I leaned over and tapped out the same message on the window glass. I still didn't hear any sound from inside the house, but there was a flutter at the window shade, as though someone had peeled back a corner to look out, and then a light blinked on behind it. I did another drum-roll on the door, and heard the bolts being drawn back. Finally a wedge of Potter's face appeared over the brass safety chain.

'What is it?' he grumbled.

'I'm a friend of Inspector O'Brien,' I said. 'I want to have a talk with you.'

'Go away,' he barked. 'I told 'em everything I know.'

'I'll go away after we have our talk,' I said.

'Who are you, anyhow?'

I fished out the two-and-a-half by four-inch photostat of my license and held it up to the crack to answer his question. He still didn't get the welcome mat out of mothballs, but his defenses were down a little when he asked, 'What do you want with me?'

'If you really want me to stand out here and tell you, that's O.K. by me, Potter, but my voice tends to carry. The neighbors may complain.'

'Alright, alright.' His face went away, the chain slid back, and then he swung open the door. Potter stood there wearing a long face and a long grey flannel bathrobe that made him look like an unemployed monk. He didn't invite me in, but he didn't throw up any roadblocks either, so I put the omission down to natural shyness and went inside anyhow. The room was a surprise. From the outside I'd have expected early flea-bag decor. It wasn't the Ritz, but it had a nice homey quality about it. The couch and chairs were Grand Rapids Early American, with plaid covers on them. The walls were freshly papered and the floors were covered with hooked rugs, and in one corner there was a grandfather clock that might really be old enough to have belonged to someone's grandfather. There was a maple whatnot with demi-tasse cups and saucers on it and some odds and ends of silver, and a whole menagerie of china dogs and cats. On all the available tabletops there were photographs in those genuine imitation-gold frames you get at Woolworth's with old publicity shots of Jean Harlow in them.

'I told the cops everything I know,' he repeated.

'I believe you,' I assured him. 'I don't think you had anything to do with Yvette LaFlamme's murder, but I still think you can help me find the man who did it. Or the woman,' I added. 'It's important, Potter, or I wouldn't come banging on your door at six o'clock in the morning. Whoever killed LaFlamme killed Alex Woods, too, and he'll kill someone else, very soon, if I can't stop him.'

Potter was finally beginning to come awake. He fished around in the pockets of his robe and finally hooked a bright green package of Lucky Strikes and a box of matches. He stoked up and breathed some smoke and then shook his head. 'I don't know nothin',' he insisted. He had a natural gift for one-liners.

The way he was eyeing me through the smokescreen told me that somewhere, far back in the dark cave of his brain, something had stirred in the shadows, the first faint hint that maybe he'd seen me before. I didn't want him to get sidetracked, just in case he had more than one track, so I tried to appeal to whatever shreds of vanity he might have left.

'A man in your position,' I said, 'always notices things. I once read about a chauffeur who made more than a million on the stock market just by listening to his boss's conversations with his secretary when he drove them to board meetings. Obviously, to be good at the job you've got to be alert, got to keep your ears open all the time, got to know what's coming next and be ready for it. And while that's happening, you're probably picking up all kinds of information. Maybe without even realizing how important some of it is. You may know a lot more than you think you know, if you sort it out. I want to help you sort it out.'

'Well ...' he hesitated.

I didn't give him time to play wallflower. 'How often do you ferry girls over from the Academy?'

'What?'

'How often does Woolcott send you to pick someone up at the Academy?'

'How – '

'Never mind,' I said. 'Let me ask the questions. It'll go quicker that way. How often?'

'Every week or so, I guess.'

'Do you pick up playmates for him anywhere else?'

'Yeah. Yeah, sometimes from hotels and different places.' He blew some more smoke and began to fidget in a way that told me he didn't like the course I had charted for us. He plucked at a seam on a cushion, and his eyes ignored me.

'Did you ever deliver Yvette for one of his very private parties?'

'No,' he answered quickly, a little more sure of himself now.

'Are you positive?'

'Yeah. The police showed me her picture. I never seen her before.'

'But maybe she looked different when you saw her. I mean, all dressed up and with her hair done in a different way, maybe you wouldn't have put that together with the photograph.'

He leaned forward to stub the cigarette out in the ashtray, and the tail-end of a sly smile flickered across his wrinkled puss. 'I recognized you,' he said, 'even if you got blonde hair now.'

So there was life in the old boy yet. 'It proves my point,' I told him. 'It proves you spend a lot of your life noticing things, but most of them aren't worth remembering.'

'I never seen that LaFlamme person,' he told me again.

166

This time I was inclined to believe him, so I adjusted the course a bit.

'Does anyone else ever run Woolcott's delivery service?'

'I don't know,' he answered. 'Moon sometimes does some drivin' for him.'

'Moon?'

'The butler. The one that opens the door. He's really like the head body guard.'

'Does Moon live on the estate?'

'Naw.' He shook his head. 'Nobody lives there. Mr Woolcott don't like it. Not even the guys that protect him live there. They come on in shifts, like at a factory.' Then he added an amendment. 'Alex lived there,' he said, 'but he was the only one.'

'What did Alex have to do with Woolcott's little parties?'

'Nothin' ...' he said hesitantly.

'If he was Woolcott's private secretary and lived in the same house, it's hard to believe he had nothing to do with them.'

We were on thin ice again, and Potter was working away at the upholstery. His face looked like someone had sifted fresh ashes onto it.

'Why didn't you like Alex?' I asked.

'I ... I didn't say ... say that!'

'You didn't have to.'

Muscles twitched in his face and his eyes roamed the room. It could have been my imagination, but I thought they paused when they came to the table next to the rocker I was sitting in. The table held a lamp that had been made from an old kerosene lantern, a milk-glass bowl, and two framed photographs. One of them showed a young girl dressed for communion, with all the usual virginal paraphernalia – white lace, veils, a prayer book and a rosary. She was trying to smile without showing her braces. The other photograph might have been of the same girl a few years later, but this time she was all in black – a gown and a tilted mortarboard with a tassle that tickled her right ear.

It was worth a try, at least. 'When did you last see your daughter, Mr Potter?'

His mouth made a question, but no sound came out. It stayed open with the question, and I could see that he hadn't taken time to put in his upper plate for me. Then the pink circle his mouth made collapsed and seemed to collapse the rest of his face too. There was a faint hissing sound, like air escaping from a punctured inner tube.

'What's her name?' I asked.

It took a while, but Potter finally forced his lips to shape the sound. 'Kathleen,' he whispered, and it came out in a slow moan.

'When did you last see Kathleen?'

'Six months ago,' he mumbled.

'Tell me about her,' I encouraged him.

It didn't take a lot of encouragement. The floodgates were opened, and I stood right in the path of the torrent. Kathleen was named for her mother, who died when she was ten. She was cute as a button, smart as a whip and good as gold. She was, in fact, every cliché a doting father ever wants his daughter to be. Holmes Woolcott had helped find a good private school for her when she was fifteen, and a couple of years later Kathleen had gotten a crush on Alex Woods, who had finished art school by then and was working as Woolcott's private secretary. When it looked like it might start to be something more than simple puppy-love, Potter had put his foot down. I could imagine it must have been a pretty heavy foot, at that. Probably he'd tried to plant a couple of them in the middle of the kid's back, and she did just what the textbooks would have predicted. She stopped being the good-as-gold daddy's darling and started slipping off every chance she had to be with Woods. She even posed for him as a model, which already proved she had more guts than I did. And she told Potter she intended to get married as soon as she was eighteen. Up to that point I could follow the story alright, even though Potter's delivery shifted from whisper to bellow, with a good bit of snuffling and snorting thrown in. From there on things got a little murky. Somehow Kathleen ended up as a party gift for one of Woolcott's business chums, and afterwards it was downhill all the way. Whether Alex Woods had anything to do with setting her up for it wasn't clear. He'd seemed to be as enraged as Potter was, but when Kathleen missed a couple of periods, he got real busy cleaning his brushes and looking in the other direction.

'Where did she go?' I asked. 'What did she do then?'

'I don't know,' Potter said, sinking his head toward his knees. His muffled voice repeated, 'I don't know.'

'Why do you stick around? Jobs aren't that hard to find anymore.'

He raised his head and looked at me, but there was a glaze on his eyes, and I knew he was only seeing the scenario he'd written in his own head. 'Because ... because maybe she'll come back there. I thought maybe Alex had sent her away, given her some money. Or the boss. I thought the boss could find out. Or one of his friends.' Then he paused and admitted, 'I don't know', in a voice full of anger at himself, at the world, at the walls that surrounded us.

The Woolcott establishment seemed more and more carnivorous all the time, and I thought I recognized the fear that must be knotting itself like a giant fist in Potter's stomach.

'I'm sorry about Kathleen,' I said, and I meant it. I was sorry for everyone who reached out for a little stardust and came back with a handful of slime. 'I'm sorry, and I don't know if I can help you, but maybe if I find out more about the case I'm on now ... maybe I'll also learn something about Kathleen. I'd like you to think again about the morning those locker keys arrived. Had anything happened – anything at all – that might have made Alex suspicious? Why was he so quick to smell a rat?'

Potter shrugged and drew the same blank he'd drawn for O'Brien.

'Was there anything else in the mail that might have upset him? Did he get any telephone calls?'

'I don't know,' Potter said. 'I was just there a few minutes, when I took up the mail, and there wasn't nobody else there. The boss was on a little trip over to Marin County.'

So much for my theory about the chauffeur's eagle eye picking up all sorts of clues that anyone else would have missed.

'And he didn't tell you anything else about the keys? Just said for you to find the lockers?'

'Yeah,' Potter said, obviously tired of having to cover the same barren ground again. 'And he said to get in touch with you if anything went wrong.'

'And that's all?'

'Yeah. He was too busy lookin' for the photos to talk to me much.'

If I'd been stumbling around in the depths of a labyrinth for a couple of weeks and suddenly saw an exit sign up ahead, it probably would have produced about the same effect.

'Photos?' I asked, trying to sound only vaguely interested.

'Yeah.'

'What photos?'

'Pictures Alex had took.'

'When did they disappear?'

'I dunno,' Potter shrugged. 'I just know Alex said he couldn't find 'em, and the boss was gonna be real mad. He was always worried about the boss gettin' upset.'

So Woods may have thought the locker keys had something to do with the missing pictures, that somebody had nabbed them to put pressure on Woolcott or some of his influential friends. Every other card you turned up in this screwy game had blackmail stamped on it.

Daylight had painted the windowshades a bright neon orange when I stood up to leave. Potter shuffled to the door with me, flicking zombie eyes in my direction. 'I'll pay you good if you find my Kathleen,' he said.

'Nix,' I answered. 'I'm doing a job for myself right now,

170

and for a friend. But if I learn anything that might help you find her, I'll let you know.'

When I glanced back at the house, he was still leaning against the door. At least they had something in common. They were both a little off their hinges.

30

I LET myself in through the front door. Vaulting the neighbor's wall and climbing back through the bathroom window in broad daylight seemed a little too conspicuous. Besides, if anyone had the house staked out the night before to see how I'd react, he'd hopefully have decided by now that I was in hibernation. There were no grisly calling cards on the doorknob, no threatening letters in the mailbox. Inside, O'Brien's coffee mug and mine were listening to a Glenn Miller concert on the radio. I took them into the kitchen, emptied them in the sink, and reheated the coffee. It was thick enough to stand a spoon up in, so maybe it would help me keep vertical for the rest of the day.

I put the telephone back in its cradle and went in to stand under a cold shower for a few minutes. I was drying off when the telephone started ringing.

'Thank God,' the voice said. 'I've tried to call you for over an hour, and the line was always busy.'

'The day got off to an early start,' I told her.

'Conchita didn't come back last night,' Ingrid blurted. 'She didn't come back at all. Is she with you?'

'No.'

'Where is she?'

'Look, kid, we can't talk about it over the phone, and try not to seem particularly concerned if anyone asks you about it. After all, girls play hookey all the time.'

'Alright,' she answered, but in a voice that had question marks hung all over it.

'I was going to call you,' I said. 'I want you to deliver a

171

message. Tell the headmistress I'll be there in forty-five minutes, and that I want to see her alone. If she can't arrange it, then I'll arrive with a friend who wears a siren on his car, and it'll bring down the tone of the establishment. Got that?'

'Yes. Isn't there anything else I can do?'

'There's one thing. I want to know about girls who've left the Academy – ones who got jobs somewhere, or ones who left in a hurry. There's got to be a mug book of some kind around, and registration records or something.'

'Maybe I could look into the matter while you're having your interview,' she hinted.

'I'll try to oblige,' I promised. 'Call Lavender if you learn anything. I'll be in touch with the office.'

By daylight the apartment was even more of a torture chamber than it was the night before. Everywhere I turned there was something to remind me of Conchita. When I opened the bedroom closet it seemed filled with her clothes, filled with the scent of her, with her sudden, dark laughter. I dressed as fast as I could and hustled outside again, where kids were already jumping rope and playing hopscotch on the sidewalk, and the neighbor's poodle was taking the first leak of the day on one of my pre-war tires.

The Plymouth answered me with a couple of belches when I pushed the starter. I pulled the choke out a little more, pumped the gas pedal, and tried again. Under the hood, somebody was grinding coffee, but the engine finally caught, backfired a few times, and then found the kind of music I was listening for.

31

MACARTHUR and Patton could have taken lessons in posture from her, but this time I knew it was all show, that Ann Shoemaker was trying to bluff us both into believing she was still giving the orders. She was even less impressed than I was.

'This is most irregular,' she blustered, fumbling with a fat bunch of keys.

'So is murder,' I said, 'and blackmail.'

It took her a few passes, but she finally got the door unlocked. I glanced into the small room that served as her office, jammed with filing cabinets, bookshelves, and a safe that would have housed a family of four. 'No thanks,' I said, 'it looks too claustrophobic.' I nodded towards the door across the hall. 'Is anyone in the parlor?'

'No.' She exploded the word close to my ear. 'But my instructions were to arrange for a private interview.'

'I'll take a chance on the parlor,' I said.

'Very well.' She pulled the office door shut and goose-stepped ahead of me across the hall.

Yes, this would be brief. No, I did not want to take a seat, and I did not want coffee. I only wanted a few straight answers for a change. As we squared off with only a few feet of broadloom between us, I knew how Gene Tunney must have felt when he took on the Manassa Mauler.

'First,' I said, 'I want to know what's in this racket for you.'

'Racket?' She spit the word out like a bite of wormy apple.

'Call it what you like, it's still a handy little service you provide. Just call us, and enjoy a fresh piece in the privacy of your very own home. What's in it for you? Are you just paying off the mortgage?'

'If you have questions about the Academy's finances, I suggest you talk to our book-keeper.'

'Do you mean the book-bender? No, I don't think we'd have a lot to talk about. Besides, I know it's Holmes Woolcott who holds the mortgage on this little sex farm. It may not say that on the mortgage, but Holmes Woolcott's speciality is owning things and people that own other things and other people, and then making them all work for him.'

Shoemaker's bottom jaw was grinding away as though

173

she were trying to flatten a few ball bearings between her teeth. She paused long enough to mutter 'Impertinence'.

'Save it,' I said. 'That dialogue's as stale as the rest of your act. If you'd prefer, I could have a chum from the police force ask the same questions.'

She laughed then, with a kind of machine-gun rattle in her throat. 'Do not make idle threats,' she said.

'The threats aren't idle, and the police know almost as much as I do. You and Woolcott are supplying the parlor games for boys who are used to eating pretty high off the hog. It may be simple community spirit, of course, but that doesn't quite dovetail with the fact that anytime someone begins to find out too much about your doubles-act, he ends up dead.' Since I didn't have anything to lose, I thought I'd make a couple of calculated guesses. 'It also doesn't explain the drugs or the photographs.'

'Drugs?' she snorted, as though I was being more imbecilic than ever, but she didn't try to deny the rest of it, and I thought a little of the curl had gone out of her sneer.

'I've got witnesses,' I said, 'but frankly I don't give a damn what kind of witch's brew you and Woolcott cook up between you. What interests me now is the whereabouts of one of your students, Conchita Gonzales.'

Her face showed that she understood the nature of my interest, but her tone was all business when she said, 'I presume she is in her room.'

'You presume wrong,' I answered, and she could tell I wasn't just guessing. 'Who does your finger work? Who whips the troops back into shape when they get out of line? Is it Moon?'

'Moon? Be serious, my dear. He is a moron.'

'Who runs the show then? Who decides when it's time to cut out a wagging tongue?'

She gave an exasperated sigh and drilled her eyes into me. 'Let me make this very clear,' she began, sending each word off on a solo flight. 'Mr Woolcott is a very old friend of mine. It may be hard for you to believe that a woman like myself might once have been very attractive to men. He helped me open this ...' She waved an imperial hand at the chintzy parlor. '... this institute because of a very old friendship, one which he still holds dear. Certain of the young women who come here are invited to spend an evening with ... seem willing enough to act as ... well, as hostesses for him. They are asked to do nothing illegal, and they are paid well for their services. That is all!' She underscored the 'all' so I wouldn't overlook it.

'And that makes you a procuress,' I added. 'It's an old profession, of course, but that doesn't make it any more respectable.' Obviously she'd been called worse things, because she let that one float right by.

'You would perhaps not understand what it is to feel indebted,' she began, and then faltered a little. 'What I wish to say is ...,' and she didn't seem at all sure any longer what she wanted to say. I shouldn't have been too surprised. After all, even the Titanic managed to find the right iceberg.

'Your story deeply moves me,' I said. 'It moves me from the bowels up, but it doesn't interest me very much. I'm not accusing you of making hamburger out of anybody, or Holmes Woolcott either, for that matter. He's too rich to have to do his own dirty work. When there's that kind of money around, there's always somebody to do it for you. Somebody who doesn't trouble you with any of the messy details.'

Shoemaker had welded herself back together again. 'I am intelligent enough,' she pronounced, 'to know that from an outsider's point of view, my arrangement with Holmes Woolcott may seem a little irregular, but it is hardly the kind of criminal conspiracy you have created in your fantasies. Holmes Woolcott is far too rich and far too powerful to resort to the kinds of tactics you accuse him of.'

'Nobody's that rich.'

'Now you are simply being childish. Of course there are advantages for Mr Woolcott in this arrangement. Otherwise he would not pursue it. He made his fortune by seeing such advantages and knowing how to utilize them, but to suggest that blackmail and murder would further his interests is simply preposterous.'

She sounded convinced, but that still just made one of us.

'Are you telling me,' I asked, 'that there's nothing Holmes Woolcott wants that money alòne wouldn't buy? Are you sure there's not an occasional patent or formula that he couldn't get his hands on just by writing a check? That there isn't some egghead he's tried to buy who couldn't be bought, and who had to be persuaded some other way? And if this whole deal is so innocent, how is it that the old disappearing act seems to be getting so popular?'

Her right hand fussed with her braids for a while and then dropped lifelessly to her side. 'I don't know,' she said.

'You don't know? Don't tell me there are really feet of clay stuffed into those size-eight Airflexes.'

'I will repeat for you, liebling. I do not know.'

The penny dropped in the slot then. I took careful aim and said, 'Thank you for the admission, Frau Schuhmacher.'

For a minute she seemed to be leaning into a galeforce wind, then she produced one of her putrid smiles and said, 'You are very clever. I knew that, of course, from the beginning.'

'Was it Heidelberg?'

'Yes,' she hissed.

'When Holmes Woolcott was a student there?'

'Yes, when he was a student there. My father had been executed just after the war as an espionage agent. He was innocent, but that fact did not make my own life any more pleasant. Holmes understood. He was kind to me then, and later he assisted me in coming to the United States.'

'The guy's a regular goodie two-shoes,' I said, and then regretted it. She and Woolcott were welcome to whatever memories they'd packed away in mothballs thirty years ago. Let them keep their visions of wurst and lederhosen and beer gardens and everything else that went with them. All I wanted was Conchita, and she wasn't even born when

Shoemaker and Woolcott had created their liebestraum.

Ann Shoemaker seemed to agree with me for once, because she said, 'I can hardly see that my past can be of so much interest to you. War always has a way of displacing persons, of ending some things and beginning others.'

'Save the canned philosophy. We're at war now, too. Your relationship with Holmes Woolcott interests me only because the two of you have spun such a nasty, sticky spider web, and someone I love happens to have gotten caught in it. I don't know how much you know about the whole mess. Maybe you really believe it's all as innocent as a Sunday school picnic. But I think you know a hell of a lot more than you're telling me. I may not be able to prove very much about your cozy organization, but I can stir up enough dust and enough suspicion to put you out of business. And I don't know how you stand with the immigration authorities, but I can check that one out too.'

'Scheisse!' she exploded. 'You have the effrontery to accuse *me* of blackmail, to fling your moral superiority in my face, to storm in here with your impertinent accusations. I would, I think, prefer to speak with your police, though they are not a breed of whom I am so very fond.' In another minute her radiator was going to boil over.

'O.K., O.K., maybe I went too far. You encourage it. But a woman is missing, and as far as I know she was last seen here. You can either help me find her yourself, or the police will do the job for me. They're pretty efficient. In fact, as I told you once, they cover a lot more territory than a P.I., and they may turn up information you'd rather read in your diary than in the morning papers. Do we play ball?'

'Vulgar idiom!' she said, but her voice lacked the old steely conviction. 'What do you want to know?' she asked finally.

'First, I want the names of everyone who would have known about Conchita's visit to Holmes Woolcott last night.'

'That,' she said, 'is almost too easy.' She ticked the

names off on her fingers. 'Holmes Woolcott, Alma Nugent, and myself.'

'And Archie Potter,' I added.

'Potter,' she sighed, 'would know only that he was to call for someone here. It is, of course, possible that Miss Gonzales told other persons of her plans, although she herself had no specific idea of her destination yesterday evening. She might have told her roommate, even though I specifically asked her to be discrete, to say simply that she was meeting a friend. She could, during the course of the day, have told a dozen people. The child had great charm, but she tended to be rather naive.'

I didn't like the past tense she was using. 'When did you see Conchita last?'

'Let me see ...' She flipped back through her memory book and then seemed to find the right page. 'It would have been late afternoon. I reminded her of the night's arrangements and promised her she could see her screen test this morning. The only other time I saw her yesterday was during the test. She seemed relaxed and untroubled, and she will have, I think, a certain magnetic quality on the screen.'

'Skip the public relations work. I'll read about it in *Variety*.'

'I can tell you no more,' she announced.

There was a fresh dose of acid in her voice when she said it, and what she'd told me got me nowhere fast. 'Who was here during the screen-test?' I asked.

She paused for a moment and then said irritably, 'Everyone.'

'Who's everyone?'

'The staff, the girls, and myself. For us it was simply a normal working day,' she replied, in a way that suggested the rest of the world probably spent the day sitting on its sweet ass.

'Can I see the test?' I asked, even though I didn't know what I expected to get out of it other than a twist to the knife that had been in me for the last ten hours.

'If it will amuse you,' Ann Shoemaker answered with a grunt of satisfaction. I'd kicked her dream around some, and now it was her turn to take a swat at mine.

32

THE screening room was Ann Shoemaker's ritzy way of describing the beaverboard box nailed into a corner of the cellar behind the boiler. There was enough room in it for a half-dozen spectators, providing none of them suffered from claustrophobia. We sat there and listened to water shuddering up through the pipes while Massimo Leone fumbled the film into the projector. I ignored him, and I hoped he could ignore me. All he had to do was let one of his secret-weapon farts in that tight space, and we'd all be goners.

Finally the projector sprayed a rectangle of light across the end wall, freckled with nail-heads. Leone pulled the string that clicked off the bulb overhead, and set the film in motion. Numbers bounced against the wall, followed by a blur of feet hammering out a slow-motion tap-dance, and another blaze of grainy white. Then a blackboard appeared, dipped out of the picture, and slowly raised into view. 'Screentest – Conchita Gonzales' was chalked on it in a kindergarden scrawl, probably Leone's own semi-literate handiwork. Then the camera pulled back to a long-shot of the garden end of the big drawing-room upstairs. It was empty for the first few seconds, and then one of the French doors opened and someone walked in out of the garden. There was so much glare from the angled door that the whole thing could have been shot in the Yukon, but then the door swung shut and the glare went away, and Conchita was standing there in a pale dress that softly wrapped and folded her, concealing just enough to make any red-blooded moviegoer want to see a lot more.

The camera tracked her as she moved hesitantly across

the room and paused beside the oak desk. She turned slowly, looking first over one shoulder, then the other, as though to be certain she was alone. Then the camera jerked in for a close-up of her staring at the desk. The delicate line of her brows was faintly distorted, as though something were troubling her. Slowly her right hand moved over to the center drawer of the desk and carefully eased it open. Now her face began to show real fear. The drawer slid open an inch, two inches, and the camera dove back for another long-shot. Conchita leaned suddenly against the desk, pushing the drawer shut, and smiled nervously at someone who had obviously just entered the room.

The scene ended there, with another of Leone's blurred floor-shots, and then seemed to begin again. Once more the French door swung open into the empty room, flashing a hot sheet of sunlight into the eye of the camera. It closed, and Conchita moved forward with a basket of flowers on her arm, chattering to someone already in the room. There was laughter in her eyes as she crossed to the desk, set the basket down, and begin to arrange flowers in a tall vase that was standing there. She held a rose up and inhaled its fragrance, then drew it in a lazy line along her cheek and smiled suggestively. I didn't have to read *Variety* to know she was good, despite the corniness of the action. She was young and fresh and natural, and she put into her performance that mixture of little-girl freshness and big-girl sexiness that I'd learned to live with. Seeing her that way, alive and happy, seemed to peel away the outer layer of my skin. The nerve ends were all screaming in protest, and I was surprised Shoemaker and Leone couldn't hear them.

With the rose still held against her cheek, Conchita glanced to the side, breaking the mood as she seemed to consult someone about what to do next. In the long-shot that followed she was tucking the same rose into the vase, and then she stepped back to admire the results. The door to the hall swung open a few inches, and was pulled quickly shut again. Conchita seemed not to notice, but turned hesitantly away from the desk and began to move toward the camera. Her walk was slow and easy, with a slight rolling sway of the hips, and the clinging fabric of the dress left no doubt about her muscle coordination. The Hayes Office probably wouldn't object to the performance, but it was a hell of a lot sexier than *Family Fun*.

The film ended with a close-up. Conchita stared straight into the camera, her eyes slightly veiled by thick black lashes, and then slowly bent her head back to reveal the taut muscles of her throat. She moved her head from side to side, teasing with glimpses of her profile, and again stared directly into the lens of the camera. Her lips were slightly parted in a wistful smile as she reached up to run her fingers through the dense masses of her hair.

The last frame clicked through the projector and the empty reel rattled like a run-away garbage-can lid. Something empty inside me wanted to answer it, but didn't speak the same language. I looked down and saw that my hands were trying to break a couple of souvenirs off the metal chair I was sitting on.

'Well,' Ann Shoemaker's voice cracked, 'are you satisfied?'

For a while my tongue seemed to be glued to the top of my mouth, but I finally loosened it up enough to say, 'Not quite.'

'She is very photogenic,' she observed. There was more than professionalism in her streamlined syllables. Somewhere, far behind it, was an inflection that on a clear day would have passed for sympathy. But not today.

I ignored her for a while, pretending to study the pattern of the nail-heads in the wall. They didn't have much to tell me.

'I want to see it again,' I said.

'Again?' she answered, as though she couldn't believe anybody was dumb enough to turn around and walk back over the bed of knives a second time.

'Yes. But just the last couple of minutes.'

She passed the information along to her technical wizard, and again Conchita was coming out of the garden to greet me. Then the film speeded up, and she was a clumsy puppet jerked violently back and forth across the wall, her lovely face twisted as a spastic's. The film slowed again, and she drew the rose along her cheek. Then it was in the vase with the others, and Conchita took two steps backward and paused to admire the results.

Just as the door to the drawing room inched open, I shouted 'Stop!' and Leone hit the switch. 'Go on,' I said, and leaned back to close my eyes and let the last scene slide by without me. It would have been too much, and I'd already seen what I wanted to see – Brand Brockaway's unmistakably oily mug shoved up to the crack in the door. Obviously he hadn't known a screen-test was going on, or he wouldn't have done the peek-a-boo routine, but from the way he jerked the door shut again, I had a hunch he wasn't bothered about blowing Conchita's scene. If there was a selfless bone in his body, it was too small to show up on an x-ray. No, my guess was he'd seen someone he didn't want to see, and I wanted to know who it was.

'Who else was in the room while the test was being made?' I asked.

'Everyone,' Ann Shoemaker helpfully informed me.

'That covers a lot of ground, lady. Whoever opened the door doesn't count as part of everybody?'

'What I mean,' she clarified, 'is that the girls were all there, in the far end of the room, and the staff, too. We often find that if there's an audience, beginners think less about the camera. Otherwise, they tend to freeze up. They've done these exercises in class, so it seems natural to have the class there, and any of the staff that's around.'

'And everybody, as you put it, was around yesterday?'

'I believe so.' She thought a minute, removing an imaginary piece of lint from her skirt while she revolved a couple of gray cells. 'I know Renate was there,' she said, 'because she helped Conchita with her make-up, and Adrianna was sitting beside me on the sofa. I don't recall seeing Ingrid Seagram, but she was certainly there as well.'

'And the staff?'

'Certainly. Our drama coach was there, and Mr Riley and our pianist. Yes, they were all there.'

It was clear the surplus of information wasn't going to help me find out what spider Brockaway had seen in the parlor yesterday afternoon, so I'd have to find out from him.

'How can I get in touch with your leading man, Brand Brockaway?'

'Mr Brockaway is normally reached through his agent,' she crisply informed me.

'Can it, lady. I'm not trying to hire him for the starring role in *The Old Testament*. I just want to ask him a few questions.'

She treated me to another of her exasperated sighs and said, 'Perhaps I can locate his private address for you.'

'Perhaps you can do that right now, and I'll just toddle off on another errand of mercy.'

'Very well.'

She led me out of the dungeons, and on the way I gave Leone a wink. 'So long, toots,' I whispered, and he looked like I'd just tapped him to play target for the firing squad.

It didn't take Shoemaker long to produce the address, and even less time to hustle me to the door. She sent me off with a bone-crushing handshake that would have done her Prussian ancestors proud.

'Be careful,' she said, and gritted her teeth to punish them for letting it slip out like that.

I hustled along the driveway to the car, parked on the street and already starting to give off spirals of heat in the morning sun. I slid in the passenger side and was dragging the door shut when I saw the hair tied to the steering wheel. It was snugged into a single, glossy bow, the kind you find on boxes of Valentine's candy.

33

THE strand of hair was locked away in the glove compartment, and in my head I tried to build a wall against it. When the wall started toppling down, I thought maybe I could prop it up again with numbers. The one Ann Shoemaker had given me was thirty-two. Multiply that by two and you get sixty-four. Square it and you get 1,024. The mileage indicator on the Plymouth said 89,752. Add that up from let to right and you get thirty-one. Add it up from right to left and you still get thirty-one. In another mile it would be thirty-two, the same as Brockaway's street number, the same as the age I'd be on my next birthday. Add my age to Conchita's and you got fifty-two. The square of fifty-two is 2,704. If one train enters a tunnel traveling fifty-miles an hour and another train enters the other end traveling thirty-five miles an hour, and the tunnel is two miles long, how long will it take someone to discover that there's only one track running through the tunnel? If a loaf of bread costs fifteen cents and a dozen eggs costs thirty cents, what color is the postman's hair? The speedometer needled up to forty-five. Square forty-five and you get 2,025. A traffic light blinked red and I slid in on two wheels, skidding up behind a laundry truck with the licence number ninety-two. Square ninety-two and you get 8,464. The square root of 8,464 is ninety-two. The square root of murder is murder.

It was a fast trip, but it wasn't fast enough. I whipped past the Chateau Moraine, hauled right at the next intersection, and came dive-bombing down in front of number thirty-two. My heart was racing faster than the motor, and it kept on racing even when I switched off the ignition. Two times two is four. Four times four is sixteen. Sixteen times sixteen is 256. Count very slowly from one to ten, I thought. Then from ten to one. I'd never known it was that hard to make the lungs pump. You reached a long way down and pulled. All the muscles strained together, twisted and dragged against flesh and only very slowly did they suck in a thin, stale column of air. It wasn't enough, and all the muscles jerked together, pulled and hauled as if they were drawing a heavy bucket up out of a very dark, very deep well. Then I took a hard grip on the steering wheel and made myself focus on the outside world – on the troops of flattened bugs that had done kamikaze flights against the windshield, the shiny knob on the gear-shift, the line of telephone poles marching off along the street, and the broken concrete walk that led up to the front door of number thirty-two. Thirty-two times thirty-two makes 1,024. Square 1,024 and you get ... Multiply 1,024 by 1,024 and you got more than I had time for now. My knees threatened to go on strike when I got out of the car, but I reminded them there was a war on, and that whipped them into shape again.

The house was the right kind of setting for Brockaway. It gave off a smell of rot and mildew and unwashed underwear that hit you in the face long before you got to the door. Fifty years ago it had probably been a decent address, but now it was just another flea-bag boarding house – the kind that's always full of newcomers who've started dreaming the Hollywood dream, and oldtimers who've stopped dreaming it. There was a ROOMS TO LET sign in the window, and the tape that held it there dated back a couple of decades. I punched the bell and it shouted at me from somewhere at the back of the house. There was no other sound, though, and so I punched it again, even though I had a feeling the team was out to lunch.

I was about to call it quits and head downtown to start dismantling police headquarters brick by brick when a woman came waddling up the sidewalk. She was taking it slow, but then she had some excess baggage to carry, and her huarachas were making a lot of noise about it.

Stripped, she'd probably weigh in at about two-hundred-sixty pounds, but she'd somehow managed to get most of it inside a rayon tent covered with palm trees and hula girls. Jammed onto her head was a hat that looked like it had been made from an abandoned desk blotter. She was so busy navigating that she'd heaved herself up onto the porch before she noticed me.

'Lookin' for me?' she asked. She squinted nearsightedly from under the brim of her hat. All her features seemed squeezed into the center of her face, leaving great barren plains and hills of swollen flesh stretching into the distance all around them.

'Maybe,' I said. 'Are you the landlady?'

'That's me. Wanna room?'

'Not exactly. I want to ask about one of your boarders.'

She sucked on her teeth and thought about it for a while. 'Don't know as I can tell you much,' she said finally. 'Ain't got but two.'

'I'm only interested in one,' I told her. 'His name's Brand Brockaway.'

'Ain't here,' she said.

'Do you know where I can find him?'

She waved an arm in the general direction of the Pacific and said, 'Who knows? Left this mornin'. Didn't leave no address.'

'I'd like to ask you a few questions about him.'

She pushed a hand through the neck of her dress and started jerking a few straps into place. 'Well, I don't rightly know,' she whined between hoistings and hitchings. 'I don't rightly know. You a girlfriend?' She squinted up at me, aiming the brim of her hat and a dose of last night's garlic in my general direction.

'Not really,' I said. 'Just call me a distant admirer.'

'Well, he's a crook!' she blurted.

I couldn't help thinking it was probably the nicest thing anybody had called the louse all week. 'What kind of crook?'

'Every kind, the son of a bitch. Skipped out owin' me three weeks rent. Flew the coop. Just like that. Bang!' She slammed a fist against the door-jamb and I could feel the house shiver.

I fished out my photostat and shoved it at her. 'I'm a private investigator,' I said, 'and you're not the only one who thinks Brockaway's a crook.'

She sucked her teeth again, found something interesting between her upper lip and her gum, and studied the card for a few minutes. 'I'll be damned,' she muttered. 'Well, I'll be damned. Knew he was a crook. Whole town's full of crooks and spies. Blowin' up factories and stuff. Damn Japs and Nazis everywhere. Whole town's full of 'em. Everybody makin' bombs. Submarines comin' right up on the beach every mornin'.'

She had a good grip on the photostat, but I managed to pull it away from her. Her hand looked like a bunch of bananas. 'Could I see his room?' I asked.

'Well, don't know 'bout that,' she fumbled. 'Don't know ...' She squinted at me again, sizing up the audience. 'How I know that thing's real?'

'Call police headquarters,' I suggested.

'Don't want to cause no trouble, honey. Sure don't want to cause no trouble ...' She gave a nice dramatic pause and waited for me to pick up the cue.

'How much did Mr Brockaway owe you?'

'Well, now, let me see. For three weeks, that'd be about fifteen dollars.'

I dug three fins out of my billfold and handed them to her. She made a little clucking sound and held each one up to study it, then rustled it beside her ear until something told her it was Uncle Sam's own moola.

'Reckon maybe you can see it,' she said, 'but there ain't nothin' to see. The bum took everythin' and run out on me while I was down to Mister Donut this mornin'. Damned crook.'

'I'd still like to see his room,' I insisted.

'Sure thing, honey, sure,' she assured me, while she excavated in her purse and looked for the house key. The purse was made of straw covered with pink seashells, and from the way it rattled it must have been full of old carpenter's tools.

She led me inside and through the obstacle course she'd built in the hall. Newspapers were tied in bundles and stacked waist-high, and there were boxes overflowing with bottles, tin cans and old shoes. 'For the war effort,' she explained with a kind of patriotic tremble in her voice.

Brockaway's room was upstairs at the front of the house, with a nice southern exposure and a few pieces of metal furniture the Salvation Army had refused to pick up. There was a double bed, a dresser, a table and a couple of chairs – all made of metal that once upon a time had been painted to look like oak but had gotten tired of the masquerade. Pinned to the wallpaper was an old girlie calendar, and stuck into the frame of the mirror over the dresser was a coupon for a free manicure at Irene's Beauty Box. There was nothing under the bed but a pound or so of dust, and nothing in the closet but a couple of empty hooch bottles. The dresser drawers were empty, too, except for a petrified bar of soap with a few hairs glued to it. I nudged it with a finger, half expecting it to show its fangs, when I spied something shiny wedged into the corner of the drawer. I levered it out with a fingernail and held it up to the light. It was the business end of a hypo.

The landlady was craning her neck and trying to get the needle into focus, but I had it tucked away in my billfold before she'd really zeroed in on it. 'Just a little souvenir,' I said. At least I had something to show for the fifteen bucks she'd skinned me for.

'When did you last see Brockaway?' I asked her.

'Last night,' she said. 'Told him he'd have to pay up or I'd call the police, the crook. This mornin' I heard him in the bathroom. Always in the bathroom, honey, always usin' up all the hot water. Used to spend hours in there and then come out with perfume all over him. The big crook. Whole town's full of crazies, honey. A girl's gotta be real careful, specially now with all them spies everywhere. Last week they try to poison all the water.' She gave me a conspiratorial squint and flapped the brim of her hat at me.

188

'Some folks says as how that ain't the real F.D.R., but some big German fella that Hitler sent over to replace the one he kilt. Say he's gonna turn the country over to them Nazis, and make everybody work in the mines diggin' coal for them German factories.'

She had a certain gift for cheering up an audience, but I thought that was where I'd come in, so I headed for the nearest exit. The monologue was still running full steam ahead when the screen door clapped to behind me.

A couple of blocks away I passed a diner made out of an old railway carriage, and my stomach reminded me I hadn't paid it any attention for the last twenty-four hours. I made a u-turn, parked out front, and went in to order myself a b.l.t. and coffee. While the maestro fired up his griddle, I made a couple of phone calls. Lavender had heard from Ingrid and she'd managed to sift a few names out of Shoemaker's confidential files while we were at the movies together. I jotted them down.

'Anything else?' I asked.

'That's it,' he sighed, in a voice that told me he'd already heard the worst of the news from Ingrid. 'You O.K.?'

'Right now I feel like I've just fought the Battle of Gettysburg single-handed, but I'm not ready to run up the white flag yet.'

'Can't I do something?' he asked.

'For now, just hold the fort, pale-face. I'll get there when I can.'

'Is it bad?'

'It's worse,' I told him. 'We can always remember it as the day the shit hit the fan.'

'I'm sorry,' he said, and I knew he meant it, but it didn't make enough difference.

'So long,' I answered, and broke the connection.

I got hold of O'Brien then and asked him what the servants of the people had turned up. They were working on it, he said, which meant they hadn't gotten to first base yet. I told him what I'd found out since he left – about Potter's daughter, the tie-in to Alexander Woods, the.

missing photographs.

'I checked out the Academy again,' I said, 'and it turns out Shoemaker is a German immigrant. She was Holmes Woolcott's mistress once upon a time, in Heidelberg. You might see what sort of file she's got with the immigration people. And I've got three names for you – girls who left the Academy in a hurry and without giving a forwarding address.' I read him Lavender's list and said, 'Check them out, too.'

'What makes you think – ' he started to ask, and I blocked him before he got over the scrimmage line.

'Also, put out a call on Brockaway. Something he saw at the Academy yesterday kind of ruffled his feathers, and the bird has flown. He's probably a hop-head, and from the sound of things he didn't have enough money for a fix. That means he could be dangerous.'

'If you'd – '

'Just a minute, O'Brien. It's my nickel this time, and I want my money's worth. When I came out of the Academy this morning, there was another love token waiting for me. This time it was knotted around the steering wheel. That means somebody knows every move I'm making, and don't tell me I'm therefore supposed to stand still and do nothing. It's against my nature. Also, if some lunatic wants to play games, I want to make it interesting for him, at least – maybe even interesting enough for him to want to play a little longer. As long as he's busy trying to cover my next move, Conchita's got a chance to stay alive. But now I just may know more than he thinks, and if you help me put it to work instead of sitting on your fat Irish ass, we've got a chance of breaking this one. Savvy?'

'Lamaar – '

'Save the small talk, O'Brien. I'm a busy girl.'

I hung up and walked back to the counter, where the sandwich sat waiting for me. The bread was limp with bacon grease and tasted a little like cardboard, but I was able to float it down with two cups of make-believe coffee. As I walked out, I noticed that the floor of the dinette was

divided into red and black squares, like a chess-board. I
didn't like the ideas it gave me. In fact, I didn't like them at
all, and I spent a lot of time trying not to think about the
fact that in the game of chess I was playing now, Conchita
was the pawn.

34

THERE was a new guard in the sentry box at Pantheon
Pictures, and from the way he rippled his cheek muscles I
could tell he was just killing time until he had his moment
on the silver screen. While he studied my press card, he
flexed his pectorals a couple of times to let me know that
nobody kicked sand in his face on the beach. Then he
drifted his watery brown eyes over me in a way that
suggested he could give me a little time later if I played my
cards right.

'Got an appointment?' he asked.

'No, not exactly. But Mr Riley said I could do a piece on
his new picture.' I hoped I had the right kind of girlish
tremolo in my voice.

'Set's closed,' he informed me, fluttering his left bicep a
little.

'I know Mr Riley doesn't usually let the press in, but I
think he'll make an exception in my case. We know each
other. And this could be a really big break for me with the
paper.'

That seemed to interest him, and he stopped studying his
own muscles to check mine out again. 'Well,' he said, 'you
can have a try. They're in Studio B.'

'Gee, thanks,' I gushed.

'Come around here a lot?'

'Once or twice a week,' I told him, and this week, at
least, it was true.

'Look me up,' he suggested. 'The name's Tom. I get off
at five o'clock.'

'Sure, Tom, I'll do that. Bye-bye now.' He flexed a bicep

for me, and I flashed him my best dimple in trade.

Pantheon Pictures sprawled over a few square miles of expensive Hollywood real-estate. It was a kind of city within a city, with palm-lined boulevards and shady back alleys and row after row of gleaming, ice-cream-colored office buildings and cottages with red-tiled roofs. Behind them, like overgrown sugar-cubes, were the concrete walls that held the sound stages, and back another half-mile or so acres of jungles and deserts and mountain ranges and Aztec temples lay bleaching in the sun. I passed a couple of Roman senators tripping on their togas and giggling about some private joke, and a geriatric case spinning along in a wheelchair and wearing a tall pointed witch's cap over her bifocals. A roly-poly man in clown-face and a bathing suit was walking a matched pair of wire-haired terriers and saying 'Now, *pee*' over and over again.

I let the signs take me to the commissary – not the one where you were likely to see Doug Fairbanks sinking his pearlies into caviar on toast, but the nickel-and-dime joint where the extras could grab a rubber hamburger between takes. The Confederate army was there, and a couple of King Arthur's distant relatives. What interested me more were a couple of frills – a blonde and a brunette – wearing a lot of skin and a few square inches of costume that was supposed to look vaguely Egyptian. I bought myself a beer and asked if I could join them. They were both pumping away at straws stuck into raspberry sodas, but they made noises that might have been affirmative.

The blonde on my left won the race, and announced it by making a lot of racket with her straw. 'Gotta go,' she said. 'I've split another damned seam.' From the size of her costume, there wasn't a seam in it you couldn't have sewn up in about two minutes. She went clattering off in her gold sandals, and left me with the brunette. Whether she was really a brunette, only mother nature could know for sure at that moment. She wore a wig cut in a blunt line just below her ears, and with bangs that hid her eyebrows. The shiny black hair was slicked down with vaseline – or maybe it was

axle grease. Otherwise she wasn't wearing much but a
snakeskin bra and panties, and what looked like the kind of
neck brace people get if they manage to live through a head-
on collision.

She was a lot more interested in the bottom of the soda
glass than she was in me, but I thought I knew how to
change that. 'Excuse me,' I said. 'I'm from the press, and I
was wondering if you were in the new Rigsby Riley film.'

She smiled up at me with eyes that were slightly crossed.
'Golly!' she squeaked. 'You're really a reporter?'

'Yes. Want to see my press card?'

'Oh, gosh, I never met a lady reporter before.'

'I'm covering the new Riley film – human interest angle,
you know.'

She patted her bangs into place with the tips of her
fingers, fluttered her lashes a little, and drew her mouth
into a letter O. Her lips were red as a new fire engine. 'How
exciting! What paper you working for?'

'I'm syndicated.'

'Gosh, how *thrilling*.'

'Are you working on the Riley film?'

'Uh-huh. But there aren't supposed to be any reporters
around – ever. That's one of Mr Riley's rules. He's real
strict about that 'cause he says it interferes with things too
much.'

'Yeah, so I hear. But we've met before and I kind of
thought he wouldn't mind if I chatted with some of the cast.
I don't want to write anything about the picture, but maybe
something about the people making it. Not the stars that
papers write about all the time. You know what I mean, all
the different types, the chorus and the grips and the make-
up people that have to work together to make a movie like
that.'

'Golly!' She was really coming alive now with the hope of
snagging a paragraph all her own. 'I just think that's the
most wonderful idea. Like nobody who's not in pictures
knows how *hard* you have to work. Sometimes we spend
days and days and *days* just to get one little scene right, and

then at the end some star steps in and they do a close-up and that's all people really *see* later. Just the big star.'

'That's the sort of thing I mean. The story behind the story's what we're after.'

'How thrilling,' she cooed.

'The new picture's called *The Loves of Cleopatra*, isn't it?' She nodded yes.

'And what role do you play?'

'Just a minute,' she said, holding up a scarlet-tipped finger to tell me I should wait. 'I'll show you!' She fumbled around under the table and came up with what looked like a gigantic salad-bowl covered in snakeskin that she hoisted up behind her head and clicked into her neckbrace. If definitely wasn't the sort of thing to wear in a gale-force wind – at least not without a pilot's licence.

'Well – ' she encouraged me.

'Well?'

'What part do you think I play?' Her dark eyes were shining with mischief – each in its own independent direction, of course.

'I give up.'

She hissed and waved her head from side to side.

'Still don't know?' she asked.

'Still don't know,' I confessed.

'An asp!' she shouted, and then sent a little arpeggio of giggles my way.

'An asp?'

'An *asp*.' She waved her head from side to side again, and I could tell that the choreography probably made a difference. I wanted to reassure her she wasn't the first dame to make an asp of herself in Hollywood, but given time she'd probably figure that one out for herself.

'Is it a big part?'

'No,' she answered cheerfully, 'but I'm also a drum majorette in the first scene.'

I thought I wouldn't strain her brain by asking for a summary of the plot.

'Are they shooting the asp scene today?'

She shook her head no. 'We did that last week,' she explained. 'We all came out of these baskets that were in a circle all around Cleopatra's bed, and we all sort of scooted on our stomachs going hiss-hiss.' She hissed a little more for me and showed the tip of her raspberry-tinted tongue. 'It was all shot from real high up, straight up overhead. This morning we did like some close-ups of different faces that'll come in and out of the overhead shot. It's called cutting,' she confided. 'Of course, they won't use most of them, but maybe they'll use mine. Knock on wood!' She clanged her knuckles a couple of times against the metal table top. 'Wouldn't that be peachy?'

'It sure would. That's the kind of story our readers want to see – the trials and tribulations of an asp.'

'I got a splinter in my stomach,' she informed me.

'A what?'

'A splinter. Scooching across the floor I got a splinter in my stomach, and it hurt like *crazy*, but when the cameras are rolling you've just got to go *on*.' She got halfway out of her chair and pointed to a spot just above the top of her snakeskin panties. 'Right there,' she said, and sat down again. 'The nurse had to pull it out with tweezers, and *that* hurt like crazy, too.'

I clucked in sympathy.

'But you can't see it,' she added, ''cause I've got some pancake on it. Anyhow, it's just an itty-bitty hole.'

'I think I can probably use that kind of detail somewhere in my story,' I suggested.

'Golly, *could* you?'

'I think so,' I said, fondling my non-existent beard and trying to look like a very clever journalist.

'But wouldn't it seem kind of *silly*? A *splinter*? In your *stomach*?'

'It's the human touch we're after.'

The kid was as soft as an overripe peach. She was beginning to pant slightly, and I felt like a heel for working over her fantasy life, but I figured there were guys around who'd do the same job with a lot heavier touch than mine.

My reasons were better, too.

One of her eyes caught a glimpse of the commissary clock then and she said, 'Oh, gosh! I've got to *run*. We're supposed to be rehearsing the finale now.'

'Mind if I walk along and ask you a few more questions?'

'O.K., but I walk *fast*,' she warned me.

We quick-timed back to the main street and turned left toward Studio B. On the way I found out the asp was called Lillian Lyles, that she was from Akron, and that she started taking dancing lessons at the age of four from someone named Etta Mae Mosby, who also taught violin and baton-twirling. I also learned that Lillian Lyles wasn't any more her real name than her slicked-down bangs were her own. 'I can't tell you what it is,' she said. 'My family would just *die* if they thought I was in pictures. They think I'm a Comptometer operator.'

There was a whole platoon of asps and handmaidens squeezing through the main entrance to Studio B, and it was easy enough to get lost in the crowd. I just missed being sideswiped by a dolly carrying a miniature of the Sphynx, and by the time I got far enough out of its path, I seemed to have lost Lillian.

Electrical cables coiled about the floor like so much black spaghetti, and the noise level would have made a steel foundry sound like quiet hour at the convent. There was obviously a contest going on to see who could shout the loudest, and somewhere a symphony orchestra was trying to drown out a team of riveters. I tried to look nonchalant, as though this sort of thing was old hat to me, but I had the feeling I was as conspicuous as a ballerina on crutches. I poked around in a few dark corners and finally came up with an electrician's manual. It had enough information on hot circuits to make good bedside reading some chilly winter night. For now, maybe it would help me look a little more official. I opened it up to a page of diagrams and tried to seem like somebody with a job to do.

All the chaos flowed in one direction – toward a mammoth sound stage knee-deep in pink sand. Rising out of the sand was a golden pyramid about five stories tall, and crawling all over it were carpenters and painters, adding a few finishing touches. A small bulldozer was grading the sand at the entrance to the pyramid, and inside, gleaming in the spotlights, was a sarcophagus covered in gold foil. The orchestra I'd heard before was on a separate stage, off to the left, and on the right there rose a kind of control tower with a room like an oblong box with plate-glass sides planted on top of it. A metal staircase zigzagged to the ground from one end, and a skinny ladder from the other, where there must have been a trap-door for emergency exits.

A voice shouted, 'Places everybody,' but no one seemed to hear it. 'Places!' The speaker system boomed so loud this time that it must have been picked up on the seismographs over at U.C.L.A. Slowly the lights began to dim down in the studio – all except for a few that were shining on the pyramid. The bulldozer backed away, the workmen came hopping down the tiered sides of the pyramid, and an army of Nile maidens hotfooted it across the sands. They were all wearing Cleopatra wigs and eye make-up, and otherwise not much but knee-length silver necklaces. They invaded the lower level of the pyramid and arranged themselves in a tight row around it.

The loudspeaker pinged and the voice called, 'Lights!' They blazed out of the ceiling in response. 'Let's hear the melody,' the speaker barked, and for the first time I caught the crumpets-and-tea inflection of Rigsby Riley's voice. The violins came soaring in first, sounding like a lot of nervous crickets, and then the rest of the band got going. 'Action!'

Their arms locked around each other's waists, a gross of Cleopatras began to do a neat military tap step that made it look as though the bottom of the pyramid had come alive and might walk off the set any minute. The loudspeaker barked, 'Cut!' There was a little chat then about pink gels and filters and camera angles, and the show cranked up again. It was done in segments. First the full chorus-line made an Egyptian daisy chain around the pyramid. Then half of them climbed up onto the next level and repeated the act. When Riley was satisfied with it, half the second row climbed up to the third row, and then half of that row to the fourth, and two hours later the whole pyramid was covered with Cleopatras, arms outstretched and hands joined and doing one-two-three-kick. Finally the lights went down until all you could really see was the silver jewelry and the casket glowing inside the tomb. If Riley could only put the same coordination into Eisenhower's troops, they'd all be sitting in Berlin having a schnapps before you could say 'Sieg heil'.

The loudspeaker gave the girls a break then, and I parked myself in a deck chair to work out the best way to get from A to B. I needn't have bothered, because B could take care of that on his own. I saw him strutting down the steps of the control tower, hands in his flannel pockets and taking it on the balls of his feet so that the performance had a jazzy bounce to it, like a good Gershwin song. Riley was used to center-stage, even up there in the crow's-nest, and I had to admit he put on a good show. Two minutes later he was standing in front of me. Even if I hadn't recognized the face, his bench-made brogues would have given him away.

'How enchanting,' he announced. 'I had not ventured to hope we would meet again so soon, Miss Ransom.' He tilted his carrot-topped head toward me and flashed a pearly smile.

'I had a job to do in the neighborhood,' I said, 'and thought I'd drop in to see you in action again. The raw material here seems a little better than it was at the Academy.' And made it that much harder to understand the time he put in on Shoemaker's prize heifers.

'It is only a matter of money, hard work and genius,' he pronounced, fluffing out his ascot with a well-manicured hand. 'The girls themselves don't really matter,' he continued. 'They are only the raw material. I mold them to whatever shape I require, just as I mold the music, the lighting, and the cameras until I obtain precisely the form I want. I control it all from up there.' He waved a pink hand toward the control booth. 'I orchestrate it down to the last detail, and *no* detail is unimportant. One must, of course, start with a vision.'

And a swollen ego, I thought, watching the way his eyes glittered as he described his kingdom.

'Would you like to join me for a cup of tea or a glass of madeira?' he asked, his voice lowering to a purr. 'I have my own trailer on the lot.'

'I'd be delighted,' I told him.

He gave me his arm, like a character out of Jane Austen, and in the best spirit of the allies I hooked a hand through it, just like one of the goody-goody sisters in Louisa Mae Alcott. As we paraded across the set, every female was looking daggers through me, and the men were placing sidebets. It all made me feel about as comfortable as a fresh cold sore.

35

THE wheels on the outside said it was a trailer, but I doubted if anything smaller than a Mack truck could have towed it away. Around the entrance, a trim little flower garden had been planted in English country-cottage style, right down to the blue herbaceous borders, and automatic sprinklers flitted silvery jets of water over them. Obviously it was only the appetizer, because the inside of the trailer was even more Rule Britannia than the outside. There was antiqued wood paneling on the walls and a pegged wooden floor. The swollen sofas and chairs were covered in flowered chintz, and here and there, wherever you were likely to stumble over them, were little needlepoint footstools. There were gas lamps with roses painted on the shades and pieces of old, slightly deformed brass that looked like they were polished at least twice a day. An antique clock was thunking out the seconds in the center of an oak mantlepiece, and in the fake fireplace lightbulbs flickered behind wads of red cellophane.

Rigsby Riley gave me a minute to check out the scenery and then said, 'Well, what do you think?'

'Very cosy,' I told him.

'Isn't it wonderfully bizarre?' he asked.

'Cosily bizarre,' I said. 'And perhaps bizarrely cosy.'

'I am pleased you appreciate my little witticism. I re-design it every few weeks, you know. Last week it was Japanese, but I found sleeping on the floor not at all to my liking. Still, one must have these little diversions. Otherwise it becomes too, too tedious. The challenge of it all,' he said with a wave of the wrist, 'evaporated long ago.'

Riley left me to browse through some old issues of *Country Life* while he went off to make tea. I used the time instead to size up the layout. There was a bedroom, complete with a four-poster that Queen Victoria could have slept in, a dressing room and a bath, all snuggled into one end of the trailer. In the center was the living room, with a dining table and chairs at the end, and beyond them the kitchen. The door we'd come through seemed to be the only way in. The windows were sealed into the body of the trailer, and air-conditioning kept the inside as cool as a thatched cottage. So far, Riley's lifestyle seemed consistent enough – a mixture of hard work and expensive tastes and an over-active imagination, all seasoned with a dash of merrie olde England.

A whistling tea kettle announced how things were proceding in the kitchen, just in time for me to get a hand out of the top drawer of an old walnut secretary. It was empty, anyhow. The man with the magical tap shoes came wheeling in a teacart with about fifty pounds of antique silver on it, and asked if I'd play mother. I didn't think I was exactly right for the part, but I tried my best to do credit to Greer Garson.

'What a pleasant surprise it was to see you on the set,' Riley said.

'Was it?' I asked, trying to sound at least marginally flirtatious.

'It was, indeed. Our first meeting was much too brief.' He edged over toward my end of the sofa and let his left arm rest on the cushion behind me. There was a faint scent of peppermint when he breathed in my direction.

'Are you comfortable?' he asked.

'Quite.'

'What brought you here this morning? It's too much to hope you might have come to see me, of course.'

'Well ...,' I hesitated, studying the cabbage-roses on the porcelain. 'Actually, I had some work to do for a client.'

The outer corners of his mouth tipped up in a smile, and his arm edged down until it lay lightly across my shoulders. 'Who would that be?' he asked, directing the question against the side of my neck.

I leaned forward and helped myself to another cup of tea. 'No one you'd know, probably. A young actress named Lillian Lyles wanted us to arrange some plugs for her in the local papers. We met at the commissary, and I came over to the set with her.'

'I don't think I know the name,' he said thoughtfully.

'She's one of your asps.'

'Well, one can't be expected to know every asp by name. There are so many, you understand.' He laughed then – a broad, jolly laugh that was full of tweeds and heather and tally-ho.

I got the teacup and saucer up in front of me and leaned against the end of the sofa, temporarily out of reach of his exploring arm. 'Do you always live on the lot?' I asked.

'Heavens, no! I've a superb beach house in Malibu. I designed it myself, and it's full of marvelous gadgets, including a kind of shoot-the-chute from the bedroom right into the sea and a roof that slides off the living room to let the sun in. Or the stars. And the kitchen is completely automated. It does everything but fetch my pipe and slippers. But when I'm working on a picture, I prefer to live here. I expect everyone working with me to be willing to put in a twelve-hour day. I put in eighteen or twenty myself, you know.'

'Incredible,' I said, because I knew it was what he wanted to hear.

'Not really. When I work, I work. When I play, I play. And my pictures are not easy to make, you know. I take charge of everything. The sets, the lighting, the special effects – each detail must have my monogram on it. The golden sarcophagus, for example, is entirely my own creation.' He eyed me slowly, to be sure I was sufficiently impressed by his jack-of-all-trades talents, then reached over, took the cup carefully but firmly away from me, and set it back on the tea-cart. 'But really, my dear, I'd much rather talk about you,' he said, inching a little closer. 'After all, I scarcely know you, and yet destiny seems bent on bringing us together.'

'There's not much to know. I'm just another working girl.'

'That I find rather difficult to believe. Yes, it really seems to me most unlikely. There seems, somehow, an air of mystery about you. Mystery fascinates me.'

'Probably it's just my new after-shave.'

'You must not be insecure about your beauty, my dear.' He reached out and touched my hair with his hand. 'You are, in fact, a very beautiful woman, though you seem to wish to conceal that fact.' His hand strayed a little, across my shoulder as he took it away and let it fall on the seat between us. The crisp cuff of his white shirt was turned back just far enough to reveal four lines scratched on his arm, four parallel grooves that could only be made by a set of sharply filed finger-nails.

'I could quite transform you,' he suggested. 'The proper make-up, different clothes. We would, of course, keep the rather masculine effect. It suits you. But it would all be softened somewhat, and there would be an unmistakable note of elegance, of understated chic. We would enhance the mystery.'

'I'm not sure it goes with my budget,' I said.

He dismissed the objection with a wave of his hand and another throaty laugh. 'We need not speak of money. Such things can be negotiated. If your present employment doesn't bring you a sufficient income, perhaps ... perhaps other arrangements could be made.'

I wasn't sure if he wanted to buy me or to buy me off, and his suave, country-gentleman style wasn't giving me much to go on.

'Is that a proposal or a proposition?' I asked him.

'My dear, you have nothing to fear from *me*. I am not the sort who pounces, or who promises screen tests to silly young girls with small brains and large breasts. It is so very boring, that Hollywood style, and so terribly *declassé*.'

'I'll bet it's not half as boring to you as it is to me.'

'Perhaps you are right. For a beautiful woman Hollywood is no doubt the best town in the world or, on the other hand, the worst.'

'And for a man?' I wondered out loud.

'For a man it seems at first a kind of paradise. One needs only to reach out and pluck the fruit from the tree.' He made a cute little demonstration of the process, and when he raised his hand for the golden apple, his sleeve slid back further. The scratches seemed to run the length of his arm. Whatever he said, he obviously still pounced every now and then – maybe just to keep in practise.

'But then it soon ceases to be interesting,' he sighed. 'One seeks other amusements.' His tongue slowly moistened his lips while his eyes searched my face. He had an air of seeming to wait for something, but all he got in reply was the rattle of the airconditioner.

'I think we might be good together,' he went on. 'There is a strength about you somehow. The women one sees every day, those little wind-up Cleopatras, even the stars who are thought to be such individualists, they are all so much putty. They are what they are told to be, or what they think the studio will buy this year. You, however, seem real. There would be depths to explore, passions to awaken, secrets to learn.'

'You flatter me,' I said, even though I thought what he was really doing was to short-change the rest of them. If girls were putty in the hands of dream-merchants like Riley, it was because the dream-merchants wrote the rule-book. I suspected Riley had a copy of it in his hip pocket right now.

'Do I interest you at all?' he asked.

'You're an interesting man,' I admitted, and that much was true. 'You're a phenomenon, an industry. The trade papers call you a blockbuster.'

'That isn't at all what I mean. Does the thought of ... shall we say of a partnership, does the idea interest you?'

'A little. After all, my field is public relations.'

'Precisely. And that means you too like to manipulate and control, to choreograph things.' He laid a cold hand on my cheek and wrapped me in a Svengali stare. 'Am I right?' he asked.

'Perhaps. But you've probably sized me up all wrong, and I'm not sure I believe in partnership-at-first-sight.'

He continued to stare hard at me and I noticed the tiny beads of sweat that dotted his upper lip, the faint nick of a razor cut on his right jaw, the way the taut skin of his nostrils, whiter than the rest of his face, flared slightly when he breathed.

'Whenever you are ready to talk further,' he said finally, 'simply contact me. It could be to your advantage.'

'Is it that simple to reach you?' I asked.

'I'll give you my private number,' he said, and went away to get it for me. When he handed me the ivory-colored card, I wondered for a minute if I shouldn't give him one of mine, but then I figured he probably had my number already.

'And now I must get back to work,' he announced. 'We're three days over schedule, and as you know, I always bring in a picture on time.' He draped his arm lightly around my waist as he led me to the door, and I could feel his dancer's body hard and lean as it curved against mine, but at the moment he didn't have time to give me more than that little sample of the good things I could expect if I accepted his offer of a merger.

He left me at the back door of the sound stage with a handshake that lingered in a come-hither way.

'Cheerio,' I said, reclaiming my fingers.

'Cheerie bye-bye.' He gave me a playful wave as he moved away. Without seeming to priss or to prance, he walked with a music-hall strut, leaning slightly forward like a man who's in a hurry, but who's just decided to take his time and let the world wait for him. With anyone else, the routine would have been played for laughs. Somehow, the way Riley did it had all the sleekness and power of a panther's stride, something taut, with muscles coiled and waiting to spring.

I headed toward the main drag, but stopped before I got all the way there. Then I doubled round a small generating plant, skirted the edge of a lily pond that had surrendered to the algae, and made my way back to the trailer. Riley's white Rolls Royce was parked behind it, and I wanted to have a gander at that famous chariot.

It had the sort of liquid gloss on it that's easy to get with about fifty coats of lacquer and a daily simonize job, and there wasn't a fleck of dust to spoil it. Obviously even the dirt knew which way the deck was stacked in Hollywood. The whitewalls were as fresh as a nurse's cap, and the grill on the front glowed in the sun like platinum. The lady mounted on top of it had her nose in the air, and that kind of bored look around the eyes that dames like to wear to cocktail parties. Just below her were the initials R.R. I remembered what Rigsby Riley had said about leaving his monogram on everything, and wondered if he still remembered there was ever a Mr Rolls or a Mr Royce sharing the same planet with him.

The door of the car was unlocked, and the registration strapped to the steering column told me who the owner was, that his legal residence was in Malibu, and that the car was five years old. There were enough dials on the dashboard to furnish a Buck Rogers extravaganza, and whole herds of cows had died to produce the creamy-white leather upholstery. On the back seat was a black umbrella, rolled into a tight cylinder, and a shirt box with nothing but shirts in it. There were a few dark spots desecrating the upholstery in the back. They could be mud. They could also be machine oil or shoe polish or blood. Or maybe somebody dropped a warm Hershey bar there.

36

LAVENDER poured rum into a pair of matched jelly glasses – a half inch in one, a half inch in the other. Then he raised his eyebrows in question marks, and I high-signed him to keep up the good work. He kept it up until my glass had a fat two fingers of cane in it. After that came a couple of slivers of ice and some coke, and we went chin-chin with the glasses, but the whole thing resembled a wake more than a cocktail hour.

'What time did O'Brien call?' I asked him for the third time.

'Just about one o'clock,' Lavender repeated.

'And he's sure it was Brockaway who got on the bus and not some other grease-ball?'

'Said it was Brockaway, and that he got the twelve-thirty bus to Reno.'

'That's no guarantee he stayed on it, though. He could have just been trying to dodge the autograph-hunters.'

'O'Brien said they'd check all along the way, that if he got off before Reno there'd be a tail on him. Said they'd put a tail on him in Reno if he went all the way through.'

'For once our Irish friend's using his head for something besides a hat-stretcher,' I admitted. 'Anything else?'

Lavender shrugged, started to say something, and then shrugged again, his shoulders hunching up in a way that told me more than a whole paragraph. His skin had a dead gray look, like he'd been dusted all over with whole-wheat flour.

Finally he asked, 'Ain't there nothin' we can *do*?'

'I've done it all,' I said. 'I've done it all twice, and every time I draw a card that says "Go to jail. Go directly to jail. Do not pass Go. Do not collect $200." Somebody's got a nice little blackmail mill going. He's collecting the dope on businessmen, maybe on politicians, too, and then leaning on them. All he's got to do is find their soft spot. They've got some interesting little sexual kink, or they're hooked on junk, or he *gets* them hooked on junk, or he photographs them playing pretzel with some floosie, and then he puts the screws to them.'

'Is that what the Academy's all about?'

'I don't know – ' I said, and they sounded like the loneliest words in the world. 'I wish I knew. Somehow Woolcott's tied into it alright. Maybe it's his way of nudging the free-enterprise system along, being sure everybody sings the right verse when he calls the tune. That would explain how Alex Woods wound up under a thousand tons of rubble – if he was working as Woolcott's finger man and slipped up somewhere along the line. It explains why somebody got hot around the collar when I started asking all the wrong kinds of questions.'

'Then you think Woolcott's really behind it?'

Wouldn't it be nice, I thought, if it could really be that simple? But there were still too many stray parts that just didn't fit. 'I don't know,' I grumbled.

There didn't seem anything else worth saying then. We both leaned against Lavender's desk and communed with the rum a while. From the corridor came the clatter of heels and a babble of voices that said another working day was over. The secretaries and typists and salesmen and book-keepers and book-makers were going home to their rented rooms and mortgaged bungalows for a dinner of fried Spam and an evening with 'The Great Gildersleeve'. Some of them would play poker and fight with their girlfriends or their boyfriends or their husbands or their wives, and maybe they'd make love afterwards. They'd tuck kids into bed, pare their toenails, unplug the toilet, polish shoes, write a letter home, have an enema, paste photographs in an album, work a crossword puzzle and feed the cat. The time would slip away and there'd be a few things that didn't get done because there are always a few things that don't. So they'd have a beer and go to bed and maybe read a little or worry about what was happening in North Africa, and then go to sleep. A few of them would get up and pee in the middle of the night. In the morning they'd go back to being secretaries and typists and salesmen and book-keepers and book-makers. And me? I'd probably still be propping up the desk and wondering how in hell I managed to louse things up like this. The elevator doors grated open and banged shut again. I imagined the elevator dropping down to the lobby, and something dropped inside me, too. It was like standing at the edge of a cliff and letting a rock fall, then listening for it to strike bottom. This time it fell and fell, and if it ever struck bottom it was so far away the sound never got back to me. Even the echo was out to lunch.

Lavender must have known just how deep the knife was twisting then, because he tried hard to take my mind off it. He started jabbering about his dimpled G.I., and how somebody spiked the orange juice at the U.S.O. with grain alcohol, and how Mamie Eisenhower spent every morning rolling bandages for the Red Cross. But he talked too much and too fast, and in the end he didn't fool either one of us. We were thinking about only one thing, and the thought kept running around in the same circle like a broken record playing the same monotonous phrases over and over again.

'Don't bother,' I said to him. 'I mean, thanks for the effort, but don't bother.'

He sighed his surrender and made a little music with his ice against the side of the glass. But he wasn't giving up quite that easily. 'What about that dancin' fool?' he asked.

'Old twinkle toes? He's one of the pieces that doesn't fit.'

'Maybe Woolcott's got somethin' on him, too,' Lavender suggested. 'Or maybe he's giving him a nice piece of change just to make the Academy look more legit.'

'It doesn't figure,' I said. 'While everybody else is collecting his pay envelope, Riley's taking his home in a bushel basket. He doesn't need the money, and he doesn't need the dames. That's why he doesn't fit, and that's why I elbowed my way onto the set with the rest of his asps, and all I got out of it was a cup of weak tea.'

'No crumpets?'

'Not even a soggy fig newton. Just tea and a nice upper-class kind of proposition – the old we-could-make-such-beautiful-music-together routine.' I ran the tea-party scene through my head again, and then corrected the picture. 'There may have been more to it than that,' I admitted. 'In his own dapper way he suggested there could be something in it for me besides the lay of a lifetime.'

'Such as?'

'We didn't get quite that far. Apparently I'm supposed to think it all over and then let him know when the urge to merge is bigger than I can handle. There's more to his act than a white Rolls and a closet full of tap shoes, but it's hard to tie that up to blackmail and murder. Riley's a pro. You see it in everything he does. He lives and breathes the movies, and with the kind of pictures he makes he's got not only the industry but the whole country by the balls.'

'Miss Ransom, your language is gettin' real seamy,' he said, shaking his head like a disapproving great aunt.

'It's the company I keep these days.'

'I *knew* it. Soon's you stopped goin' to Wednesday night prayer meetin', I thought, devil gonna catch that gal.'

'He caught me,' I admitted, 'and he's holding on fast, and I think I need another drink.'

Lavender took my glass just as the telephone shrilled, and so I reached over to answer it. It seemed to take a long time for my hand to get there.

'Lamaar?' the voice asked.

'Yeah, O'Brien. What's the good news for the day?'

'You heard about Brockaway?'

'I heard he's on his way to Reno, or pretending to be. Which doesn't prove much, of course.'

209

'You wanted us to check Shoemaker out with the immigration people.'

'Well?'

'Clean as a whistle,' O'Brien said. 'She's been here since 1928. Never in any trouble. She got her citizenship papers five years ago.'

'Which also doesn't prove anything – not with her connections. What about the three fillies?'

'Nothing much there,' he suggested after a short pause. 'There's no lead at all on one of them. The second moved to Seattle and married a grease-monkey.'

'And the third?' I asked, hoping he was saving the best for last.

'Stella Forbes. Last heard, she was working as a cocktail waitress in Fresno, but that was nearly six months ago. She seems to have disappeared after that.'

'Does it strike you, O'Brien, that the old disappearing act is becoming the new national sport? It may even replace baseball.'

'Sometimes people have good reasons for disappearing, Lamaar. Sometimes they disappear from one place because they've got something to do somewhere else, or because they just don't like it where they are.'

'Save the philosophy, O'Brien. We'll play Socrates and Plato next time you've got a day off. How is it you know this little chickadee left Fresno within the last six months?'

'Because she quit her job, all fair and square, with two weeks notice, and packed her suitcases and went away. She didn't leave a forwarding address, and we don't know where she went to from there. When I said she'd disappeared, I didn't mean – '

'Hold it, handsome, and back up a little. I just want to know how you found out even that much about Stella Forbes. Is she on the blotter, or is she in your little black book?'

'I don't have a little black book,' he growled, and I made a note to send him one for St Patrick's Day.

'Then what was she charged with?'

'She wasn't,' O'Brien said. 'The grand jury subpoenaed her six months ago.'

'For serving a martini without an olive in it?'

'They were looking into a fire at the electronics plant in Fresno. The D.A. had an idea it was espionage.'

'What's the connection to Stella Forbes?'

'None. At least, that's what the D.A. decided. But the manager of the plant claimed her as his alibi.'

'A night at the Bide-a-Wee Inn, huh?'

'Something like that. He told his wife he was at a Kiwanis dinner in Bakersfield, and was staying overnight, but it didn't check out.'

'And what about Forbes? Did she confirm his alibi?'

'She confirmed it.'

'Which gave the D.A.'s prime suspect a clean bill of health, I guess.'

'Not exactly. They still suspect collusion of some kind, but there wasn't enough evidence to bring charges.'

'How bad was the fire damage?'

'Total. The fire started in a warehouse area where some explosive chemicals were stored. The whole place went up with a bang. Apparently you could see it as far away as Tulare.'

'And what was being manufactured at the plant?'

'Radio systems for B-29s, bomb sites, precision instruments. Also, some new kind of firing mechanism for bombs. Most of it top-secret stuff.'

'What's the manager's name?'

'Lamaar, I don't see – '

'Skip it, O'Brien. I'll explain later. Just give me the sap's name. I presume it's not classified information.'

'His name's Andrews. Arthur Andrews. But you're not going to get very far in that direction. The grand jury heard evidence for two weeks, and it didn't get them anywhere.'

'I've got a different set of tricks, O'Brien.'

'Now, Lamaar,' he said, putting on his neighborhood-bully manners, 'don't go off half-cocked. It's too big for you in the first place. In the second place, it probably doesn't have a damned thing to do with Conchita's disappearance.'

'I'll decide that for myself. Thanks for the tip. Now be a good boy and go polish your buzzer.'

'Lamaar, for Christ's sake, don't do anything stupid.'

'Have you ever known me to do anything stupid, O'Brien?'

'Hell, yes!' he stormed.

'Then don't think you can teach an old peeper new tricks,' I said, and dropped the telephone back in its cradle.

Lavender was still holding the jelly glasses. 'Skip the drinks,' I said. 'Just grab your lipstick and comb. We're going to make a little run up to Fresno. You're in the co-pilot's seat, and from now on you're getting time-and-a-half for overtime.'

'What's one-and-a-half times nothin'?' he asked, scratching his head.

'Damned if I know,' I told him. 'I was always lousy at arithmetic.'

37

ON the left of the road was a sign that announced YOU ARE NOW LEAVING LOS ANGELES. To the right stood a two-story billboard with a picture of Uncle Sam wearing a striped top hat and a permanent scowl. 'Is This Trip Necessary?' he asked. The answer was that I didn't know, but I was willing to gamble my last gas coupons to find out. Lavender and I didn't say much because there wasn't much to say, and neither one of us had any interest in kibitzing about the celebrated California scenery. We pushed north while the sun slowly disappeared like a fat navel orange somewhere over the Pacific, and by the time we hit Bakersfield there was nothing left of it but a faint glow silhouetting the telephone poles. As the heat of the day began to drain away, the Plymouth found its stride and hummed along at a good, steady sixty-five. I knew then that

we'd make it as long as the tires held out. They were all as
bald as Daddy Warbucks, and not much younger.

Fresno sits on the eastern slope, almost halfway up the
San Juaquin Valley, and on a clear day you've got the
Sierra Nevadas for a picturesque backdrop. It's mainly
farm country, the stuff the Oakies were dreaming of a few
years back, but they got about as cheery a welcome as the
Wobblies who were trying to give the fruitpickers new
ideas a couple of wars ago. The moon was riding high by
the time we rolled down the main drag and found a
telephone booth. I shut myself into the sweat box and let
my fingers do the walking. They found Arthur Andrews
sandwiched between Alcoholics Anonymous and Balis
Andrews, Undertaker. At least he was keeping good
company these days. The address was Oleander Lane, and
I left the phone booth to find someone who could give us
directions.

There was a handkerchief-sized park at the next
intersection, with a couple of rusting benches and a bronze
statue of some pioneer ancestor who'd probably once come
limping up out of Death Valley, across the Sierras, and
down into the long green valley. These days he wasn't
doing much but standing on a granite cube and showing off
a fresh coat of pigeon shit. Probably he couldn't have told
me much about Oleander Lane anyhow, but nearby was a
checkered cab with its lights off and a couple of feet sticking
out of the passenger's window, and that looked a little more
promising.

The cabbie didn't like being hauled back from the land of
nod, and he liked it even less when he found out there
wasn't a fare in it. He blinked a lot and scratched himself,
stuck a cigarette in his face and lit it with his trusty Zippo.
Then he finally allowed as how I might be able to get there
if I took a right and then kind of bore to the left. I thanked
him for his hospitality, promised to write him a letter of
recommendation to the Chamber of Commerce, and
hotfooted it back to the car.

'It's about five minutes from here,' I said to Lavender, 'so

213

start looking tough.'

'Tough?'

'Yeah, I wouldn't want the Andrews punk to think he could take advantage of a defenseless broad.'

'I'll scowl a lot,' Lavender suggested.

'Do that,' I told him, 'and keep your ears tuned. I may need you as a witness.'

Oleander Lane was lined with oleander bushes, and even though spring had finished doing her stuff a long time ago, there were enough blossoms left to lay a thick blanket of perfume on the night air. The house I was looking for was a two-story shingled job, with a comfortably middle-aged, middle-class spread about it. It was set back about ten yards from the street, with a row of gas lights along the walk and a cast-iron jockey to hold your horse. The gas lights were blacked out now, in case some crazy slit-eyes was trying to aim a bomb into the oleander, and the jockey was looking a little tired just standing there with the hitching ring in his hand. We could both have used a good night's sleep.

I jabbed the doorbell, and when that didn't produce any action I tried using the side of my fist against the knotty-pine door. After a couple of minutes someone came thumping down the stairs, and I braced myself for the old flying wedge tactic that used to score so many points for Notre Dame. It got me into the middle of the entrance hall a couple of seconds after the door opened, and Lavender wasn't far behind. Arthur Andrews stood there in gray-and-white-striped flannel pyjamas, and his face was full of questions that I didn't give him a chance to answer. Instead, I flashed him my photostat and told him I was asking the questions. He dropped his bottom jaw and blinked a few times before he remembered who was lord of the manor.

'This is preposterous,' he spluttered. 'You can't come barging into my house in the middle of the night. Who are you?'

'I'm Lamaar Ransom,' I answered, shoving the photostat

214

his way again, 'and this is my assistant, Mr Trevelyan. We believe you can help us in some inquiries we're making.'

'You have n-n-no right – ' he began.

'Never mind. I'm sure you want to do all you can to see that the principles of law and order prevail in this hour of trial. That the sword of justice can do its stuff.' I was advancing on him and backing him toward what seemed to be the living room. 'A man in your position has a special obligation to contribute to the national welfare, to take vitamins for peace, to hoe your Victory garden regularly, to have meatless Tuesdays and fishless Fridays, and to tell me everything you know about Stella Forbes.'

He stopped backing up then and started salivating. By the time he got his vocal chords functioning again he was mad as a wet hen and ready to turn us over to the cops for illegal entry. Before he got to the telephone to play outraged citizen, I was stripping off my blouse. 'Don't touch me!' I warned him. 'Don't you dare lay so much as a finger on me, you brute!'

'Don't what?' He stopped in mid-stride and looked at me with eyes that could have passed for saucers.

'Don't touch me!' I made it a little louder this time, and started messing up my hair.

'For-for-G-G-God's sake,' he pleaded. 'My *wife's* asleep upstairs. And my k-k-kid.'

'Outrageous!' I said, looking at Lavender.

'Outrageous,' he agreed, and hid his face behind his hands as though he couldn't bear to witness such an infamous scene.

'When my assistant heard my screams and came rushing in from the car, where he was awaiting me, he too was outraged that a married man would attempt rape with his own wife and child sleeping upstairs. You see, Mr Trevelyan had a very sheltered childhood, and I promised his mother to shield him from the coarser things of life like forcible entry.'

'You can't do this!' Andrews snarled, but without much conviction.

I began to unzip my fly just as a sleepy voice piped out from somewhere overhead, 'What is it, Arthur?'

The man slouched over to the bottom of the stairs and called up, 'Never mind, honey. It's just somebody from the plant.' Then he shrugged in a way that told me I'd just won the first round.

I reassembled my wardrobe and we all tiptoed into the living-room like a trio of conspirators. Andrews switched on a table-light, closed the door to the hall, and checked to be sure the draperies were shut all the way. He wasn't liking it any better, but he wasn't going to fight it either.

While we all made ourselves comfy, Andrews took a last stab at playing his trump suit. 'I told the police *and* the grand jury everything I knew about Stella Forbes,' he whined.

'Maybe,' I said, 'but Mr Trevelyan and I were busy that day and couldn't hear your testimony. How about a little summary just for us?'

He sighed, rubbed some more of the sleep out of his eyes, and threw in the towel. 'What do you w-w-want to know?' he asked.

'Where did you meet her?'

'She was – ' he began. 'There's this cocktail lounge on the north side of town, not f-f-far from where the plant was. The old plant,' he added. 'I used to – to sometimes stop in for a drink. On my way home from the plant. Sometimes I worked late and I'd stop in just to unwind a l-l-little.'

'That's not what I asked you. I know the Forbes cookie was a cocktail waitress, and I know she was your alibi the night of the fire, so you can spare me all that. I asked where you met her.'

'At-at-at this cocktail lounge – '

'Cut the shit, Andrews.'

He was silent then, staring at me with a face you could have used in science class to demonstrate the laws of gravity. Andrews was on the downhill side of fifty, and his flabby face sagged so much it could have been trying to arrange a merger with his flabby neck. The bags under his eyes were like matched elephant-hide luggage.

'Talk,' I said. 'I haven't got much time.'

'B-b-but my wife – '

'Yeah, sure. Your wife's upstairs, and she doesn't know a thing about it. Or she only knows some cockeyed version you dreamed up. And she's a lot younger than you,' I guessed, 'and she'd leave you flat if she knew what you'd been up to. Fine. Whatever you tell me, Andrews, I'll keep to myself – or as much of it as I can. I'm not interested in busting up your little honeymoon nest, and I'm not trying to help the D.A. solve riddles. My guess is he'll get you sooner or later as an accessory, but he can do it on his own time.'

Andrews chewed his lip and thought about it a while. Finally he said, 'I met her in L.A.'

'Where in L.A.?'

'At a party,' he edged.

'Whose party?'

'J-j-just a party.'

'Let me help your memory a little, Andrews. You met this skirt at an exclusive kind of open-collar, hair-down supper given by Holmes Woolcott. Am I right?'

He didn't say anything, but he gave a little groan that told me I was on target. Lavender whistled in appreciation.

'Did Woolcott own the electronics plant here?'

He shook his head. 'No, but we did some subcontracting for Woolcott Industrials.'

'Fine. That's the kind of precision we like. So you met Stella Forbes there and she fell for you in a big way. Am I right?'

He shrugged, and I had a little trouble translating his sign-language.

'Let me rephrase it, chump. You met Stella Forbes and she pretended to fall for you in a big way – lots of leg, up-from-under looks, and a kind of catch in her voice when she said your name. Right?'

'Some-some-something like that,' he admitted.

'Whose idea was it for her to come to Fresno?'

'Hers,' he answered.

'And what did you think about it?'

'I did-did-didn't,' he stuttered. 'I-I didn't want – want her to come here. It was all her idea.'

'But she came anyhow.'

'She came anyhow,' he echoed.

'What kind of hold did she have on you?'

'What do you m-m-mean?'

'You'd eaten grapes from the same bunch, you'd used the same toothbrush, right? You'd maybe had a tumble in the hay together. That'll do for starters. But what was she using for leverage?'

Andrews was busy studying his bare feet, like he'd forgotten there was anybody else in the room but himself and his corns.

'Did she have photographs?'

'Pho-to-graphs?' he wondered, making nice wide O's with his mouth when he said it.

'That's it. You know the slogan: "You press the button and we do the rest." Did Forbes have a plain brown envelope with a few eight-by-ten glossies in it? A little souvenir of the pair of you making the two-headed beast?'

He made a slight nod with his head.

'Did you get that, Mr Trevelyan?'

'From here it look like he tryin' to say yes. Maybe tell him to paw the ground once for yes and twice for no.'

Andrews sent what probably passed in tonier circles for a withering glance toward Lavender's corner of the room.

'Well?' I asked.

'Yes,' he sighed. 'She had pho-pho-photographs, and she said she'd send them to my wife if I didn't help her find a place here, if I didn't keep seeing her. She said – she – she – said she was in love – love – with me, couldn't let me – let me go.'

'Did you tell the grand jury that?'

'N-n-no,' he whined.

'Why not?'

'Be-be-cause – I was – .' He paused and finally shoved

the word out: 'Afraid.'

'Who were you afraid of, the Forbes dame?'

'N-n-no.'

'Who?'

'I don't – don't – know.'

'Come on, mister. Fish or cut bait. Who was it?'

'I don't *know*,' he insisted. 'My – my –, th-th-things happened.'

'What things?'

'The day – the day I was supposed to – to – to testify, I went out to the car and there was – was – this doll.' He shuddered and dragged a hand across his forehead as though he was trying to wipe away the memory, but now that he had started he seemed relieved to be telling it to someone. 'I've g-g-got this daughter,' he said. 'She's only five. My wife's a lot younger than me, you know. Well, on that morning I went – went – out to the car and there was her favorite doll, the one – the one – she always sleeps with. It was on the f-f-front seat of the car, and its head was cut off. It was all covered with something that looked – looked – like – like b-b-blood.'

Somebody walked across my grave when he said it. I recognized the pattern.

'So you told the grand jury just what Stella Forbes told you to tell them?'

'Yes,' he said. 'I t-t-told them I met her after she came to Fresno, that I was at her place the night of the fire.'

'Were you?'

'Yes.'

'And where was she?'

'There. There with me. She g-g-gave me back the photographs. S-s-said I'd been a good boy and she didn't want to cause me any trouble.'

'What caused the change of heart?'

'I – I – don't – don't know what you mean,' he whined.

'I think you do. What did you give her in exchange for the photographs?'

'I – I don't know – '

219

'Listen, bub, and listen very closely, you motherless bastard. I don't have much time, and I want a complete set of straight answers. You shit in your own nest, and you're going to have to clean up the mess. That doesn't interest me. And I wouldn't sleep any better if I knew your ass was behind bars. Anyhow, Fresno's out of my jurisdiction. It's a case in L.A. that I'm trying to solve, but I need to know as much as I can about how the set-up here worked. I'm tired of playing the rape scene, but I'm equally tired of your waltzing around. Do I get the answers?'

The eyes he turned on me looked like last week's left-overs set in aspic. 'She wanted – she wanted – ' he began. Then he blurted it out. 'She wanted the combination to the room where the chemicals were stored.'

'The combination?'

'The door – the door had a combination lock, like on a safe. It was a lead door with a special l-l-lock on it.'

'And when did you give it to her?'

'That afternoon,' he answered. 'The afternoon of the fire, and she said I should c-c-come that night. To her place. She said if I came that night, she'd give me the pictures. I was – was – there when we heard – heard – the explosion.'

I leaned back into the stuffed cushions and let my neck rest on the chairback. I was tired, and I was fed up with having to sort through everybody's dirty laundry, and I needed a drink and a nap and a shower and a fresh start in life, maybe. But they weren't in the cards. Not now, at least.

I pulled myself back up, pulled the living-room with its freestyle stone fireplace into focus again, and asked, 'Was anyone else in touch with you?'

'No,' Andrews said, in a lost, lonely sort of way that told me he wasn't hiding anything now.

'So Stella confirmed your alibi with the cops and with the grand jury, and then she packed her bags and left town.'

'Yes.'

'And you haven't heard from her since?'

'No.'

'And did Forbes also present you with the negatives of those snapshots?'

'Yes,' he said, and his voice held the kind of relief the condemned must feel when the governor's pardon comes through.

'And you haven't heard anything from the guy sitting on the second set of negatives? The ones made from the positives?'

The little color that was left in it suddenly drained out of his face. It was like pulling the plug in the bath-tub. He started to say something, but his tongue wasn't cooperating.

'Don't crap your Doctor Dentons,' I said. 'They've probably written you off a long time ago. You served your purpose. But that's what's wrong with the blackmail business. You pay and you pay and then you pay again for the same thing you paid for in the first place. It's like a hamster running around inside a wheel. He never really gets anywhere. But forget it. You delivered the goods, and it's all ancient history now. What about Woolcott Industrials? Have you heard from them?'

He seemed relieved to be able to talk about business instead of monkey-business. 'They're giving us technical advice on b-b-building the new plant,' he said.

'And you'll be doing the same kind of work?'

'Yes. Government stuff – electronics, mostly.'

I tried to tie the loose ends together in my head, but a couple of them were still too slippery to get hold of. 'Let me ask you a hypothetical question,' I suggested. 'If you were interested in getting your hands on a single industrial secret – something in your own field – some electronic device, some gizmo that's maybe still in the development stage, what would it be?'

'I don't know,' he said slowly. 'I d-d-don't know. I'm just an engineer. We were making radio parts,' he added.

'And some new kind of super-duper explosive device for bombs,' I reminded him.

'There's a dozen different plants in California making

221

them,' he informed me.

'I don't mean anything that's being manufactured now. I mean something that's still on the drawing-board, or something that's still at the prototype stage. Something people would spend a lot of money to find out about, or that they'd use blackmail and murder to get hold of. Think about it.'

For a minute or two his face showed as much expression as that of a day-old corpse, but then there seemed to be a little flicker there, as though an idea had just tripped across the dark cave of his skull.

'There is – ' he began, and then seemed to dismiss it.

'*What* is there?'

'Well – ' he fumbled. 'It's just a theory, really.'

'Let me have it.'

'There's been some talk about different uses of radar.'

'Radar?' I wondered out loud.

'Radio detecting and ranging devices,' he spelled it out for me. 'We make some parts for them, but just the consoles. The different elements are usually made in different plants, then assembled somewhere else.'

'And?'

'Well,' he began, and he was on home ground now. He even forgot to stutter. 'A radar beacon sends out a high-frequency radio beam that bounces off objects, and you can tell by the way it bounces the size of the object, or how fast it's moving if it's an object in motion. It's the same way bats get around in the dark.'

'And what else could you use it for?'

'That's the point. You can't. It's still pretty new, but there's a theory that you might be able to send messages with it.'

'You can always send messages with a radio beam,' I told him, just in case it had slipped his mind.

'Not that kind.' He shook his head like he was dealing with a backward student. 'The theory is that by controlling the vibrations you can cause changes in the object that the beam strikes.'

'What kind of changes?'

'Molecular changes. The idea is that the message could cause the molecular structure of the object to rearrange itself.'

I guess I didn't look convinced, because he added a short paragraph of clarification.

'Molecules,' he said, 'are bunches of atomic nuclei and electrons held together by electrostatic and electromagnetic forces – '

'Skip the physics lesson,' I said. 'Just put it in layman's language.'

'The idea is that with an electronic beam you send a signal that interferes with the existing magnetic field. It causes the molecules to lose that kind of glue that holds them together.'

'And what would the result be?'

'They'd fall apart – the same thing that happens when a piece of wood gets old and brittle. Or even a piece of steel. Only this would work a lot faster.'

I turned to Lavender. 'Are you thinking what I'm thinking?' I asked him.

'Sho *is*, Miss Scarlett. I'm thinkin' about Rembrandt Woods and a certain office buildin' over in Santa Monica.'

'Bull's-eye!' I told him.

'What would it take to make something like that?' I asked Andrews.

'Just to build it? It wouldn't take much. That is, the nuts-and-bolts part of the work, that's all pretty standard by now. What's missing is the formula,' he said.

'What formula?'

'The formula that determines the frequency, that says just what the right kind of vibrations would be. I don't know anything about all that. I'm an engineer, not a physicist, and the kind of machine you're talking about doesn't exist.'

'Are you sure?'

He shrugged his shoulders. 'Maybe it exists,' he confessed, 'but I don't know anything about it.'

223

'If it did, how big would it be?'

'I don't know. Big, I guess. You'd need a big console and radarscope, and a pretty powerful sender.'

'So you couldn't carry it around the way Buck Rogers carries his ray gun?'

'Definitely not,' he shook his head. Now that we were steering a clear course away from his sex life, the creep was getting talkative. I wouldn't have been surprised if he'd broken out a bottle of pre-war Haig and Haig to lubricate the wheels of knowledge a little.

'Where would you install it?'

'You'd have to install it someplace high,' he said. 'The top of a tall building maybe. If the building itself was on ground high enough above sea-level. Or you'd build a special tower for it.'

'Could you use a regular radio tower?' Lavender asked, giving me a wink that told me he was due for a raise.

'Maybe.'

I thought it through, and it seemed to make sense, even if it did sound like something to pad out the Saturday afternoon double-feature. 'Would anybody dare to use it?' I asked.

'What do you mean?' Andrews answered.

'Would anybody risk turning it on? Wouldn't all hell break loose?'

'No. You could beam it, control it, so that you caused the results you wanted, where you wanted to cause them.'

You might use it to get rid of a suspicious private secretary, I thought, but then I realized it wouldn't be worth the bother. An ice-pick in the neck would work just as well and involved a lot less technology. Besides, Woods was dead before he got stashed in the cellar. There had to be another reason for turning the beam on that particular building – like giving a demonstration to a prospective client. Getting rid of Woods would be just a fringe benefit. But why get rid of him at all? Was it because he suspected a frame-up when the locker keys arrived, and went galloping off to protect his boss? The idea of protecting Holmes

Woolcott sounded like protecting a boa constrictor from a litter of kittens. So maybe Woods was just being taught an unforgettable lesson because he screwed up the photo archives.

'I think that's all I wanted to know,' I told Andrews finally. 'But I'd like to use your phone before I go.'

The way I read it was probably too simple, but I had to play with the cards I'd drawn. They didn't follow suit, but they included one dead physicist, a science-fiction disintegrator ray, a tycoon who collected radio stations and a dame who provided meat on the hoof for a blackmail syndicate.

It took a while to reach the Academy, and a while longer before somebody finally hauled Ingrid to the telephone. I had only one question to ask her, but it was the sixty-four-dollar question. 'Was your father doing any kind of research with metals?' The answer was just what I expected.

We left Andrews to wash the sweat off and climb back into the connubial couch. On the drive back to L.A., Lavender sang to keep me awake. He knew all the verses of the theme songs for the Army, the Navy, the Coast Guard and the Marines, but his Ink Spots imitations were even better. I dropped him off near his apartment building and went home for a fast shower and a quick change into battle dress. By then, I'd been awake for exactly forty-eight hours, but the bed didn't tempt me. Whenever the two of us got together again, it was going to be on my own terms.

38

THREE walls of the room were covered with bookshelves that climbed all the way to the vaulted ceiling, and halfway up there was a kind of catwalk for anybody who wanted to browse among the loftier titles. Probably the place didn't get too much walk-in trade, though, and it was just as well;

from the look of some of the leather bindings, they wouldn't survive a brisk sneeze. There were nice little Gothic touches everywhere – gargoyles jutting out of corners, and doorways set into the bookcases with cute little pointed arches over them. There weren't any flying buttresses around, but maybe they were out for a brush-up and press. The fourth wall was all window, made out of diamond-shaped panes of glass tinted a pale lilac color, with ridges of lead between them. It overlooked a walled garden with a fountain bubbling and frothing in the center, and not far away stood what might have been a piece of modern sculpture; the only other possibility was that Holmes Woolcott had leased the garden to a junk dealer who specialized in rusty automobile bumpers.

There wasn't much furniture in the room other than a few hand-tooled leather armchairs and a desk made out of a quarter-acre slab of polished onyx. The desk was supported by chrome bases cast to look like overweight lightning bolts. Maybe it was there to remind the owner he was living in the twentieth-century – like the discrete little ribbons of light that glowed from behind cornices on the bookshelves. The top of Woolcott's desk showed the kind of down-home clutter you can get away with only if you've got at least five digits in your annual income. There were a couple of dozen silver trophies, all looking like they were freshly made that morning – some with golfers getting off a stiff wood shot, some with crossed tennis rackets, and even more with streamlined airplanes zooming away to unknown destinations. Scattered around between them were grape-fruit-sized chunks of raw amethyst and rose quartz and a ten-pound cube of jade with a grinning face chiseled into each side. There were enameled boxes and lacquer ones, and an ivory crucifix so split and stained it could have been carved a day or two after the event took place. Next to the telephone, which seemed to have a button for every day of the year on it, was a dictograph machine with a half-wound spool of wire. There wasn't a pen or a pencil or a pad of paper in sight. Obviously Woolcott pampered his wrists, and let other people do the hard labor for him.

I'd cooled my heels for nearly twenty minutes. Counting the half-hour it had taken to bully and threaten my way past Woolcott's home guard to get even this far, that was more minutes than I felt like giving away. Still, in the name of good-sportsmanship I'd round it out to an hour, and if Mr Aviation hadn't made his appearance by then, I could try to solve the riddle of the telephone and get O'Brien up here to help speed the finale along. A bunch of newspaper clippings, stapled together in the upper left-hand corner, was sticking out from under one of the geological specimens, and I tugged it loose. They were all about Alexander Woods – not about his big smash in Santa Monica, but the one which he was supposed to have made at the tower Gallery in Beverly Hills. Someone had used a red pencil to underline the important words and phrases – things like 'tour de force' and 'genius' and 'intensity of composition' and 'vibrant, sensuous impasto'. I was wondering if I'd maybe seen a different exhibition when a muffled clicking sound interrupted me. A section of the bookcase slid outwards into the room, drifted to the side, and made way for Holmes Woolcott.

He blinked when he came into the room, like something emerging from a cave after a very long hibernation. His thinning salt-and-pepper hair was brushed sleekly back from his temples, and he had the look of a man whose valet has just pulled out all the stops. There was a freshly razored glow to his cheeks, and with a three-way stretch of the imagination you could even reconstruct the handsome mug that used to appear regularly in all the popular magazines, before he got so camera-shy. The toughness wasn't there anymore, though. The face looked like one of those complex shapes folded in tissue-thin Japanese rice paper. Woolcott took a few steps into the room and the bookcase closed up again with a little hiss of contentment for another job well done. He seemed ill-at-ease in the dark pinstriped suit, but it wasn't the fault of his tailor. Every dart and pleat and buttonhole had been worked with an old-master's nimble fingers. A braided gold watchchain with a dull orange glow was draped across his vest; where he should have had his Masonic doodad hanging there was a gold spoon too small to eat porridge with. He managed to ease a little farther into the room, like someone not quite sure if the right messages are getting through to his legs. He had the air of a man waiting for something, but I decided to let him have the opening line, since I'd already decided I was going to have the last one.

Woolcott brushed a hand in front of his face, waving away imaginary flies, and then checked his chin, to be sure the barber had earned his tip. He started to speak, thought better of it, and his eyes surveyed me from stem to stern. Given his history, maybe he was checking me from cockpit to tail as well. Then his lips crinkled into a smile. 'I like you better as a blonde,' he said finally, in a voice that resembled a cheap phonograph playing a few doors down the hall. Its faintness seemed to startle him, and he shook his head a few times to jar the cobwebs loose.

'We could talk better sitting down, I think.' He gestured me toward a leather armchair and waited for me to sit down before he lowered himself carefully into the one facing it.

'I am not accustomed to holding business conferences at such a barbaric hour,' he pronounced, and before I could think of a wise-crack about Attila the Hun, he read the rest of the riot act to me. 'I also resent having my staff bullied and pushed about. They are paid to represent my interests, and one of my interests is in remaining as private as possible. You came here first as an impostor, as a spy, and now you return like some hysterical fury, some wild harridan predicting the day of doom. Neither role becomes you. Under any other circumstances, I would simply have telephoned the police.'

Obviously the staff had elaborated things a little when they reported my entrance, but I wasn't going to bring suit for defamation of character. They'd helped get me where I wanted to be.

'You can skip the etiquette lessons,' I told him. 'In this case the end justifies the means. It's a rule you seem to know pretty well. In fact, it wouldn't surprise me if you'd written it yourself.'

'Business is business,' he muttered, glancing at me sideways from underneath hooded lids.

'For some people, murder is business – and kidnapping and blackmail, too. How's business, Mr Woolcott?'

'Do not talk in riddles!' he snapped, his board-room instincts cutting through the fog in his head. 'What's your fee?' he demanded.

'My fee? Do you mean my price?'

'Fee. Price. Whatever you want to call it.'

'Has everybody got a price in your world?'

'For God's sake, young woman, stop your infantile philosophizing. And spare me any Calvinistic rhetoric. You are a private detective, I believe.'

'A licensed gumshoe. Yes.'

'Then obviously you have some scale of charges for your customers.'

The idea of a financial transaction had put his prefrontal lobes back in working order again. Still, the scenario I'd rehearsed on the way back from Fresno was going a little haywire. I'd come to beard the lion in his den, but apparently the lion had other ideas about things, and they weren't making a lot of sense to me yet.

'Why not ask a satisfied customer?' I suggested to him. 'You could start by asking Ann Shoemaker.'

'Don't be absurd. Ann Shoemaker squeezes every penny until it screams. She will never get value for money. She retains too much of the peasant mentality of her ancestors.'

'I noticed.'

'Since you seem so reluctant to name a price, I will offer you $100 per day as a professional fee, plus $50 for general expenses. Naturally, I would expect to pay any extraordinary expenses as well, and would not insist on their detailed itemization. In addition, I am prepared to offer a bonus of $5,000 when the case is closed. Would you prefer cash or a check?'

'Back up,' I said, 'and hold your horses a minute. When the numbers get that high the air starts thinning out, and I forgot my oxygen mask. I'm working on a case anyhow, and I don't think you're going to like the punch line. It just may dissolve our partnership arrangement before the ink is dry on it.'

'There is no conflict of interest,' he pronounced slowly and carefully. 'I want you to find the murderer of Alexander Woods.'

There was something strange in his tone — a note of pleading that probably hadn't been there for the last three decades, and that could have used a good dusting off. Unless he was a better actor than the whole Barrymore clan rolled together, it was genuine, and if it was genuine it shot my neat solution of the case all to hell and back. On the other hand, maybe Woolcott was only playing a variation on the old guilty theme-song: the best defense is a good offense.

'Let's get one thing straight,' I said finally. 'I'm not for sale — at any price, and my services aren't for hire right now. On the other hand, I'm interested to know who killed Alex Woods, but the reasons aren't professional any longer. They're strictly personal. Every lead I've got points to Woolcott Industrials,' I told him, and watched his face closely as I said it. There wasn't even a flicker of response. Maybe Woolcott was playing an elaborate game of cat and mouse with me, but I had to gamble that he was on the level now. There wasn't anything else to do, and there couldn't be much time left to do it in.

'First of all,' I said, 'I need to know more about the kind of jobs Woods did for you.'

'He was my private secretary,' Woolcott answered.

'How private?'

'He did the first, preliminary sorting of the mail and called to my attention any letters that needed my personal attention. The remainder were distributed to various aides and secretaries. Now and then there was some kind of errand for him to run. And he occasionally played backgammon with me. Otherwise, he spent the day in his studio. He was a very dedicated painter. A very gifted one.'

I let the lesson in art-appreciation float by. 'What role did he play in your little soirées?'

Woolcott snapped his head to the side as though I'd slugged him with the question. 'None,' he grunted.

'You mean he didn't even design the invitations?'

'He did nothing,' Woolcott repeated in a voice that set the words in italic type.

'No follow-up assignments? No darkroom chores?'

Woolcott sighed like a man who'd had a little too much of life and said, 'I had the impression you were in a hurry. I therefore find your oblique methods rather puzzling – and more than a little irritating. Alexander Woods was my – well – was what you might perhaps call my protegé. He assumed certain minor and entirely routine responsibilities only because he was too proud to live from my charity, and because his tastes were much too expensive to be satisfied through the sale of his pictures. Does that answer your question?'

'Not quite. Apparently some of your guests get caught with their pants down – get caught without a chance to smile for the birdie or say cheese. I don't know if it happens here or somewhere else. Maybe only the first contact's made here, and the lights-action-camera stuff comes later. It doesn't matter. Candid photos like that can be very persuasive sometimes.'

'Preposterous!' Woolcott spluttered. 'Utterly preposterous! I respect the privacy of my guests as much as I wish my own privacy to be respected, and blackmail is far too clumsy a device to be of any appreciable use to me.'

'Then what's in it for you?'

'For me?' he wondered.

'Yeah. For number one. Don't tell me the sex buffet is just another of the charities you support.'

'For all your somewhat cynical manner, you are quite tiresomely naive,' Woolcott said.

231

'Spare me the character analysis and answer the question. What's in it for you?'

His fingers drummed lightly on the arms of the chair, and he answered in a bored monotone. 'My lifestyle and my wealth,' he said, 'make it possible for me to entertain in a somewhat – let us say – in a somewhat unconventional manner. My guests seem grateful, however, for what I offer them. That gratitude puts them in my debt, and in turn makes them rather more amenable to various business arrangements. If that sounds to you like some sinister undertaking, let me assure you it differs little from the cocktail parties given by junior executives to impress their superiors, or from the pathetic little spaghetti dinner concocted by the wife of a young university lecturer for his overweight department chairman. I do not like cocktails of any kind, and I have no talent for cooking spaghetti. I entertain in a different way, and it amuses me.'

Woolcott was papering over a lot of cracks, but he was at least making a neat job of it. 'The other possibility,' I said, 'is that Woods was doing some moon-lighting, that he had his own portrait business set up.'

Woolcott shook his head. 'No,' he said. 'No, I – I – think not. I hope not. He could have had anything he wanted.' His voice trailed off into silence.

'Somebody was blackmailing your cronies,' I informed him, 'and they were plugged directly into the fun-and-games you were organizing here. It's the only explanation that makes sense.'

'That is your interpretation,' he sighed. 'And yet I know every member of my staff, every close associate, better than most husbands know their own wives.' The comparison didn't exactly impress me.

'Ann Shoemaker, for example?'

'Ann Shoemaker best of all. I loved her once.'

'But she loved your dollars better,' I guessed.

'There weren't so many dollars then. But she was obsessed by her father's trial and his execution. She blamed the Americans for it – *all* Americans. She blamed me, even

232

though the event was long past when I met her.'

'If she hates Americans so much, why did she start pledging allegiance to the stars and stripes?'

'Life was not easy in postwar Germany, even for young women with families to support them. It was even harder for an orphaned child.'

'And by then you had more dollars,' I suggested.

'She was not interested,' he said, in a way that told me the fact was still a bitter pill for him to swallow. 'Over the years we have made a series of business arrangements that are to our mutual advantage. Like Alex, Anna was never interested in charity.' The way he pronounced 'Anna' seemed to soften it and sweeten it, to give Shoemaker a whole history I'd never have credited her with.

'It seems to me that most of the so-called arrangements in your life turn out to be strictly business.'

He shrugged as if to say he had gotten used to it a long time ago, but his right hand began to play nervously with his 14-carat coke spoon.

'What about your arrangement with Alfred Leslie, the physicist?'

'I admired his work,' Woolcott said promptly. 'I once utilized some of his research on metals stress in an aircraft design, and various companies in which I hold interest have consulted him from time to time, I believe. He was a brilliant physicist and, I am told, a very likeable sort of man. I wouldn't know. I never met him.'

'Then how is it that your name appears in his calendar for the day he killed himself?'

'I have no idea. In any case, it is many years since I visited anyone. The only appointments I keep are ones in this house, and those are increasingly rare.' He seemed to puzzle over it a minute and then asked, 'How do you know my name appears there – in Leslie's calendar?'

'That's confidential information,' I said.

'Have you seen the entry yourself? No, you needn't tell me. That, I presume, is another piece of confidential information.' He didn't need an answer. He'd planted the first seed of doubt, and he could let it sprout all by itself.

The pattern was right. That much I was sure of, because there was only one ugly little explanation that made all the dirty pieces fit together. The problem was that I had tried to put them together with a couple of the pieces upside down.

'Do you know anything about the research Professor Leslie was doing at the time of his death?'

'More of the same, I presume. He was interested in the molecular properties of metals – particularly in metal stress and fatigue. The latter costs the aeronautics industry alone a few billion dollars a year.'

'Would his work have included any radar experiments?'

'That's out of his area.'

'Maybe I don't mean radar itself. Could his experiments have applications to radar technology?'

'His work would have almost unlimited application. He was engaged in pure research, you understand, not in applied research. It would be up to other people to make the applications.'

'What do you know,' I asked, 'about some kind of science-fiction device, some gadget for causing molecules to come unstuck?'

A glimmer of recognition brightened his eyes then, and he sniffed a couple of times, like a predatory animal on the scent of really big game. 'A molecular implosion device,' he said. 'It doesn't exist, but it could – at least theoretically. And if that's your question, Leslie's research would have a direct bearing on the development of such a radar potential.'

'If you could build a gizmo like that and wanted to conceal it, what sort of location would you pick?'

He thought a minute and then gave me the same answer I'd gotten from Arthur Andrews. 'In a radio tower, perhaps, or on top of a tall building – high enough so you could direct the beam without anything obstructing the path.'

'How big would it be?'

Woolcott shrugged. 'Who knows? The size of a radar sender, but they're getting smaller all the time. The technology is being developed at incredible speed because of its military potential. But the console would certainly be large and complex, and it would take a lot of extra power to run it. You couldn't just plug it into a, normal wiring system.'

Even that little piece of information fitted into the puzzle, clicked into place down in the lefthand corner where the blue of the old mill stream crossed the green of the pasture.

'Thanks,' I said, and made for the exit without waiting for anybody to see me out. Woolcott was still levering himself out of the tooled leather chair when I last saw him, and his face was wearing a fresh question mark.

The convertible snorted a couple of times, pawed the ground and tore off down the drive, spraying gravel into the tea-roses. The black Caddy, long and fat as an executive hearse, must have been on my tail soon after I hit the main drag, but I never noticed it. If I had, it wouldn't have made a damned bit of difference.

39

A FLAGPOLE was planted in front of the main entrance to Studio B, flying a red wigwag that did a hula in the breeze. Over the door a red light was blinking on and off, on and off, and beside it a bell was ringing steadily. Supervising the sound-and-light show was a beery-faced guard in a khaki uniform. His fat jowls were stretching his freckles thin, and his stomach was restaging Custer's Last Stand, with his shirt buttons as the cavalry. He was hiked back in a straight chair, leaning against the wall, with a cap shoved to the back of his head to show his greasy curls.

I looked at my watch, looked at the light winking on and off over the door, looked at my watch again, shook it, held it to my ear and screamed, 'Oh, no!' The guard flopped his chair down onto all four legs and looked at me like I'd just dropped the collection plate in church. I repeated the little pantomime for him and then shrilled, 'This is *terrible*. I'll be fired!'

He cocked a weary eye at me, mumbled something about scatterbrained dames, and hoisted himself out of the chair. He still wasn't convinced though, and just stood there with that dumb, bored look on his face that seems to grow on guards and nightwatchmen like scum on a pond.

'Mother of God!' I cried, eyes to the heavens and hands clasped to the bosom. It was something I remembered from a Bing Crosby movie.

It took two fat keys to unlock the door, and a lot of fat leaning on it to make a hole big enough for me to squeeze through.

'Bless you,' I said. 'Bless you, my son, and Erin go brae.'

'Meshuga,' he muttered.

I was in what looked like a tunnel, and the only light came from another red lightbulb over the door at the opposite end. I eased the door open a few inches, enough to see that Riley's three-ring circus was in full swing today, and that the panic-factor was high enough for me to slip in without being noticed. By staying in the shadows, with my back against the wall, I could cover a fair amount of ground. I'd forgotten to tape up my dog-tags, but given the decibel level in the studio, I figured no one would notice.

I covered maybe a hundred yards, moving away from the pyramids and the watch-tower from which Riley surveyed his domain, when a pile of lumber got in the way. Straight ahead was a double row of cubicles, like whitewashed outhouses, that I figured were dressing rooms for the hoi polloi, and right on cue a squad of Nile maidens descended on them, clucking and squealing like a henhouse with a stray fox in it. Lillian Lyles wasn't among them, but she came limping along a couple of minutes later, wearing only one sandal and carrying the other in her right hand, the heel she'd broken off of it in her left. As soon as she pulled open the door to one of the dressing rooms and hobbled in,

I took off in a sprint and had my hand on the door handle even before it had clicked shut.

'Oh-h-h!' she shrilled. 'Oh, gosh, you scared the pee-pee out of me.' She leaned against the pint-sized dressing table and held a hand to her chest to stop the heart palpitations. 'Wow, I thought I'd never *see* you again. How've you been?'

'Fine,' I lied. 'I lost you the other day, and I thought maybe I could do a little follow-up on that story we were talking about.'

'Gosh,' she cooed, 'how thrilling!'

The air in the dressing room was so thick you could have sliced it with a knife and sold it as anesthetic. It was Hollywood's very own secret combination of sweat and powder and coldcream and broken promises.

'We're shooting the finale today,' Lillian told me. 'And I had to go and lose this darned heel.' She held the two pieces up like a kid who's just broken a new toy and wants daddy to fix it.

'Let me have a look,' I said.

She handed me the sandal, and it didn't take long to make a diagnosis. 'I think you'll have to shoot it,' I said.

'To *what*?' She made a nice little cupid's bow with her mouth when she said it.

'Skip it. Just remember one thing.'

'What?'

'Remember that I owe you a bus ticket to Akron, and if I haven't got the dough, I'll carry you there piggy-back.'

'Gosh,' she fluttered, 'I don't know what you're *talkin'* about.' She tilted her head to the side and batted her lashes under her Cleopatra bangs. Her chin was pushed slightly forward, and there was a cute little dimple right in the center of it.

'Never mind,' I said. 'I'll explain later.' Then I made a fist and took careful aim. I got a bull's-eye, square in the dimple, and Lillian Lyles went to the mat like a boxer with a glass jaw. I hustled her out of her knee-length necklace, then a set of silver lamé snakeskin-patterned underwear, and covered her up with a faded plaid bathrobe that was hanging on the door. After I'd done my quick-change act, I piled my hair on top of my head and poked a couple of bobby-pins into it. Then I reached down and pulled off Lillian's wig. Her own hair was mouse brown, and it was getting a little thin on top.

I had to leave my bag in the dressing room, hanging on the door under my shirt and slacks. It meant I had to leave the Mauser there, too, but there was no other choice. You couldn't have concealed an aspirin in the costume I had on.

Outside, the chorus line was still enjoying its coffee break, but a few of the girls had already started drifting back toward the set, and I tagged along. When we got there, a few more were sitting on the bottom tier of the pyramid, sipping coffee from Dixie cups. A team in coveralls was raking the sand, and overhead a couple of daredevils were hanging from the I-Beams, adjusting lights. Nobody seemed particularly interested in where I'd left my sandals.

Rigsby Riley wasn't anywhere in sight, so I guessed he was still up in the crow's nest, but I had to be sure of that before I made my move. I mingled with the crowd a while.

'Christ,' somebody was saying. 'I fell flat on my *ass*.'

'Watch out,' a voice piped out. 'You could break your nose that way.'

'Oh, but he's too, too dreamy for words. He gives me the shivers all over.'

'I will absolutely never – no, *never* – understand the male species,' a baritone voice announced with a lot of long vowels.

'Say, honey, have you got a light?' This time the voice was speaking to me, and I told it no. I wondered where she kept her cigarettes, but I was too well-bred to ask.

There was a sudden crackle of noise from the loudspeakers and then the single word 'Mac!' came blaring out. 'Mac!' it repeated. A man with a necklace of earphones went trotting by and started clanging his way up the metal staircase to the control tower. The maestro was safely aloft, then, giving orders to some trouble-shooter, so I could reconnoiter for a while without catching his eye.

I decided to take an unguided tour, and the sand felt good between my toes. It was a little like the old days out at Malibu, when there wasn't any garbage coming in on the tide, and when kids dug for private treasure on the beach without turning up rusty sardine cans with every shovelful of sand. Now I was the one doing the digging, and there was only one logical place to stash a five-foot-two Mexican-American treasure.

Riley's tinsel town pyramid had only three sides. The fourth wall stood open, and inside you could see a tangle of beams and struts that looked like something put together by a lunatic with a giant erector-set. I scrambled through and made my way up to the front, where three plywood walls formed the golden tomb Cleopatra's sarcophagus was standing in. A ladder was propped there, leading up to the bank of lights that illuminated the burial chamber. I climbed it, looked over the top, and wondered what to do next. It was at least a fifteen-foot drop down the other side, and the floor was concrete. There weren't even a couple of inches of sand or a pair of P.F. Flyers to cushion the fall. I hiked one leg over and checked the scenery again, but the floor hadn't gotten any closer. Then I got the other leg up and felt the plywood edge bite into my semi-bare fanny. The wall began to shimmy a little, and the two-by-fours that braced it up started to get into the act too. I got a grip on the top of the wall and eased myself over. Dangling there, I remembered the old show-business motto – 'Break a leg' – and then my hands slid away from the wood and the floor jumped up at me. Somebody drove a nail into each heel and it shot up into my legs, vibrated my knees, got lost somewhere in the stomach, just as a huge fist grabbed hold of my spine and gave it a good shake. I lay on the floor for a couple of minutes, maybe longer, trying to guess how many of the fractures were compound. I tried wiggling my toes, but there must have been a short-circuit somewhere, because the message wasn't getting through. I raised up on my elbows, stared them in the face, and said, 'Move, you bastards!' They moved a little, and then the ankles moved, and then the knees, and I knew there wasn't anything wrong with me that six months in traction wouldn't cure.

I rolled onto my stomach and inched over to Cleopatra's tomb, commando-style. The sarcophagus sat on a platform raised about a foot above the floor. Both of them were sprayed gold and covered with phony jewels big as goose eggs. What interested me more was the neat little row of holes drilled just under the lid of the mummy case. I dragged myself until I was close enough to get an elbow onto the platform, and then reached up and knocked. Apparently nobody was at home. I knocked again, and the same hollow echo answered me, but I somehow knew I couldn't be wrong – not only because of the ventilation holes, but because the sarcophagus was just the kind of ghoulish touch that went with the Halloween-party mood of the whole damned case. And it would be too risky to stash Conchita where he couldn't get to her in a hurry – either to knock her out again, or knock her off. Then, just for a moment, I thought I might be as fruit-cake as everybody else involved in this screwball business. Otherwise, what was I doing crawling around the concrete in snakeskin B.V.D.'s? That's when I heard the scratching sound. It wasn't much, and it didn't last long. It was about what you'd expect a weak kitten to make, or a woman shot so full of hop the most she could get into action was a couple of finger nails.

I pushed up as hard as I could on the lip that stuck out on the top of the mummy case. It had a mind of its own, though, and pushed back even harder. Then I stood up, got it in a half-nelson, and tried to heave it to the side. It didn't matter now if anybody saw me raiding the tomb, because I'd found what I was looking for. But I still hadn't found the way to get the lid off. I gritted my teeth and muttered 'Open sesame', but that didn't help any either. There had to be a lock somewhere, or a concealed switch that released the top, but it didn't seem worth looking for. A pick-ax or a cold chisel would do as well. 'Hang on!' I barked through the ventilation holes.

This time I used the front door of the pyramid instead of the servants' entrance, and left my tracks in the sand. An old codger in bib-overalls watched me come out, shook his head to show what he thought of the manners of chorus girls, and started raking my trail away. That's when Riley and the type with earphones draped around his neck came down the stairs from the tower, moving fast. I got out of their flight path and put a few lamp stands between us. Riley was talking a mile a minute and using his arms like semaphores. It was obviously crisis time, and his face was as flushed as a late-summer sunset. Still, his eagle eye wasn't missing much. He stopped to watch the geriatric case raking sand in front of the entrance to the tomb and shouted something at him. The old man turned, cocked an ear in Riley's direction, and then started shuffling over, dragging the rake behind him. I didn't wait to eavesdrop on their little tête-à-tête. Diversionary action seemed the order of the day, and I thought I could provide some.

The metal steps were icy cold on my feet, and there were more of them than I had thought. By the time I got to the bird's nest I was breathing heavily, and my legs were asking for a furlough. The door at the top had a metal strap bolted to it, and on the jamb to the right was the metal ring the strap fitted over. An open padlock was dangling there. Riley must have been feeling pretty sure of himself to fall asleep at the helm like that.

The inside of the control room would have made Dr Frankenstein turn pea-green with envy. The place had more shiny knobs and switches and dials and levers than the Hoover Dam. One whole panel of them had steel rods across it, holding all the switches in the same position and fastened in place with the same kind of padlock that was hanging beside the door. Overhead was a silvery glass disc, with a neat little row of knobs under it. I thought I'd skip all that and aim for a few special effects closer to home. The first two switches I threw made pretty blue sparks, but not much else. The third one worked wonders, though. It got a lazy monsoon off its feet and back to work. Water gushed from sprinklers in the roof and sent Nile maidens and technicians running for cover. From that high up they looked like an hysterical ant colony. The whole scene got even more interesting when I had the wind machines working, stirring up some wet sand, and when the fog machines cranked into ˙ action. Setting off the Roman candles just behind the orchestra was a mistake, though. I think they were left over from another picture.

I figured I could probably dismantle the whole set now without attracting too much attention, and I was looking around for something to do it with when the trap-door flopped back and a hand caught my ankle. I looked back to see Rigsby Riley's face twisted into a very nasty expression just before he jerked my leg out from under me and sent me sprawling across the steel plates bolted to the control-room floor.

'You stupid, meddlesome fool!' he screamed.

'Don't be a sore loser,' I advised him, getting up onto one bruised knee.

'Bitch!' he roared.

'The party's over, Riley. It's not just your movie that's being washed down the drain out there. It's your whole filthy racket.'

'Is that so?' he asked, suddenly calmer and more in control of his facial muscles. 'Is that really the case?' he wondered. 'I think not, my dear. What a pity. You were my only interesting adversary.'

I don't know where he got the gun. I only remember it was small and that it had a pearl handle to match his manicure. I was staring down the stubby nickle-plated barrel, and the hole in it wasn't any bigger than a pea-shooter. It looked like it meant business, though.

'All the rest were so dull,' Riley muttered. The tail end of a smile jerked up the corners of his mouth. 'Dull,' he repeated. 'Dull, dull, dull,' he said, and then the gun exploded. Bouncing around the control room, the noise sounded like a howitzer going off, but you could still hear the little crunch the bone made when it broke. Riley did the old vaudeville double-take, skipping backwards and making a pair of wide eyes at the audience. But his eyes couldn't see the hole in his forehead. At first it was just a black circle, like a beauty spot pasted there, but suddenly a jet of blood spurted out of it and drained down onto his white silk shirt, carrying bits of bone and a few fleshy grey lumps with it that resembled congealed oatmeal. Then Riley took a long, hard dive at the floor.

Holmes Woolcott leaned against the metal doorframe. His spiffy pinstripe suit was soaked with water, and a little puddle of it was spreading around his feet. He wasn't looking at me, and he wasn't watching the occasional spasm that was flopping Riley's custom-made two-tones around. His pale gray eyes were fixed on something that even the radar beacon on the roof wouldn't have located.

'Alex – ' he said, as though he was trying to explain something, and then there was a rush of air that sounded like the far-away moan of a wounded animal. 'Alex was – ' He strained to get the words out, but they stuck in his craw, and he was strangling on them.

I levered myself up off the floor and walked over to him with knees that buckled like a drunken marionette. His whole body was trembling, and his teeth were chattering as if an Arctic wind was blowing through the room. He tried again, but all he got out was the one word, 'Alex.' I finished it off for him. 'Alexander Woods was your son,' I said.

He seemed to get me into focus then, and his head nodded just enough to tell me I was on the right track.

'And he never knew,' I guessed.

He didn't respond, but his face looked as wasted as the back-side of the moon, and I knew I was right.

'Whose idea was that?' I asked him. 'Was it yours or Ann Shoemaker's?'

'W-w-what?' His lower lip hung slack as the village idiot's, and there was a froth of saliva on it that dribbled down in a shiny stream across his well-shaven chin.

'Whose idea was it not to tell Alex, to let him grow up

243

thinking of himself as a glorified charity case?'

He answered only with a kind of gargling sound, far back in his throat, and then his head collapsed onto his chest and the gun fell from his hand. It clanged down the steps with a racket like a blacksmith pounding an anvil, and then everything got very quiet. The only sound was the phony Hollywood rain blowing against the windows.

'Skip it,' I said. 'Forget I asked. It's none of my business anyhow. Besides, I've got a friend downstairs who's in kind of a tight spot, and I need to put some clothes on before I catch pneumonia.'

I was halfway down the stairs when I heard his voice. 'Anna,' he said. Then it rose to a wail that ended in the same two syllables: '*An-naaa.*'

40

SHE was wearing a mauve linen suit with a short jacket snugly belted at the waist and softly padded shoulders that stressed her long, sleek, streamlined shape. On her right hand was a topaz ring with a stone fat enough to choke an elephant, and peeking out from under her cuff was a discrete hint of old-fashioned gold – something sentimental, something inherited from a great-aunt or grandmother, and something that was probably signed by Louis Comfort Tiffany himself. She looked fresh as a spring garden, but she looked older, too. Part of it was because her hair was pulled back and gathered into a snood, but it was more than that. Her eyes had never been more intensely blue, but they seemed older as well.

Before she sat down, Ingrid laid her purse on the desk – a trim snakeskin job with gold fittings. She nodded at it and said, 'I thought I should settle my account.'

'The account's settled,' I told her. I shoved my elbows against the arms of the chair and hoisted my butt up a little, then resettled it on the leather cushion to give another bruise its day in court.

'It's still open in my books,' she answered with that teasing little Mona Lisa smile she worked so well.

'Better fire your book-keeper.'

'He's already been called to the colors,' she laughed, 'and I've taken on the job myself. If you won't tell me how much I owe you,' she added, 'I'll have to work it out for myself and send you a check.'

'I'll send it back.'

She shrugged as though she knew a hopeless case when she saw one, and said, 'Don't be so proud. We made a business arrangement, pure and simple.'

I wasn't sure those were the adjectives I'd have picked, but I let it ride. 'I wasn't trying to find out anything about your father's death,' I explained. 'In the end, I was only working for Conchita, and for myself. It wouldn't be right to get paid for that. Every time I turned a corner in this case, somebody else was being bought or sold. It's kind of nice to have a different set of motives.'

'But that doesn't pay the rent,' she reminded me.

'No,' I agreed, but I didn't tell her just how on target she was with that one.

'And you've had expenses,' she said.

'Not many. A few tanks of gas, a couple of phone calls, a few dog-meat hamburgers.'

'What about this Lillian Lyles? Won't you need a lawyer to answer the assault charges?'

'She dropped them. She was so tickled to see her name in all the papers that she decided I was her bosom buddy.' I remembered something about a viper in the bosom, but it didn't seem relevant right then.

She sighed and said with a brisk nod, 'I'll think of something.' Then the little lines puckered up between her brows again. She looked down at her hands and began to toy with her topaz. Muscles twitched slightly under the golden surface of her cheeks, like summer lightning on the distant horizon.

'Do you know – ' she began. 'Do you know what Riley

found out about my father?'

'No,' I said, 'and that's the truth, the whole truth, and nothing but the truth. He had lots of different ways of working his fact-finding missions. With Brockaway he probably threatened to put out a bulletin on an old homicide charge, or to tell the world he was hooked on junk. Maybe Riley was even supplying it and threatened to cut off the flow if Brockaway didn't cooperate in whatever ghoulish little party game Riley had dreamed up. But the tie-in to Woolcott was the most elaborate one, and the one that produced the most results. Riley must have played on Alex Woods' vanity, his need for ready cash, his feelings of inferiority. Woolcott doled out the booze and the chicks and the happy-powders as part of his own cockeyed idea of public relations, and it was a perfect set-up for someone like Riley – so long as he had a contact man who could fill him in on the vital statistics.'

'And then Riley blackmailed them?'

'No, it wasn't quite so neat or simple as old-fashioned blackmail. There wouldn't have been any kicks in that for a guy like Riley. He wanted adventure, wanted to tinker with things and choreograph them the way he did one of his own pictures. It was all strictly big-league, too. He went after industrial secrets and sold them to the highest bidder, or he arranged firework parties like the one up in Fresno. Getting hold of your father's formula, that must have been the real *pièce de résistance*. Whatever he learned about Alfred Leslie's past, he sprang it on him in Princeton last December. He was in New York then, arranging financing for the new picture, so it was easy. Maybe he disguised himself to look older. He was a whiz-kid with the make-up too, you know. Maybe he didn't even bother. Holmes Woolcott's name was enough to get him the appointment with your father, and that was all Riley needed.'

'I knew – ' she said, and then paused for a minute. There was a slight tremble to her lips, but she got it under control and went on. 'I thought I knew my father so well,' she qualified it, 'and I've gone back over everything I ever heard

246

about him, everything his friends ever said. I can't imagine what some blackmailer could have learned that would have persuaded him to – to – '

Her voice trailed away, and she started fiddling with her ring again.

'Whatever it was,' I told her, 'it probably happened a long time ago.'

Her blue eyes pleaded with me. 'But if my father had given Riley what he wanted, why would he – why – why would he kill himself?'

'Because blackmail doesn't ever finish anything. It's only the beginning. Think of the kinds of defense research your father was involved in. Riley went home and made his new toy and played with it a while, but he would have gotten bored with it sooner or later, or found a buyer, and then he'd need another, deadlier toy. Your father did the only thing he could – not to stop Riley, but to stop his own collaboration in Riley's schemes.'

'But why didn't he just *tell* me? Why would he have cooperated in the first place?'

'He should have told you. He should have told Walter Winchell, too, and sent a press release to Ripley's *Believe It or Not*. That's the only way to throw a monkey wrench into the blackmail mill. My guess is your father wanted to protect you, not himself. Maybe he was wrong, but he was willing to die to do it.' I let that sink in for a minute and then I asked her, 'Do you really want to know what it was?'

For what seemed like a long while, the only sound in the room came from a few nasal car horns that drifted up from the street below. Then Ingrid raised her eyes to mine and gradually the deep furrows between them faded away. 'No,' she said in a hoarse whisper. 'It's not that I'm afraid to know,' she added, 'but I don't seem to *need* to know any more.' She was made of championship stuff, and you can't keep a champ down for long.

'Remember that,' I advised her. I was full of free advice today – on everything from parent-child relationships to tips on how to stretch a pork chop to feed a family of five.

'But it's all so awful – and so stupid – that so many people had to die just because of the ego of one little man.'

'That's what war's about a lot of the time, too.'

'Maybe,' she said, not quite sure she could buy the cracker-barrel philosophy. 'I don't know. But he was only playing *games*,' she stressed.

'That's right. Very dirty, very deadly games. Otherwise, he found life too dull.' I heard Riley's rasping voice again, the way he had spit the words out: dull, dull, dull.

'But I don't understand why he should want to kill his own partner, why he'd have gotten rid of Alex Woods.'

'Maybe he didn't like his pictures,' I suggested. 'Or maybe the goose that laid the golden egg laid a square one. Woods was a neurotic type anyhow.' He didn't have much choice, I thought. 'He seems to have misplaced some photographs, and maybe he was scared the whole thing was getting out of control. At any rate, Riley probably sent the locker keys to put a scare into him, to whip the troops into shape by showing what could happen to anyone who got a little out of line. Or it could be that Riley was just trying to throw suspicion in Holmes Woolcott's direction, and that Woods was grateful enough for what Woolcott had done to try to protect him. Obviously Riley and Woods had a show-down of some kind, and the dancing master decided to make the funeral service a real extravaganza. But somewhere along the line, Woods learned I might be called in to look for LaFlamme, so he picked me as the patsy in case the locker keys proved too hot to handle.'

'But who would have told him you were going to be asked to find Yvette?'

'There's only one candidate – old sweetness-and-light Shoemaker.'

Ingrid's perfectly arched brows wrinkled a little. 'Why would she confide in Alex Woods? Even if she was worried, she doesn't seem the type to ... to ...'

'To show a little old-fashioned human weakness? You're right. But don't forget that Alex was her son – and that he had his own reasons for worrying about LaFlamme's vanishing act.'

'It's so stupid,' Ingrid said finally. 'It's such a waste.'

That seemed to sum it up pretty well, and I couldn't think of any editorial remarks that ought to be added. Riley's monomania had a high price-tag on it, and Holmes Woolcott had taken his percentage, too. Archie Potter's daughter was among the victims, but she'd gotten off easy – hidden away somewhere with a broken heart and an illegitimate kid. 'Yeah,' I muttered, 'it's a waste.'

Ingrid picked her purse up off the desk and said, 'I'm still going to send you a check.'

'Save yourself the postage.'

She laughed, then, and there were silver bells in the air.

'Furthermore, I'm going to send it air mail – from Princeton.'

She walked to the door, and I got up to hobble along behind her. 'You're going home then,' I said.

'Yes,' she answered with a bright smile. 'For better or worse, I'm going home. I don't know what it means, but I'll have to find that out for myself. There are father's papers to put in order – a lot of things to be done.'

I waited with her while the elevator grated up to the sixth floor. As she stepped in, her legs making a little silken whisper, I told her, 'Be happy! That's an order, and remember that I outrank everybody in the whole damned regiment.' The doors shimmied shut before she could answer, and I watched the indicator overhead needle its way down to the ground floor.

When I limped into the outer office, Lavender was studying himself in the compact I'd gotten as a reward for letting Holmes Woolcott have his way with my shoe. He patted his finger waves into place and eyed me over the top of the mirror. 'Don't forget Conchita wants you to bring home a dozen eggs,' he said, smoothing his eyebrows. He clicked the compact shut and added, 'Hey, you forgot to bring back my earrings.'

'Damned if I didn't. I'll tie a string around my finger and bring them in tomorrow.'

'Don't forget,' he said. 'I want to wear 'em on Saturday night with that Roman thing – the one with the gold belt.'

'Got a big date?' I asked.

'Uh-*huh*!' he beamed. 'I sure *do*. Almost six-foot-three.'

'I thought you were being awfully frisky today, but I figured maybe you'd just gotten hold of some loco weed.'

'No, *m'am*. This time it's a hot one.'

'Congratulations.'

'Thanks!' He put down the compact and began to snap out a jazz tempo on his fingers. He bobbed his head to the rhythm and started chanting, 'When you're hot you're hot, and when you're not you're not.'

I didn't stick around for the finale. Instead, I went back to my meditation chamber, got my feet up on the desk, and counted a few sheep. The first three or four made it over the fence. I'm not too sure about the rest of the flock.

250